ZANE PRESENTS

ALLISON HOBBS

TAMING MADAMM

Dear Reader:

Thanks for taking the time out to read *Taming Madam M*. All I can say is, "Whew!" Allison Hobbs has truly reached the top of her game with this one. Sexy, intriguing, provocative, freaky and scandalous with a whole lot of drama. What a powerful combination! Allison has kept her audience captivated for well over a decade but this one tops the cake. Even I was shocked by her erotic muse and that is saying something.

Enter the world of Madam M, whose humble beginnings and the luck of meeting the right man who would do anything for her, give her the opportunity to run a training camp for sex slaves. People from around the world pay her high fee to have their "pets" properly trained. In *Taming Madam M*, we meet those who actually desire to be degraded, bound, and humiliated by various people all in the name of sexual gratification. Wanting to please their masters and receive the coveted certification that will increase their value, they are willing to do anything and everything to be reach their goals.

As always, thank you for supporting myself and the authors of Strebor Books. We appreciate the love and we will continue to try to bring you the best and most prolific writers on today's literary scene. You can find me on Facebook @authorzane or email me at zane@eroticanoir.com.

Blessings,

Zane

Publisher
Strebor Books
www.simonandschuster.com

ZANE PRESENTS

ALLISON HOBBS

TAMING MADAMM

SBI

STREBOR BOOKS

NEW YORK LONDON TORONTO SYDNEY

Strebor Books
P.O. Box 6505
Largo, MD 20792
http://www.streborbooks.com

This book is a work of fiction. Names, characters, places and incidents are products of the author's imagination or are used fictitiously. Any resemblance to actual events or locales or persons, living or dead, is entirely coincidental.

ISBN 978-1-59309-578-9
ISBN 978-1-4767-5911-1 (ebook)
LCCN 2015934963

First Strebor Books trade paperback edition October 2015

Cover design: www.mariondesigns.com
Cover photograph: © Keith Saunders/Keith Saunders Photos

10 9 8 7 6 5 4 3 2 1

Manufactured in the United States of America

For information regarding special discounts for bulk purchases, please contact Simon & Schuster Special Sales at 1-866-506-1949

The Simon & Schuster Speakers Bureau can bring authors to your live event. For more information or to book an event, contact the Simon & Schuster Speakers Bureau at 1-866-248-3049 or visit our website at www.simonspeakers.com.

To my sweet bae, Johnathan Royal.
So loving and giving; you are my hero!

CHAPTER 1

Striding with impeccable posture, the butler made his way to the kitchen. With his nose turned up as if assaulted by a foul odor, he cast a withering gaze upon the head cook and her two helpers who were gathered around a large oak table sipping coffee and leisurely perusing various sections of the newspaper.

He clapped his white-gloved hands together to draw their attention. "Have you slackers completely lost your minds? You people are not paid to laze about and browse through Madam's newspaper." Clucking his tongue in disgust, he promptly gathered the spread-out sections of the newspaper and reassembled the publication, smoothing it out to give an untouched appearance.

Azalea, the head cook and the only member of the household staff who didn't cower in the butler's presence, glanced at her watch. "It's only seven-twenty; plenty of time before Quintoria is up and ready for breakfast. She always eats precisely at ten."

"I passed Madam's quarters a few moments ago and heard her and her guests stirring."

"I had no idea Quinnie had guests," Azalea said, worry replacing the impertinence in her voice.

"There's a lot you don't know, Azalea. And please refer to the lady of the house as Madam and *not* by her given name! Now, prepare two extra plates and be quick about it. Heads will roll if Madam isn't served breakfast before her feet hit the floor." The butler clapped his hands together sharply, urging the kitchen staff to get moving.

Realizing that despite her close friendship with Quintoria Stevens, she would be called to the carpet if her employer experienced a single hunger pang before her breakfast was set before her, Azalea jumped to her feet.

"Get busy, girls. Madam has risen," Azalea barked. "Darcie, I want you to begin the batter for crepes. Edwina, you can start preparing the fresh-cut fruit and ricotta cheese filling."

"Yes, ma'am," the two young women replied in unison. In a flurry of motion they bustled around the kitchen, creating a commotion as they swung open cabinets and drawers.

The kitchen now throbbed with life and Azalea quickly tied on an apron. She stroked her chin thoughtfully. "Hand me that gourmet cookbook next to the fridge, Darcie."

"Yes, ma'am." Darcie searched through the stack of books and grabbed *Quick and Easy Gourmet*.

Squinting, Azalea thumbed through the pages. "Along with the crepes, Madam and her guests will enjoy crispy potato galette with poached quail eggs and caviar, and of course a pot of green tea for cleansing and serenity."

Satisfied that the kitchen staff was handling their duties satisfactorily, the butler turned on his heels to exit.

"Mr. Hardwicke, I could use an extra pair of hands in here. Would you please send in one of the scullery maids to assist in the kitchen?"

"The scullery maids are quite busy attending to other duties, today," the butler replied haughtily and left the kitchen.

The cooks worked in silence until the sound of the butler's heels clicking against hardwood could no longer be heard. Once they were certain he was out of hearing range, the chatter began.

"I wonder if that hot actor, Deon Provost is upstairs with Madam," Edwina said, wearing a dreamy expression.

"Deon Provost! I didn't know Madam hung out with a big star like him," Darcie exclaimed in a hushed, awestruck tone of voice.

"Yep, I heard she discovered him. She produces his movies, but they're also friends with benefits," Edwina informed.

"I realize that she's involved in making movies and whatnot, but I didn't know her celebrity friends came to the house. I had no idea that famous people were into Madam's freaky lifestyle," Darcie whispered as she whipped the crepe batter.

"About a year ago, I personally served breakfast when Deon Provost stayed overnight," Edwina whispered conspiratorially.

"For real?"

"Ohmigod, yes, girl. His body was crazy with muscles everywhere. It took all my willpower not to touch one of his biceps."

"Was he naked?" Darcie asked excitedly.

"Mm-hmm. And even though the sheet was covering him from the waist down, I could still see his dick print. Whew, chile, that dude is packing. But here's the nasty part…he wasn't in bed alone with Madam."

"Who was with him?"

"There was this Asian chick laying up in the bed. She was in the middle of Madam and Deon. Both her hands were under the sheets and she was moaning and squirming like she was about to cum. I thought she was fingering herself, but when I looked closer, I realized the heifer was stroking Deon's package and playing between Madam's legs at the same time."

"Oh, Lawd!" Darcie exclaimed.

"While the Asian girl's hands were rustling underneath the sheets, Deon and Madam leaned toward each other and started kissing. It was freakiest shit I'd ever seen. I tried to act normal and not stare, but I was so hot and bothered, my hand started shaking as I poured Madam's tea."

"Would you have joined in if Madam invited you?" Darcie inquired.

"I damn sure would have," Edwina said, laughing.

"Wow! Madam is a bigger freak than I thought. But I'm not mad at her at all. Hell, I admire her for being a rich bitch and a boss who gets it in wherever and with whomever she pleases."

"I know, right? The next time my husband pesters me about a threesome, I'm gonna tell him I'll do it as long as it's me, him, and another dude—someone hot like Deon Provost," Edwina said wistfully.

"Men are selfish. They want the pleasure of smashing two chicks, but they ain't tryna share their woman with another man," Darcie continued.

"True. My husband would whip out his pistol if I tried to bring a dude into our bedroom. But a girl can dream, can't she?"

Darcy stopped stirring and cut an eye at Edwina. "I wonder if Deon Provost is upstairs with Madam right now."

"I doubt it. I read on a blog that he's dating one of those Jenner girls."

"Ugh! That family irks the hell out of me. Always snatching up our black men like it's their birthright since they have Armenian blood."

"Those Jenner sisters aren't even Armenian, the Kardashians are. They're straight-up white girls with Bruce and Kris's… Oops, I mean Caitlin and Kris's regular, Caucasian genetics."

Edwina and Darcie laughed.

"Ladies, ladies," Azalea interrupted. "I've heard quite enough chatter about sex and celebrities. Show some respect while you're working in Madam's kitchen. Furthermore, you two have a lot of gall gossiping about Madam and her lovers when she's the person who signs your paychecks."

"I'm sorry, Miss Azalea. I forgot that you and Madam used to be real tight back in the day."

"We still are. We're best friends; the only difference is that I work for her now," Azalea corrected. "Now, listen to me. I want you girls to keep Madam's business out of your mouths. Don't forget the confidentiality agreement you signed when you started working here. She could sue both of you for everything you've got, which isn't much," Azalea added.

"It's not like we're selling Madam's information to *TMZ;* we're only talking amongst ourselves," Edwina reasoned.

"Focus on your work and not Madam's personal affairs. And don't let anyone in this house hear you speaking with all that slang talk the way you do in the streets. This is Madam's home and you must follow the house rules when you're alone and also when you're around the guests. Proper English at all times. Do you understand me, ladies?" Azalea said firmly.

"Yes, ma'am," Edwina and Darcie said at the same time.

The butler, who had only gone a few yards down the hall before tiptoeing back toward the kitchen, had overheard the entire conversation. He made it a point to eavesdrop on all the staff. Being a dutiful head servant, he made sure the household staff held Madam in the same high regard as he did.

He lived to please her for she was more than merely his employer; she was also his astonishingly beautiful wife.

The butler wheeled the breakfast cart over the marble flooring in Madam's private quarters. When he reached the master bedroom, he rapped sharply on the double oak doors.

"Enter," Madam said gaily.

With her perfect pair of breasts on display, Madam was propped up by pillows, sandwiched between two pale-skinned, hard-bodied young men who both looked like Scandinavian male models. They had white-blond hair that curled against their necks, clear green eyes and were obviously identical twins. The only way to distinguish between them was by the small silver rings that adorned the nipples of the twin on the left of Madam.

Completely smitten with Madam, the brothers murmured in Norwegian as they fussed over her, nuzzling her neck, caressing her shoulders, fondling her breasts, and suckling her deep dark-colored nipples.

Always the consummate professional, the butler averted his gaze as he announced the morning menu.

Madam scowled. "The menu sounds dreary and unappetizing, but it'll have to do. These boys will need some kind of sustenance to keep me satisfied," she quipped.

"I'll inform the cook that Madam finds the menu completely uninspiring and demands to be wowed with excitement and creativity in the future."

Madam nodded. "Well said, Jamison." She usually referred to him as Butler, and only called him by his given name when she was experiencing fond feelings toward him.

Earning a compliment from Madam caused the butler's heart to flutter and he could feel a twitching sensation in his loins. Taking his mind off his growing sexual desire, he pushed the cart to the left side of the enormous bed, reached over one of the muscular, white-haired boys and began setting up Madam's silver breakfast tray. He placed a covered dish in the center of the tray and then began pouring tea into a floral-print teacup.

"I acquired these two delectable pieces of eye candy from Norway.

They don't speak a word of English but we've had no trouble communicating, for the language of love is universal," Madam said wisely and then bestowed her husband with a brilliant smile.

Keeping his head down, the butler continued working. Being in his wife's presence, if only to serve her, was one of his greatest pleasures. Basking in the glow of her smile was more than he could handle, and his blossoming erection was hard to conceal.

"You look uncomfortable, Butler. Is something wrong?" Madam inquired.

He cleared his throat. "No, there's nothing's wrong that I can't manage."

"But you look absolutely tortured," she said, her sensual lips forming into a devious smile.

"I'm fine," he said in a weak voice. He set the newspaper on Madam's tray and bent over to pick up a breakfast tray for the blond twin on the left side of the bed.

"Put the tray down, Butler. I won't have you working for me if your health is impaired," Madam said sternly.

"My health is fine. Please, Madam, allow me to serve you."

"No." She cast a glance at the lump in his pants. "Obviously you can't work in your current condition."

The butler opened his mouth to protest, but Madam held up a hand, silencing him.

"Open your pants and show me your cock. I'll be the judge of whether or not you're capable of carrying out your duties."

"If it pleases you, Madam," he said pitifully and then pulled from his fly a large, veiny dick that writhed in the palm of his hand.

"Stroke yourself," she commanded.

"Yes, Madam," he replied breathily. His eyelids fluttered closed and his hips bucked forward as he grasped his hot, rigid flesh.

Mid-kiss and mid-suckle, the twins stopped administering to

Madam and gazed wide-eyed at the butler as he pleasured himself.

"Why are you boys gawking? It's breakfast time, so help your-selves to some tasty sausage." Madam released a burst of laughter.

The twins didn't understand Madam's verbal command, but when she nudged her head toward the butler's thickening dick, which jutted out from a jungle of dark pubes, they realized what was being offered to them.

Madam moved aside, allowing the twin on her right better access to her husband's bloated penis.

The butler squirmed at the unexpected sensation of soft lips on the head of his dick. He gasped and his body jerked when a second mouth engulfed his scrotum. One warm tongue licked the under-side of his dick head while another wet tongue lathered his balls. The exquisite dual sensations were maddening and he squeezed his eyes closed and clenched his teeth, desperately trying to stave off the exploding pleasure. He wasn't gay, nor did he have homo-sexual tendencies. He hated it when his wife challenged his sexuality. In her opinion, if his dick grew hard for another man and if he ejaculated into another man's mouth, then he was at the very least, bisexual.

The butler disagreed. He was straight, goddammit. He couldn't control how his dick behaved when it was inside a hot mouth.

"Hurry up and suck off the butler before our breakfast gets cold," Madam implored in a steely voice. Realizing the twins did not comprehend her words, she irritably grabbed a handful of white-blond hair and sped up the process, causing the head of the dick-sucking twin to bob up and down rapidly as she force fed him the full length of the butler's massive dick.

Wanting to win Madam's approval by outshining his brother, the other twin became creative. Flipping onto his back and with his mouth wide open, he tea-bagged the butler's scrotum.

The butler was a virile man, capable of sixty minutes or more of sexual stimulation before succumbing to an orgasm. And although Madam had commanded her Scandinavian lovers to bring her husband to a swift orgasm, he realized that she took pride in his uncanny stamina.

Thrusting into the wet mouth, the butler squeezed his eyes shut and gritted his teeth to stave off the urge to ejaculate. Gasping, he balled his fists as the dual stimulation from the twins threatened to bend his will.

Weakening, the butler began to quiver and shake. Feeling helpless, he cracked his eyes open and sought out his wife's lovely face.

The smile she cast held no warmth, but it was still a smile, nevertheless. Bewitched by her beauty, enchanted by her smile, he let out a primal sound as he flooded the mouth of his wife's lover with torrents of hot passion.

CHAPTER 2

"I'm disappointed in you, Butler. You lasted all of five minutes," Madam said disdainfully, dismissing him with a wave of her hand.

The butler could feel a flood of red-hot shame rush to his face. He was grateful that his dark complexion concealed the degree of his humiliation. Managing to appear stoic, he zipped his pants and gave a slight bow. Straightening his back, he pivoted and left the bedroom, allowing Madam and her lovers complete privacy to dine and continue fornicating.

Outside Madam's chambers, unable to breathe for a moment, he fell against the door, panting. The degradation of being ordered to participate in sordid sex acts with not merely one of his wife's illicit lovers, but two, had stolen his breath away.

Madam delighted in humiliating her husband—in causing him to suffer the indignity of accepting her never-ending parade of lovers, both male and female. After forcing the butler to be molested by the pair of perverted twins, she'd dismissed him wearing a grimace of contempt, as if he were nothing more than an inept circus act…or a court jester who had displeased the queen.

But the butler had only himself to blame. When Jamison Hardwicke had first met Quintoria Stevens he'd been an affluent man, the sole heir of the Hardwicke Paint Company fortune, and one of the city's most eligible bachelors. Beautiful women came a dime a dozen for a man of his stature. Yet, from the moment he'd set eyes on Quintoria, he'd been drawn to her. Looking back, he wished she'd never applied for employment at his thriving business.

At twenty-eight years old, she should have already been established in a career instead of applying for an entry-level position as his personal assistant, but he was too blinded by lust to probe her about her limited work history. He'd been too horny for her to find out exactly what she'd been doing with her life for the past ten years. Had he known then that she'd disrupt his life and turn it upside down, he would have dismissed her before the interview had ever gotten started.

Indeed, she was a shockingly beautiful woman with dark velvety skin and mysterious slanted eyes, and she had a raw sexuality that seemed to permeate the air around her. But that shouldn't have mattered since an entire staff of attractive women was at his disposal.

Being gratified by his female employees was one of the many perks that came with being the head honcho of the company. None of the women had ever claimed sexual harassment and he would have been shocked to be hit with such a frivolous lawsuit. Any woman who'd ever become intimate with his large sex organ quickly realized that she'd been bestowed with an amazing honor.

The moment Human Resources completed Quintoria's paperwork and granted her an employee identification badge, it occurred to him to bend her over his desk to begin her orientation. But something stopped him. She had a way about her—a haughtiness and sense of entitlement that both intrigued and annoyed him. It would be exciting to knock her down from her pedestal and watch her grovel and beg for his immense dick. All in good time, he'd told himself back then.

A week into Quintoria's employment with Hardwicke Paint Company, he found it difficult being in her presence without needing to relieve himself. She was such an unusual beauty, tall and lean with skin like black satin, high cheekbones, and dark, luminous eyes that had an Asian slant to them. He often wondered what her pussy looked like, and the very thought was maddening.

On numerous occasions during business meetings outside of his headquarters, thoughts of Quintoria had caused his dick to stir restlessly in his pants, forcing him to have to interrupt important discussions of commerce to go jack off in the restroom. Often while driving, his desire for her would become so strong, he had to pull over on the side of the road and take out his big pulsing cock and then pacify it with rapid hand strokes.

At the office, his sexual need had become so strong that in order to manage his erections, he had to find contentment between the thighs of up to four or five female employees in the course of a single workday.

Quintoria seemed oblivious to the fact that her boss often stared at her—molesting her with his eyes. She seemed unaware that it took all his willpower not to reach out and cup her firm ass cheeks and pull her onto his elongated pleasure pole.

Seated at her desk outside the boss's office, she was always so hard at work, prying into the financial aspects of the company, she didn't seem the least bit curious or suspicious when he held numerous private meetings with female staffers throughout the day.

She was an eager employee—quite ambitious—and seemed to want to learn all the ins and outs of the paint industry. Jamison considered himself merely humoring Quintoria when he listened to her suggestions on how he should run his business.

He noticed that she became sullen and withdrawn whenever he disagreed with any of her ideas, and he soon found that agreeing with her proposals garnered a smile. And when Quintoria spread her succulent lips into a smile, it drove him wild.

He was more than ready to humble her by pinning her down on the couch in his office, throwing her long legs over her head, and then power-ramming his big juicy cock into her snug cunt. But realizing that once he'd defiled her she'd no longer be considered special, he decided to put off the inevitable.

Quintoria was extremely ambitious and she asked innumerable business-related questions throughout the workday. It was obvious to him that in due time she'd spread her legs for him, most likely in the hopes of furthering her career. But while climbing the ladder of success, she'd also have to climb on his dick, and she would not be prepared for the craving she'd acquire. He smiled at the thought of how pathetic she'd become once she began her desperate obsession with his big, unruly dick.

That craving for his dick meat happened to every woman who experienced the sensation of having it slammed inside her. As refined and beautiful as Quintoria was, her pussy was no different than any of the other pussies he'd conquered. Her cunt would be in a constant state of arousal—yearning and throbbing for him.

On a lark, he invited Quintoria to the theater. To be on the safe side, he also bought a ticket for Monica from the tech department and instructed her to meet him in an obscure location to clandestinely take care of his carnal desires during intermission.

But his plans were foiled when Quintoria declined his invitation, stating that the date and start time of the popular Broadway play interfered with the part-time job she was forced to work in order to pay for a convalescent home for her sickly aunt.

Inwardly, Jamison seethed, but managed to produce an insincere smile and to inject compassion into his tone as he offered to pay for her aunt's care. To his astonishment, Quintoria refused his generosity, stating that she was too proud to accept charity. She suggested a salary increase, boasting that her contributions to his business warranted triple the salary she presently received.

"A fair salary will permit me to care for my aunt in the manner she deserves and also allow me the dignity of managing my own financial affairs without needing anyone's assistance," she said with hard insistence in her voice.

It was a preposterous idea. Who did this nobody-assistant think she was? Never had he encountered such gall, such unparalleled self-aggrandizement. He was so outraged, his dick grew stiff and it took a huge amount of steely willpower not to tear open her dress, toss her on the leather couch in his office, and pound into her relentlessly until all the tension had left his loins and flooded her body.

Although she wasn't at the beck and call of his sexual urges yet, she soon would be. Quintoria had only worked for him a few weeks and he wanted to keep her around a bit longer, and so taking a deep breath, he gathered his composure. In addition to being beautiful, Quintoria was obviously gutsy. In a warped way, he admired her self-possession. With so many wimpy women in his employ, it was refreshing to meet someone who dared to challenge him.

Reluctantly, he tripled her salary. He certainly could afford to— at least temporarily. He refused to allow the new assistant or any other employee to manipulate him into paying an excessive salary that wasn't deserved, but he went along with Quintoria's ridiculous demand with the intention of firing her immediately after gutting her pussy until her insides were nothing more than pink mush.

Once he filled her cunt with juicy penile meat, Quintoria wouldn't be so special anymore. She'd be no different than any of the other women who had tried unsuccessfully to fuck and suck their way into his favor. It wouldn't be long before pompous Quintoria Stevens would drop to her knees in his presence, grateful for the opportunity to oblige him with an open mouth and a relaxed throat.

Of course he'd soon tire of her and send her packing like all the personal assistants who had preceded her.

Despite their level of education and job qualifications, all the female employees who worked for the Hardwicke Paint Company were expected to be on call to lower their panties for their tyrant boss whenever he summoned them. He didn't believe in sharing office pussy, and therefore, workplace romance was prohibited among the staff. All the cunts on the premises belonged exclusively to Jamison Hardwicke.

On one occasion, his big, ravenous dick had begun to throb uncontrollably when a new employee, a big-bosomed young woman named Kelly, had strutted over to the water cooler. The urgent manner in which his dick pulsated informed him that there was no time to verbally communicate his desires to the new staff member. Whipped into a frenzy of arousal, he was fully engorged, too far gone to waste the precious time it would take to shepherd the woman back to his office. His dick, a wild dark beast, acting on its own accord, twitched inside his pants as it desperately sought to inhabit a warm, wet place.

He had no choice but to feed the dark beast right there on the spot.

"Lift your skirt," he demanded hoarsely. There was no better time than now to let her know that pleasuring the boss was part of her job description.

"Excuse me?" Kelly muttered, unaware of office protocol.

"Stop your dallying and pull up your skirt, woman," he said with impatience.

"But…" Eyes filled with fear and confusion, Kelly's gaze swept the area, imploring her coworkers to help her. But no one came to her rescue. They all seemed to be frozen in place, gawking at the salacious scene taking place right before their eyes.

Irritated by the new employee's dawdling, Jamison pressed down on her shoulder, forcing her to bend over.

Startled employees, who had been moving about the office, stopped in their tracks and stood transfixed. Those who were seated at their desks gaped and rubbernecked as if witnessing a horrible car accident. They'd all grown accustomed to their boss helping himself to every vagina on the premises, whenever the mood struck him, treating the most intimate part of a woman's body as if it were nothing more than a portable potty. But he usually committed these offenses in the privacy of his office. Or in darkened stairwells or in a cubby area behind one of the copy machines. Never had he copulated so openly and so violently in such a high-trafficked area for all eyes to see.

"What are you slackers looking at? Get back to work," Jamison bellowed.

Obediently, the beleaguered employees quickly averted their gazes and busied themselves with work obligations.

"Oh, my God! What do you think you're doing? Stop it!" the accosted woman whimpered as her boss unzipped his pants and roughly tugged her panties down. Within seconds, her protests turned into soft moans of pleasure as the huge shaft stabbed into her. Suddenly, she widened her legs, accepting the intrusion. Her vaginal walls constricted, becoming a possessive warm sheath that clutched desperately at the massive, pounding appendage.

"Your greedy pussy loves being fed big, juicy dick, doesn't it?" Jamison demanded in a coarse voice. "You want me to stuff this big sausage down your throat, don't you?" He continued the revolting dialogue as he thrust hard and deeply.

Although staff members did as they were told, keeping their eyes fixed on their computer screens, their ears were perked as they waited to hear Kelly's response.

"Yes! Yes! Yes!" Kelly cried, launching into a high-pitched squeal as ecstasy rocketed throughout her body.

After the scandalous occurrence, many female staffers, having developed what seemed to be an unquenchable thirst, began to loiter around the water cooler. Separating herself from the pack that hung around the water cooler, Kelly found an excuse to visit her boss in his private office.

Looking up from the papers that were outspread on his desk, he gazed at her with cool indifference. "What can I do for you, young lady?"

Kelly dropped her eyes self-consciously. "I was wondering if you wanted to, uh, you know…" she said in faltering speech, shifting from foot-to-foot.

"You came to get some more juicy dick meat, huh?" Jamison said with a prideful chuckle.

She gave a twitchy smile and nodded quickly.

"Don't be shy, Kelly. You have to ask for what you want. I'm sure you've heard the expression, 'a closed mouth doesn't get fed,'" he remarked, leaning back in his chair and unzipping his pants.

"Can I have some… Oh, God. It's so weird putting it this way." Fidgeting, she laughed uncomfortably.

"You want some thick dick meat, right?"

"Yes."

"Then say it. Tell me exactly what you want and also your reason for wanting it." From his sharp tone, it was obvious he was grow-ing impatient with Kelly.

"I, um, I'd like some more dick meat because…well, because my…my cunt is so hungry," she stammered, red-faced.

"Let me explain something to you, Kelly. I'm a successful man because I run my business efficiently. Do you think you're the only woman in my employ who enjoys getting this big juicy slab of dark meat lodged in her cunt?" he asked in a firm tone of voice while caressing his erection.

Captivated by the sight of her boss's swelling dick, Kelly couldn't speak. She shook her head in response to his question and unconsciously licked her lips.

Suddenly, he picked up the phone on his desk and pressed a button. "I want to see you in my office, Adrienne," he said. He returned the phone to its base and looked at Kelly. "I don't know what you've been accustomed to with former employers but here in my place of business, no one gets preferential treatment. There's a rotation in place and you won't get the opportunity to get your greedy cunt filled with this stiff dick until your turn comes around again. Is that clear?"

Kelly swallowed hard. "Yes, Mr. Hardwicke."

"Good. I'm glad we have an understanding."

Adrienne, a waiflike woman from the accounting department, entered the office and crinkled her brows. "Should I come back when you've finished with Kelly?"

"No, no. Kelly was just leaving. Weren't you, Kelly?"

"Yes," Kelly replied unhappily.

"Before you go, Kelly, come over here and kiss my dick goodbye." He gripped his cock, aiming it upward.

"You want me to kiss your cock goodbye?" she asked, baffled by the odd request.

"Did I stutter?"

"No, sir." Kelly made her way to other side of the desk, knelt down and kissed the head of his dick with the reverence of a Catholic kissing the Pope's ring.

Kelly left and Jamison pulled Adrienne to his lap, lifting her dress and impatiently yanking her panties down as she awkwardly spread her legs to accommodate him.

Thoughts of Quintoria invaded his mind, sending surges of rippling flames straight to his loins. He'd never wanted anyone as badly as he wanted her. Yet he sensed that she believed—for some unknown reason—that she was too good for him. *How dare she?* The heat in his loins kindled by sudden rage set off an orgasm of volcanic force. He thrashed and groaned; his body writhed as he pretended that Adrienne was Quintoria. He imagined himself plowing into his new assistant's tight pussy with such vigor that he had to wrap his arms tightly around Adrienne's tiny waist to anchor himself and prevent them both from being flung from the chair.

CHAPTER 3

Uppity Quintoria Stevens had no idea the kind of man she was toying with. She had no clue how well-endowed he was. She was completely unaware that women became instantly addicted to his big cock. There were so many dick-addicts in his employ that Jamison Hardwicke had no choice but to ration out his penis.

His female employees, with their insatiable desires, would suck him dry and fuck the skin off his dick if he didn't run a tight ship. Of course there were times when he broke his own rules—times when he was so distressed by the throbbing in his pants that his brain turned to mush. During those times when logic escaped him, he was forced to surrender to the pressure of his tightly coiled genitals. Forgetting about his well-planned rotation system, he simply grabbed whoever was close at hand and dragged her to the nearest private or semi-private location.

Quintoria was too brash and too conceited to realize what an honor it was for him to bestow upon her the privilege of wrapping her luscious lips around his lengthy cock. But she'd soon find out, and after he unleashed the dark beast upon her, he had no doubt she'd gladly accept a sizeable pay cut for the privilege of being in close proximity of his big, pulsing dick.

He smiled as he imagined himself stretching out Quintoria's snug little pussy while she clung to him, shuddering and crying out in unabashed passion.

But things hadn't worked in his favor. Quintoria turned out to be a shrewd and ruthless woman who enjoyed the sexual pleasure of both men and women. She was a hedonist, and no amount of debauchery could satisfy her perverted desires. She was quite a challenge, and Jamison never backed away from a challenge.

In hindsight, he should have walked away. He'd still own his business and wouldn't be dressed in a butler's uniform if only he'd been satisfied with all the wet office pussy that had been available to him. Succumbing to his desire to add Quintoria to his list of conquests had been a life-altering mistake.

Oh, how far the mighty had fallen.

Quintoria turned out to be the worst assistant who'd ever worked for him. She refused to do simple tasks such as bringing him his morning coffee, picking up his dry cleaning, and keeping his cigar box full. She let his office phone ring continuously before bothering to pick up.

Although he showered her with expensive gifts, she never seemed appreciative. In fact, she always appeared bored by the wonderful presents he bestowed upon her. She was so hard to please, it was exasperating. One day during a moment of extreme frustration, he told her that he'd fallen in love with her. He didn't actually mean it, but hoped the false confession would help him gain entry inside her lacy panties.

"If you love me, then prove it," she responded dully.

"I'd be happy to prove it. What do I need to do?"

"First, I want you to stop whoring around with the female staff."

"Okay, that's not a problem."

"Second, I want you to impress me with your willpower by becoming completely celibate."

He scowled. "For how long?"

"The time span is to be determined," she said with a wicked smile.

"Have it your way. I'm going to prove that I love you," he said with the utmost sincerity, though he planned to revert back to his old habits the moment he'd had his way with Quintoria.

In an attempt to prove his love, he took her on a romantic vacation in Paris. When they arrived at the hotel, she insisted on separate rooms. She ignored him for most of the trip, choosing to spend her time in the company of several swarthy, French-Algerian men, sharing breakfast with one and dinner with the other.

Her rejection of Jamison only intensified his obsession with her. Crazed with the desire to be near her, he blurted out a marriage proposal, and she accepted, though she continued her affairs with her two Parisian lovers.

When they returned to the States, she married him in a small ceremony with only the preacher and her best friend, Azalea, present. None of the staff from the paint company or any of his golf buddies were invited. In fact, she ordered him to give up his favorite sport altogether and insisted he devote his time thinking of ways to worship and adore her.

"You want me to give up golf?" he asked, incredulous.

"You'll do it if you love me," she said.

Argh! Grrr! What a ballbuster this bitch was. But in a perverted way, he liked it. Her audacity made his dick as hard as granite.

On their wedding night, Jamison finally got to touch her when she allowed him to massage her feet. He ran her bathwater and fed her grapes while she reclined in the tub. Showing the devotion that was slowly but surely becoming a real emotion, he knelt before her when she stepped out of the tub, telling her that he was her loyal subject, willing to do anything she desired. Humbling himself aroused another dark part of his soul that he never knew existed. Overcome with emotion, he begged her to order him around and treat him like a lowly servant.

Quintoria's eyes lit up. "I have an idea."

"What is it, my dearest darling? There's nothing I wouldn't do for you."

"I want you to take a trip to Europe."

He winced. "A trip without you? Why?"

"Don't question my motives," she said sharply.

"Of course, my dear. I'll follow your orders and go to Europe."

She smiled approvingly as she dried her wet body.

"May I dry you off, my darling?" he asked, reaching for the towel with trembling hands.

"No, you piece of scum. You're not fit to touch me."

Ahh! He shuddered lustfully. It was preposterous but true…the more she degraded him, the more aroused he became.

"While you're in away in Europe, I'll handle the family business."

"That's fine, my dear," he said breathily, yearning to touch himself.

"Do you want to know why I'm sending you to Europe?"

"Yes."

"You need help."

"What kind of help?"

"Help in learning how to serve me in the manner I deserve. I plan to enroll you in an intensive eight-week training program at the International Butler Academy in Valkenburg, Netherlands."

He covered his mouth in shock. "Th-that seems rather extreme, my dear. I'm sure there's an online course I can take."

"No, I want you to become proficient at bowing and scraping when you're in the presence of your betters, such as me. At that elite butler school, you'll also learn how to meet the demands of running a modern household with confidence, grace and style."

"But that's absurd. I don't need classes to know how to serve you. And I've always managed my housekeeper quite well."

She sighed. "I intend for us to move into a much larger home with a full staff. So, until you've received accreditation from the butler academy, my legs are closed to you."

"But this is our wedding night, and I've waited so long to lie in bed with you. Darling, please. My manhood is so unusually big and powerful that I wouldn't dream of forcing it inside your sacred little temple…at least not yet. But if you would allow me to penetrate you with a finger or my tongue, it would make me enormously happy."

"I don't care about your happiness, Jamison, and neither should you. If you don't want to devote your life to pleasing me, then we should annul this marriage immediately." Her dark eyes bored into him, challengingly.

"I don't want an annulment," he admitted.

"What do you want?"

"I want to be your butler and your devoted servant." He couldn't believe the words had come out of his mouth, but she was the most remarkable woman he'd ever met. It was the first time he'd ever felt the strong urge to worship anyone. The desire alone was an aphrodisiac beyond anything he'd ever experienced.

Unabashedly naked, Quintoria strutted across the bathroom floor and began brushing her hair while gazing at her image in the mirror. He stood behind her with an erection blooming in his pants.

"Kneel behind me and kiss my ass while you relieve yourself. You can thank me for the honor after you cum."

That was the night the tables had turned on him, and thirteen years later, he was still striving to turn them around in his favor, but doubted he'd ever succeed. Madam owned him. He was her fool, her lap dog, and her willing servant.

When he returned from Europe, possessing all the knowledge one needed to perform the duties of a professional butler, he discovered that Quintoria had sold his family business and squandered the proceeds on a mansion and a few business investments. Everything she'd acquired was in her name only. Overnight, he had virtually become a pauper.

At that point, she informed him that he was no longer allowed to refer to her by her first name. While he was training in the Netherlands, she had joined a community of sexual deviants and now went by the moniker, Madam Midnight. She wanted to be referred to as Madam by her husband and the household staff she'd hired, which included Azalea. Azalea was the only person Madam allowed to call her Quintoria and sometimes Quinnie, for short.

CHAPTER 4

The butler made his rounds through the massive estate, checking on the pleasure-slaves who were being trained to do hard labor and also to excel in providing sexual pleasure. In the grand foyer, he happened upon two young women from the United Kingdom—Marnie from Ireland and Brynne from Scotland. They were supposedly busy scrubbing the marble floor, but were doing more giggling and gossiping than actual work.

Except for the cook and her two helpers (who were local women and also paid staff) the other members of the household were all willing pleasure-slaves from different parts of the United States and Europe. After completing an apprenticeship in Madam's residence the pleasure-slaves were given certificates and were considered distinguished and qualified to serve the wealthy elite, dignitaries, powerful politicians, and even European royalty.

The butler caught the tail end of the girls' conversation and from the gist of what he'd heard, he determined that Madam's personal handmaiden, Lyza, an exotic creature from Rio de Janeiro, Brazil, was involved in a torrid affair with Hugo, the stable hand. Hugo was a redneck from Alabama, much too uncouth to be intimate with Madam's favorite pleasure-slave.

On Madam's behalf, the butler would put a swift end to that filthy romance! It boiled his blood to think that someone who worked on such a personal level with Madam would be literally rolling around in the hay with a vulgar stable hand. The idea of the two of them copulating like animals during the course of the workday riled the butler enormously. He'd see to it that both Lyza and Hugo were severely disciplined, but he'd have to bide his time and punish them in secret.

Despite the Brazilian tart's unforgiveable transgression, Madam would not appreciate the butler chastising her personal property.

Making his presence known, he cleared his throat, startling Brynne and Marnie. He gave them a stern look that caused them both to tremble.

"No fraternizing among the staff," he harshly reminded the young women.

"Yes, sir," Brynne responded, her face flushed as she hurried to the other side of the large room. She busied herself by dusting a porcelain vase.

"Careful with that vase," he admonished. "It's from the Ming Dynasty—a rare Chinese work of art that should not be defaced with a feather duster. I want you to hand-wipe it lovingly—demonstrate care and reverence in every stroke."

"Yes, Mr. Hardwicke." Brynne put down the feather duster and retrieved a square of cloth from the pocket of her uniform.

"You're getting excellent training here, are you not, Brynne?"

"Yes, sir, I am."

"It would be a shame if your apprenticeship was suddenly terminated, wouldn't it?"

Brynne lowered her eyes and nodded. "A terrible shame, sir," she said in a voice that was hesitant, on the edge of a nervous stutter.

Satisfied that Brynne was sufficiently contrite, the butler turned his attention to Marnie. It was on the tip of his tongue to send her to the kitchen to help the cooks by peeling potatoes or scrubbing pots and pans, but he decided against it.

Azalea, with her disrespectful attitude and smart mouth, didn't deserve any extra help. She took advantage of the fact that she was Madam's childhood friend, but one of these days he was going to stuff his erection between Azalea's impertinent lips and teach her a thing or two about showing respect to her superiors. Until that day, he'd have to continue to come up with devious ways to chastise the cook.

"I want you to go upstairs and scrub and polish the floor in the linen room, Marnie."

"But I haven't finished in here, sir."

"Brynne will finish your duties down here. Now, off with you." He made a shooing motion with his hand.

The butler watched Marnie climb the palatial staircase and found himself distracted by the seductive sway of her hips. Marnie was a petite Irish beauty with alabaster skin and long raven hair that cascaded down her back. He briefly considered following her to the linen room, but a cursory glance at Brynne changed his mind. With a white cloth in her hand, Brynne fondled and caressed the exquisite vase in such a sensual manner there was a sudden and violent stirring in his loins.

With the stealth of a panther he crept behind Brynne and rubbed his hardened organ against her round bottom. She gave a soft gasp as his gloved hands cupped her outrageous D-cup breasts and lightly bounced them up and down.

"Keep working," he whispered as he ripped open the front of her uniform, delighting as buttons popped off and rolled over the marble floor. With her breasts exposed, he raked gloved fingers across her extra-large areolas and tweaked her nipples.

The stiff fabric of the gloves against Brynne's delicate skin evoked a moan from her lips as she continued to wipe Madam's cherished vase with a shaky hand.

"It's been awhile since we've spent quality time together, hasn't it, Brynne?"

"It's been a very long time, sir," she responded dutifully.

"The life of a lowly maid must be horribly depressing," he said as he gave her nipple a sharp pinch.

Brynne let out a tiny whimper and nodded briskly. "Yes, sir."

"In this household of over a dozen pleasure-slaves, you and Marnie work the longest hours and have to endure the harshest and most backbreaking chores. You girls are at the bottom of the heap," he said, shaking his head piteously. "Luckily, fortune has smiled upon you. I considered closeting myself in the linen room with Marnie, but my pity for you has given me a change of heart. I realize I'm a stern taskmaster, Brynne, but moments like this I find myself prone toward acts of kindness."

"You're very kind, sir," she said with her back to him, clutching the edge of the table while he groped her body, paying particular attention to her voluptuous breasts, which were as round and firm as cantaloupes. He toggled her dark rose-colored nipples until they became erect.

"Hopefully my kindness won't be taken for weakness," he said solemnly. "As you know I have a rotation system in this household, but I'm fond of you, Brynne. For your hard work and dedication, I want to give you a special treat. Now, bend over and spread your legs and allow me to brighten your otherwise dreary day."

With an arm around her waist, he thrust his sex into her, moving her golden brown hair to the side as he bit the back of her neck, softly growling as he imagined himself plunging into Madam. If his bitch of a wife happened to come traipsing down the stairs, catching him behaving so recklessly with a pleasure-slave and in such close proximity to her precious vase, there would be hell to pay.

Madam didn't allow the butler to squander his seed or share his magnificent cock with the domestic help or anyone else. Unless he was under the precise orders of Madam to fill the mouth or stab into the cunt of one of her many lovers, the butler's dick was supposed to stay zippered inside his pants.

The idea of Madam catching him in the act incited him to drive his shaft into Brynne as deeply and harshly as possible. As far as his wife knew, the butler found other women repugnant. No matter how many pretty servant girls were available, Madam believed it was beneath her husband's dignity to dally with any of the domestic help.

Imagining his wife's shock at finding him engaged in such illicit intimacy with a lowly scullery maid aroused him to the point of madness. With his nine-inch cock deeply embedded inside Brynne's hungry little cunt, he bit into the flesh of her neck and plowed into her, knocking her into the table that held Madam's treasured vase. A sudden and tremendous crash coincided with the butler's explosive climax.

Brynne's deep blue eyes bulged in horror as she gazed down at the shattered vase. "Oh, my God! Madam's vase is broken," she said in a quavering voice.

The butler continued stroking, as if trying to revive his softening member.

"Madam's vase is broken," she repeated in a terrified shriek.

Annoyed that she'd broken his concentration, the butler cursed as his dick plopped out of her. He whipped out a white hanky from his pocket and wiped off his glistening cock, and then stuffed it back inside his pants. Following Brynne's downward gaze, he stared at the jagged pieces of the porcelain vase that lay scattered around the room.

"Madam is going to be absolutely livid," he whispered in Brynne's ear. "No doubt, your apprenticeship will be terminated," he said gravely.

"B-but it was an accident," Brynne replied.

"I'll speak with her and try to persuade her to keep you on—at least on a part-time basis."

"But I need full-time training. My master sent me here for intense and rigorous training. He'll be furious with me if I return home without getting a certificate from Madam."

"You should have thought about that when you were carelessly handling Madam's most precious possession."

Shocked, Brynne turned around and faced the butler. "But I didn't break it; you were—"

"Madam doesn't tolerate impudent pleasure-slaves who lie and refuse to admit to their wrong doing."

Realizing that the butler expected her to take the blame for the broken vase, Brynne dropped her head in defeat and mumbled, "I take full responsibility, sir."

"Good. Wait here while I go deliver the disconcerting news to Madam."

There was a twinkle in his eyes as he headed toward the staircase. He was delighted to have a valid reason to break up his wife's despicable ménage-à-trois. As he ascended the stairs, he gazed out the floor-to-ceiling windows and noticed the darkening sky. A loud thunderclap preceded a sudden downpour. The bad weather set the tone for the grief Madam would experience after she discovered that her priceless vase had been destroyed.

Naked, Madam leapt from the bed and stared at her husband in utter shock after receiving the appalling news.

"I can't believe it! After two years of negotiating with the seller and after investing a small fortune, my beloved vase is ruined?"

The butter nodded grimly. "It's beyond repair, Madam—smashed to smithereens." He reached out a hand toward her. "Come see for yourself."

"I don't want to see it. Have that beast of a girl clean up the mess and then send her to me."

Madam's two blond playthings sat on the bed looking troubled. Although they couldn't understand the conversation between Madam and the butler, they sensed that the mood had shifted from erotic to somber. With the intention of lifting Madam's spirits, the brothers climbed out of bed and stood next to her, looking like beautifully sculpted bookends. They stroked her hair, rubbed her shoulders and breasts, but she pushed their hands away, finding their touches to be more annoying than soothing.

"Lips and tongues—not hands," she said, using one of the few English expressions the twins understood.

The boys immediately dropped to their knees. Christoff, the twin with the nipple rings, knelt before her lapping at her clean-shaven mons and sucked the protrusive fat clit that poked through while his brother, Arnoldus, assumed a position in the rear with his face flush with Madam's firm ass.

How the butler wished he could trade places with either twin. He gazed at his wife's jutting, chocolate-tipped nipples with intense yearning; his entire body in a state of sexual hunger.

"Madam, may I?" he asked in a tremulous voice, nervously biting his bottom lip as he stepped toward her.

"May you what?"

He cleared his throat. "If it pleases Madam, may I join your guests in providing you pleasure? Your beautiful breasts are being neglected and I, your devoted servant, would love nothing more than to lavish them with attention."

"I'm sure you would, Butler," she said with mocking laughter. "But your particular skillset is better suited in dealing with household matters. Now go downstairs and supervise those crude trainees who obviously have no business working inside a civilized home."

Suddenly Madam gasped and thrust her hips forward as Christoff began rolling the tip of his tongue over her jutting clit. It was a struggle for her to talk during the onslaught of dual pleasure. Gasping and undulating, she said to the butler, "Bring the klutzy girl who broke my vase to my chambers. I want to have a word with her in exactly thirty minutes."

"As you wish, Madam." He bowed elegantly and with unfailing courtesy, he backed out the doorway.

Outside Madam's chambers, he massaged his dick, wincing as he attempted to relieve some of the coiled tension inside his pants. He pulled out his pocket watch and scowled—he had less than twenty-nine minutes to grab one of the pleasure-slaves and have his urges satisfied.

CHAPTER 5

At the end of the corridor, the sound of a scrub brush scratching against hardwood flooring drew his attention to the linen room. Striding with purpose he made his way to the area of the house where Marnie was working.

Hearing the butler's approach, Marnie's heartbeat quickened. Sensing him standing there, silently looming in the doorway, no doubt critiquing her work, she dared not look up. She wiped back a curl that was plastered to her sweaty forehead and began scrubbing harder than ever.

The butler cleared his throat and Marnie reluctantly looked up.

"I'm disappointed in you, Marnie. The time you wasted blathering with that idiot, Brynne, could have been spent perfecting your cleaning skills." He scowled down at the floor. "Your work is sloppy—quite unacceptable. You're slow and inefficient, you stupid, wretched girl."

"I'm sorry, sir."

"You should be finished scrubbing and on to polishing by now." He looked at her through narrowed eyes. "If you want certification from House of Stevens, then you'd better start taking pride in your chores."

"Yes, Mr. Hardwicke," she said dipping the scrub brush into the bucket of soapy water.

"That's enough scrubbing! It's time to move on to polishing," the butler said impatiently.

"But…I can't polish the floor until I've finished giving it a thorough scrubbing, sir."

"I'm not referring to the floor, you worthless moron."

Marnie parted her lips to utter an apology but no words emerged. With her pretty face flushed in humiliation and her lips trembling in fear, the butler found her to be absolutely enchanting. He could feel heat surging through his body as he imagined her pretty lips puckered around his mighty weapon. He freed his cock from his pants, and it throbbed so violently, he had to tussle with it to keep it within his grasp.

"What are you waiting for?" the butler raged.

Wearing a confused expression, Marnie held up the rag she had planned to use to polish the floor. "Do you want me to stop scrubbing and begin polishing the floor?"

The butler made a scoffing sound. "Forget about polishing the floor, you blithering idiot. You won't need that rag to polish my cock!" With his hand locked around the base of his dick, he took steps toward the terror-stricken girl.

Wearing a doomed expression, Marnie took a breath and shifted her position in order to rise from the floor.

"Stay put," he said sharply and pressed down on her shoulder. "As I've told you in the past, the best knob-jobs are performed with the maid on her knees. And remember, it is your duty to suck me off with grace and poise."

Performing in the manner in which she had been taught, Marnie inched closer to the butler, tilted her head back and stretched her mouth open. Striving to accommodate his enormous length and girth, she closed her eyes and did her best to relax her throat.

But no matter how many times she'd endeavored to suck the butler's gargantuan dick with grace and poise, she always gagged. Tears always spilled from her eyes. And this time was no different.

He grabbed her by the hair and pulled her head back further, spearing her throat with his massive cock.

"Massage your neck to relax your throat," the butler instructed as he pushed a few more thick inches down her throat.

Gasping for breath, Marnie obeyed, frantically rubbing the front of her neck in an attempt to relax her throat muscles so she could successfully deep throat her superior. But her gagging and choking interfered with the butler's pleasure. Agitated, he yanked his dick out of her mouth. "You're hopeless," he said vehemently.

"I'm sorry, sir. Let me try again."

He eyed his pocket watch. "There's no time to monkey around with you. Do you realize that the female servants in this house all vie with one another for the opportunity to suck my cock?"

"Yes, I'm aware, sir." Marnie's long lashes fluttered as she lowered her eyes in humility.

"You have absolutely no appreciation for the time I've taken to instruct you in the art of fellatio. By now, you should be a highly skilled cock sucker."

The more the butler raged at her and called her names, the wetter her tight little cunt became. "I'll get better at it, sir. I promise."

With a grunt of disgust, the butler gazed at his pocket watch and then grabbed Marnie by her dark hair and yanked her head back. "I can't waste any more time with you. Take in as much dick as you can manage and then suck on it with vigor."

With half of the butler's hard dick gliding in and out of her mouth, Marnie sucked and slurped, licking around the smooth crown as if her very life depended on it. The moment his cock began to pulse and quiver, she parted her lips as wide as possible, offering the warm soft inside of her mouth as a convenient cum-receptacle.

But the butler had other ideas. He gripped the base of his heavy dick and aimed for Marnie's face, splashing her alabaster skin with his secretion. Hot cum spurted into her nostrils and burned her eyes, but she didn't utter a word of complaint. "Thank you, sir," she whispered, her tongue darting out and lapping up the drippings that encircled her mouth.

With his handkerchief, the butler wiped away saliva and traces of cum that glazed his flaccid dick. Marnie watched with a lustful gaze. "Shall I lick it back to life, sir?" she asked, her small delicate hand easing between her thighs, her caressing fingers circling her firm clit, striving to dull the throbbing ache.

"No, that'll be all for now, Marnie. We'll continue your deep-throat lessons in a week or two."

Panic shone in Marnie's eyes. "A week or two, sir?"

"Yes, I'm taking you out of rotation."

"Why, sir?" she asked with pleading eyes.

He met her gaze with a cruel glint in his eyes. "At the rate you're going, you're never going to finish your apprenticeship, and Madam will never write a letter of recommendation for you. How do you expect to be accepted for service inside an affluent household if you're unable to perform proper fellatio on the master of the house as well as his distinguished friends?"

"I'm trying, sir. By the way, sir… Marnie paused. "I'm not training to work in an affluent home."

"What are you training for?"

"To be sold on the auction block. My master is a heavy gambler; whenever he gets low on funds, he auctions me off for six months."

"Then what's the problem? Why'd he send you here?"

"I don't have a good reputation with other masters in Ireland. I'm considered crass and ill-trained, and I was sent here to become refined enough to get a good price for my master."

"I see. And if your master is that down on his luck, then who is paying for your apprenticeship here at House of Stevens?"

"I'm a charity case, sir. But if I become well-trained, Madam will take sixty percent of the profit when I'm sold at auction." Marnie swallowed. "It's important that I learn all that I can. My master can be a cruel man when he has money troubles."

Hmm. So my greedy wife is not only earning a small fortune from training pleasure-slaves but she's also earning income from sales at the International Underground Auction Block.

The butler checked the time and lifted a brow in alarm. "I must report to Madam. Meanwhile, I strongly suggest that you take some initiative and begin practicing on bananas, elongated cucumbers, and hefty eggplants. At the rate you're going, you'll never get sold."

"Mr. Hardwicke, would you be kind enough to…" Marnie's voice trailed off and she gave the butler a pleading look as she slowly lifted her uniform, revealing a nest of glossy raven pubic hair.

"Lower your uniform, you brazen little trollop. You're getting above yourself, flashing your greedy little cunt at me without permission. It is horribly smug of you to presume that your selfish desires would possibly matter to me."

Marnie quickly dropped the skirt of her uniform and apologized profusely.

The butler shook his head disgustedly. "I'm of a mind to give you a sound spanking, but lucky for you, I simply don't have the time. However, the next time you disrespect your betters with such wanton behavior, I shall bend you tightly over my knee and spank you until you beg for mercy."

The butler's threat caused tears to spring to Marnie's eyes. He looked at her without pity. Groaning and rolling his eyes in frustration, he said, "Pull yourself together and get on with your work."

Shoulders squared, head held high, he marched out of the linen room. He always felt good about himself and was better able to endure his wife's abuse after chastising a servant or two.

CHAPTER 6

Madam studied Brynne with disdain. "The vase you destroyed was a priceless heirloom. It took months of negotiation for me to acquire it."

"I'm truly sorry, Madam." Brynne spoke with her eyes lowered.

"Your apology is worthless. How foolish of you to hand-wipe such a treasure. Any nincompoop with half a brain should know that one should very carefully feather dust such a remarkable work of art."

"I was ordered to hand wipe the vase."

"Ordered by whom?"

Brynne lifted her eyes and cast a glance at the butler. He met her eyes with a scathing gaze, prompting her to drop her eyes. "No one ordered me, Madam. I took it upon myself. I wanted to please Madam by giving the vase a spectacular shine."

"Then you're a spectacularly stupid girl. Clumsy and untrainable in my opinion. Pack your things; you're going back to Scotland."

"Please, Madam, don't send me back. I'll do better. I'll work harder than ever if you'll kindly give me another chance to finish my apprenticeship."

"Why should I? You've proven yourself to be utterly worthless. In fact, you're a terrible liability." Madam glanced downward, examining her fingernails. "I prefer to cut my losses—leave this house at once!"

"I beg you to reconsider, Madam. I'll do anything to continue training in your fine home."

"My reputation would be tarnished forever if I were to send an inept and clumsy girl such as you to work inside the refined homes of my esteemed acquaintances. You only have yourself to blame; now pack up and go," Madam said with finality.

"But I have other skills, Madam," Brynne blurted in desperation.

Madam lifted a brow. "Such as…"

"I can take a harsh whipping, Madam. And…and I can vigorously suck and deep throat cocks of various sizes."

Madam looked at Brynne with renewed interest. "I've never taken the cane to you, so how is it possible for you to withstand harsh whippings?"

"My step-mum, Madam. She caned my ass regularly."

Madam nodded. "And what about the dick sucking—is your step-mother responsible for teaching you that skill as well?"

Brynne blushed and cut an eye at the butler, prepared to reveal that since the beginning of her apprenticeship, he'd been teaching her the art of fellatio. But when the butler glared at her, Brynne thought better of tattling on him.

"I'm ashamed to admit that back in Scotland, I was somewhat of a floozy." Looking contrite, she swallowed nervously. "Dick sucking is second nature to a slut like me. I can take a cock all the way down my gullet. Two cocks at once if it pleases you, Madam."

Having second thoughts about casting Brynne out, Madam leaned forward. "If you can successfully suck off two cocks at once, then I might consider keeping you here."

Overcome with gratitude, Brynne rushed toward Madam, dropped down to her knees and pressed her lips against Madam's slipper. "Thank you, ma'am. I won't disappoint."

"I'll be the judge of that." Madam lifted a silver bell and jangled it. Almost instantaneously, the blond twins entered the bedroom, completely naked.

"Here's an opportunity for you to flaunt your skills," Madam said to Brynne and then gestured for the twins to step forward.

The boys grasped their rigid cocks and Brynne sighed with relief. Blowing the twins would be easy; their two cocks combined didn't equal the size of the butler's huge dick. Confident she could win the approval of the mistress of the house, Brynne moistened her lips and scooted over to the twins. She parted her lips invitingly and sucked in Christoff. Taking the initiative, she reached out a hand, encouraging Arnoldus to join his brother inside her warm and willing mouth.

Once Arnoldus had squeezed his cock inside her mouth, she reached around and cupped both boys' asses, pulling them in more deeply. Putting on a show for Madam, Brynne made loud, sucking sounds while swirling her tongue along the slits of their dicks, inciting the twins to gasp and buck their hips while speaking Norwegian.

Trickles of perspiration slid down the sides of Madam's face. She gripped the sides of the wingback chair as she viewed the tawdry exhibition.

Eager to cater to Madam, the butler retrieved a tissue from her vanity table and stood by her side, devotedly wiping droplets of sweat, while being careful not to obstruct her view. Madam emitted a soft sound of distress and the butler glanced at her, noting how she'd slumped in her seat wearing an expression of distress.

"It would be an honor to assist you, Madam," said the butler.

Grimacing, Madam shook her head and kept her gaze on Brynne and the twins. When Brynne began making gurgling sounds as if being strangled by the two prodding dicks, Madam crossed her legs and moaned.

"There's no reason for you to suffer for even a moment when I, your devoted servant, am at your side ready to serve you."

With a sigh, Madam nodded.

In an instant the butler was down of one knee. Kneeling at the side of her grand chair, with his back erect, eyes looking straight ahead, he reached out an arm and snaked his hand beneath Madam's dressing gown. It had been so long since he'd been allowed to probe her juicy wet cunt with a thick finger, it took every ounce of the butler's willpower not to cry out in gratitude and passion.

Madam humped on the butler's finger for a while and then widened her legs.

Eager to cater to his wife's every whim, he obliged her by inserting two additional beefy fingers inside her hot cunt. Amazingly, he maintained a stoic expression throughout the duration of the three-finger-fuck session.

On the edge, both Christoff and Arnoldus cried out and began shuddering violently. In sync with the twins, Madam thrust her hips forward as she spurted silken cream all over the butler's fingers.

After Madam's breathing returned to normal, the butler slowly and tenderly removed his fingers and brought the cream-covered digits up to his lips. But before he had the opportunity to lap her juices from his fingers, Madam said sharply, "Where are your manners, Butler? The dessert on your fingers is for my guests."

"Please, Madam." He choked out the words, clearly distressed.

She glowered at the butler. "Feed my guests!"

Forlorn, he rose to his feet and took elegant strides across the room where the twins lay in a heap on the floor, panting from the double orgasm they'd received from Brynne.

It tickled Brynne to see Mr. Hardwicke, who tormented her on a daily basis, being treated with such contempt by Madam, whom she'd heard through gossip was actually the butler's wife.

The butler knelt down and finger-fed each boy. He thought about sneaking the third cum-coated finger into his own hungry mouth until Madam interfered. "I believe the maid should be rewarded with the remainder of the dessert."

Begrudgingly, the butler poked a finger inside Brynne's mouth. His dick hardened unbearably as the maid greedily slurped up Madam's delicious juices.

Feeling both irate and horny as he escorted Brynne back to the grand foyer where Madam had instructed her to continue her chores, the butler decided to make a pit stop to his bedroom, which was a dreary and uninviting space in the attic. All the other servants were housed in dormitories on a lower level of the house.

Making long and swift strides up and down a series of corridors, he steered Brynne to his private chamber. When they reached the remote stairs that led to the attic, a worried look crossed Brynne's face. "What's up there?"

"Paradise," the butler said with a sneaky grin.

"Uh, Madam has put me on probation, and I don't want to agitate her further by not finishing my chores."

The butler smirked at Brynne. "There's plenty of time to finish your chores. Now do as I say."

Reluctantly, Brynne followed the butler up the creaky stairs and into the attic that had been transformed into a bedroom. She gave a shudder when she entered the claustrophobically small area. Squinting in the gloom of the ill-lighted room, she immediately noticed that the room was immaculate with every item neatly in its place. She scanned the butler's private chamber, noting that the bed was made up so tightly a quarter could bounce off of it. His grooming items were lined up in a neat row on top of the bureau, and displayed on a rack were extra pairs of shoes that shone so brightly they seemed to provide illumination to the dim room.

The walls were beige and bare and the sparsely furnished room was devoid of anything decorative. Figuring it poor taste to openly gaze around the butler's personal space, Brynne kept her head bowed, hands folded in front of her, furtively stealing glances. From her peripheral vision she saw a hook next to the bed from which a doubled leather strap dangled ominously. Sensing that the butler had brought her to his room for nefarious reasons, Brynne shrank back and wrapped her arms around herself fearfully.

He gave a wry chuckle as he closed the door and engaged the lock. "Don't pretend to be demure and innocent when you're nothing more than a vulgar little tart. Despite your whorishness, I'm aroused by the idea that you were raised to withstand harsh whippings." He rubbed his gloved hands together and gazed at Brynne with sinister delight. "Let's find out how much punishment you can actually endure."

The butler crossed the room and removed the strap from the hook and began to caress it.

Brynne's eyes became large as she experienced a frisson of fear. "Mr. Hardwicke, sir, you misunderstood me. My step-mum never beat me with objects—she always used her open hand across my bare ass. She was a strong woman and she didn't need to use any kind of device to inflict pain upon me."

"Hush! Not another word from you, you despicable girl. You destroyed Madam's most cherished possession and it's my duty to ensure that you're appropriately punished."

"But Madam already punished me!" Brynne's voice scaled up in fear.

"The lewd exhibition that took place in Madam's bedchambers wasn't punishment at all. I saw a glint of pleasure in your eyes as you guzzled those twin dicks." He shook his head and frowned. "Madam is much too lenient with the trainees and that is why I must take the liberty of dispensing harsh punishment when necessary. Now remove your uniform—I want the sting of this leather to directly connect with your naked skin."

In a panic, Brynne whirled around and futilely tried to unlock the door. Unable to disengage the heavy bolt, she began pleading for mercy.

Angry, the butler stalked toward her with the looped strap in hand. "Be quiet," he hissed. "Hysterics will not be tolerated. Over time, you'll learn to welcome our discipline sessions. Your whory cunt will drool in anticipation whenever I raise my strap."

Brynne recoiled, her face wrinkled in a grimace.

"You need to realize that it's not Madam who rules this house—I do! Madam's nothing more than a figurehead. Although she barks out a litany of never-ending demands, I'm the one who gets into the trenches with you novices. My hands-on approach transforms ordinary submissives into highly sought-after pleasure-slaves. I train you people to serve in the most prestigious households around the world. Madam has more interest in her self-indulgences than in actually taking the time to instruct the trainees that are under her tutelage. She's so self-centered—so egotistical," he said, shaking his head bitterly. "She has no idea of the lengths I go through to ensure that this household retains its stellar reputation for turning out the finest pleasure-slaves from anywhere around the globe. Now, quit your whining and strip out of your uniform."

Brynne slowly removed her uniform and stood naked before the butler. Biting her lip despairingly, she gave him an utterly defeated look.

Unmoved by Brynne's forlorn expression, he impatiently gestured for her to turn around, and when she didn't move quickly enough, he gripped her by the shoulder and physically jerked her around, slamming her against the door. She let out a surprised screech as the first blow of the strap caught her on the back of a thigh.

"Silence," he implored, landing an even heavier blow across her rounded buttocks. Aiming with expert precision and brute force, the butler struck her relentlessly while Brynne, flinching and twisting, tried to avoid the harsh sting of the belt.

Craning her neck she caught sight of the angry red marks that had begun forming on her buttocks. "Please, master. Please don't hit me again."

The crimson welts on Brynne's white ass deeply aroused the butler, but it was the manner in which she pleaded that truly stirred his loins. No one had ever called him *master* before and the sound of the esteemed title so greatly affected him, he groaned and involuntarily lowered the arm that was raised high and poised to strike again. His fingers unfurled and the belt dropped from his hand. Overcome with lust, he snatched off his gloves and flung them on top of the neatly-made bed.

Breathing heavily, he hastily unzipped his pants. "Madam should have cast you out of the house after your deplorable behavior, but you impressed her with your remarkable fellatio skills. Now, I want you to impress me. Turn around, Brynne."

Brynne immediately turned and faced the butler.

"I want you to suck my dick as if your very life depends upon it."

Grateful that the flogging session was over, she nodded and sniffled, wiping tears from her eyes. Then she drew in a deep breath as she prepared to give an unforgettable performance.

Using both hands she gingerly held the butler's dick and took in the sight of it and then kissed the head worshipfully. "Thank you for having pity on me, master," she whispered seductively, having caught on to the fact that being called 'master' was pleasing to the butler's ears.

"You're a wretched little Scottish cunt—not worthy of sucking this juicy dick meat," he said in a husky tone that was a combination of desire and disdain.

"You're right, master. I'm unworthy of the privilege of sucking your cock." Brynne smiled with satisfaction when she noticed pre-cum bubbling out of the small opening in his cock. Surely, he'd never beat her again if she gave him an excellent blowjob. Leisurely, she licked the shimmery droplets and murmured, "Mmm, your dick meat tastes delicious, master."

Worked into a frenzy of desire, the butler thrust himself so deeply his dick hit the back of Brynne's throat, causing her eyes to fill with tears. She pulled back, sucking only half of his huge cock. Trying to make up for her inability to swallow him whole, she bobbed her head up and down enthusiastically, sucking his beefy dick with fervor, swirling her tongue around the head and making loud slurping sounds.

"Suck the whole thing," he demanded and grabbed two fistfuls of her hair, forcing her head to remain in place as he drove his thickness past her comfort zone and caused her to heave and choke. "My dick is twice the size of those little-dick Nordic twins, isn't it?" he demanded to know, but Brynne, gagging violently was unable to speak.

The butler's dick pulsed ferociously as it stretched its way down her throat. Annoyed that Brynne was slumped to the side and unresponsive to his question, he thrust into her windpipe with such force, she made a gurgling sound as her eyes began to roll into the back of her head.

It filled him with pride to realize that his dick was so immense and powerful, it was a lethal weapon with the ability to end Brynne's worthless life if he so chose.

On the brink of an orgasm, his body shook. "Suck this good dick, Quintoria, you bitch," he bellowed, using Madam's first name instead of Brynne's. After verbalizing his festering resentment toward his wife, he released a torrent of cum into Brynne's mouth. Suddenly, her eyes popped open as she was brought gasping back into consciousness.

Smiling with satisfaction, he shook off the last drops of creamy cum onto Brynne's lips, which she greedily lapped up as if the cumdrops were a highly sought after elixir.

He watched her polishing off the head of his dick with her warm tongue and he felt god-like in the knowledge that his big almighty cock was capable of restoring life as easily as it could take it away.

CHAPTER 7

Christoff and Arnoldus had been sent to Madam by Countess Inga Hedvig—a hedonistic woman who was willing to pay a small fortune for the boys to be properly tutored in the art of submission before being presented at the Royal House of Norway.

But Madam wasn't happy with the arrangements. Why should she use her great skills to train the boys so that the countess could curry favor with Norway's royal family? Though Madam's vast wealth was derived from many sources, a large part of her fortune came from training willing submissives into perfect servitors for their affluent owners. Oddly, the submissives came from not only the lower classes but from all walks of life.

A year ago, she'd trained a beautiful Oscar-winning Hollywood actress who enjoyed being subservient. That actress was sold on the underground auction block for a billion dollars. Madam's training fee for the actress and the commission she earned after the sale had been her largest profit to date.

But in the situation regarding the twins, it wasn't merely about money. It was also about power. Madam yearned to associate with members of the Norwegian monarchy. She envisioned herself partying regularly at the palace in Oslo, Norway. She intended to socialize with the king and queen on such a personal level that wherever she went, she'd be whisked either by motorcade or helicopter. Powerful people did not have to sit in traffic. It was her biggest fantasy to have the king and queen eating out of the palm of her hand. All she needed was an introduction and she'd take care of the rest. With her powers of seduction it would be easy to have the king nibbling on her chocolate-tipped breasts while the queen feasted between her legs.

Oh, the very thought was intoxicating!

Therefore, if Countess Hedvig didn't see fit to arrange an introduction between Madam and the Norwegian monarchy, then Madam wasn't interested in providing formal training to the twins.

Although the blond hunks were wonderful eye candy and were completely obedient, she was willing to suffer the loss of their beautifully docile presence as well as a sizeable sum from the countess's bank account to get the ultimate prize: the opportunity to rule a country—behind the scenes, of course. Real power was always wielded behind the scenes.

And she should know. The preeminent filmmaker, Renauld St. Jacques, who was notorious for instilling terror in actors, the film crew, and who thought nothing of resorting to intimidation tactics to keep studio heads in line, was putty in the hands of Madam Midnight. She recalled fondly how he'd stormed off the set immediately after throwing one of his infamous tantrums. Holed up in his trailer where he was assumed to be sulking, the petulant director was actually catering to Madam's every whim and being spanked soundly when he didn't live up to her expectations of devotion and obedience.

The tyrant director had returned to the set with an ass so profoundly sore it prevented him from sitting in his director's chair. For the duration of that day, he worked cinema magic while standing on his feet for many hours. He often told Madam that he was able to create some of his best work after being disciplined by her.

Through her association with Renauld St. Jacques, Madam had wormed her way into the film industry. The prominent director's influence had opened doors for her and now she was a notable producer with a host of A-list celebrities clamoring for her attention.

After conquering the film industry and after securing numerous successful business ventures, she was ready to take on a new challenge. She gazed at the twins who were now dozing in her massive bed, their tousled heads nestled together. *You boys are going to get me the keys to the castle*, she said to herself while smiling fondly at the beautiful brothers.

Wearing a loosely knotted red silken robe, Madam Midnight sat in an ornate high-back chair with a phone pressed against her ear.

"Yes, I agree the twins are a novelty," Madam said, speaking to Countess Hedvig of Norway, the owner of Christoff and Arnoldus. "But being a novelty doesn't make one suitable for a life of servitude."

Bored, Madam glanced at her nails as the countess prattled on and on about being willing to increase the payment they'd agreed upon if only Madam would transform the twins into pleasure-slaves with qualities so superior as to delight dignitaries as high up the social ladder as the Norwegian monarchy.

Madam's ears perked when the countess mentioned her close relationship with the royal couple. "Countess, we agreed that I would spend two days evaluating the twins and I've concluded that they're obstinate, clumsy, and completely untrainable."

The countess gasped. "But they're not obstinate. They're dear, sweet boys…always eager to please in every way they can."

"Listen, I'm the expert and I say that working with them would require more time than I'm willing to expend. I'm willing to for-go the fee for the evaluation and put them on a flight back to Norway this evening. I'm sure you can find someone with more patience than me who'd be willing to continue their training."

"B-but no other training academy can hold a candle to House of Stevens. Do you realize I was put on a six-month wait list merely for you to evaluate the twins?"

"I'm well aware," Madam said dryly.

"There's an exclusive party in Sweden at the end of the month in which I had planned to present the twins. Everyone who is someone will be in attendance with their most beloved submissives. My boys need extensive training in order to keep up with the well-trained pleasure-slaves being presented by elite members of society: business tycoons, entrepreneurs, corporate executives, financiers, socialites, star athletes, actors, actresses, and super models. The best of the very best! I have no problem doubling your fee if you'd please get the twins trained in time for party."

Madam sighed audibly. "I'm not easily persuaded but..." She paused, taking an extended breath. "If you could finagle an invitation for me to attend a social gathering hosted by the queen of Norway, I'd be willing to make the sacrifice of training your uncivilized twins. Oh, and you'd also have to double my fee."

"The royal family is very particular about who gets invited to their festivities, but you're more than welcome to accompany me to...uh...perhaps afternoon tea with the queen."

Madam frowned but injected a smile into her voice. "How soon can you arrange a tea date for the queen and me?"

"I'm not sure. Special appointments have to be made. To merely speak to the queen's secretary can be an exercise in fortitude. But I promise you that I will work tirelessly to obtain an invitation for tea with her royal majesty."

"I'm looking forward to it. Meanwhile, the twins will begin training on Monday."

"Splendid! Thank you so much for accepting them into your program."

"Bear in mind that you won't be able to visit them or even speak with them over the phone during the intensive six-week apprenticeship."

"Six weeks? No, no, that's entirely too long. As I told you, I need them to be ready to accompany me to the party in Sweden at the end of the month."

"And as I told you, my program lasts for six weeks. Take it or leave it," Madam said firmly.

"I'll take it."

After getting off the phone with Countess Hedvig, Madam pressed a button on her phone and shortly afterward the butler rapped softly on her door.

"Enter, servant," she said in a strong and tightly controlled voice.

"I'm at your service, Madam," the butler responded. He yearned to be ordered to kneel before her and kiss the bejeweled slippers on her feet. He ached with the desire to sniff between her firm, velvety thighs and to dip his tongue into her syrupy pool of juices. He moistened his lips as he imagined being bestowed with the extreme honor of licking her slit clean and then sucking her distended clit.

Madam nudged her head toward the twins. "Get those lugs out of my bed and drag them to the servants' dormitories. They'll be joining the new recruits on Monday morning, but in the meanwhile they can help out in the stables."

The only sign that the butler was disappointed that Madam hadn't requested him to attend to her more intimate needs was a slight twitch in his face. He straightened his posture and assumed a stoic expression as he strode toward the sleeping twins. Taking his frustration out on the pretty-faced boys, he grabbed two handfuls of blond curls and yanked them out of bed.

Shocked by the unexpected aggression, the twins struggled to break free of his grip. Frantic, they spoke Norwegian and stared at Madam beseechingly.

Madam gave the twins the thinnest of smiles. "Sadly, you two have failed to meet my high standards and now playtime is over—it's time for you boys to begin learning to behave like proper pleasure-slaves." She made shooing motions with both hands. "Get these miserable good-for-nothings out of my face. I'm exhausted from struggling to communicate with them. I don't want to see them again until they've learned to say in impeccable English, 'Yes, Madam' and 'It is my pleasure to serve you, Madam.' Do you understand, me, Butler?"

"Yes, I understand you perfectly, Madam." The butler tugged the twins along.

Being the most daring of the two, Christoff suddenly broke free and shot across the room toward Madam. Flinging himself at her feet, he sobbed openly as he begged in his native language to stay with her in her private quarters.

Madam glowered at Christoff, who had taken the liberty of kneeling before her without permission. She tried to snatch her slippers away from his kissing lips, but he clutched at her ankles.

"As you can see, Butler, this one has atrocious manners. His mistress has spoiled him rotten and he obviously doesn't know his place."

Christoff spoke to Madam in rapid Norwegian and there was panic in his voice. Judging from his stunned expression, he didn't understand why Madam had suddenly begun to treat him with such disdain.

Madam kicked at Christoff, but the audacious young man insisted upon tearing one of her slippers off and covering her foot with adoring kisses.

Livid, Madam leaned downward and gave Christoff a sound smack across the face. Shocked, he placed a hand over his reddened face and then awkwardly scooted backward, rejoining his brother.

Madam turned her gaze upon the butler. "I'm overwhelmed with running my various corporations, and I can't seem to muster the energy it takes to properly train students anymore. Those two Nordic beauties are expected to service aristocrats and perhaps even members of the royal family of Norway. But if I don't get them up to speed, I fear my prominent standing in the fetish community will be greatly diminished."

Seizing the opportunity to be of service, the butler cleared his throat. "Madam, if I may…"

Madam made a noise of exasperation deep in her throat, and then nodded her head, reluctantly granting the butler permission to speak.

"I realize I've only been useful in overseeing domestic matters. However, over the years I've observed the superb work you've done with multitudes of poorly trained submissives and I sincerely believe that if you allow me to take these twins under my wing, I can smooth out their rough edges and enhance their level of training until they've been completely transformed into magnificent pleasure-slaves. With rigorous training I can program them to only become sexually aroused when they're in service to their betters."

"I couldn't possibly entrust you with such a vital role in their training when your sexual experience during the last thirteen years has been so utterly limited. Let's be honest, Butler, you're practically a 'Eunuch.' If I didn't allow you the occasional dalliances with my pleasure-slaves, you'd have no sex life at all—well, aside from the manual release you enjoy when you're alone in your attic-abode. I find it preposterous that you think yourself capable of training the twins to do anything other than clean and serve meals."

Her words dripped with contempt, shooting down his suggestion and callously ridiculing his virility. The butler felt a rush of shame along with a thrilling sensation coursing through his system. He dropped his head and bit the inside of his bottom lip. It was all he could do to try to prevent an erection. It was so pathetic—the way his wife controlled him. She could get his dick hard by merely spewing cruel words and making a mockery of him. He placed his hands over his growing embarrassment and bit down even harder on his lip.

Madam's gaze went from the butler's shamed face and down to his concealed crotch. "Remove your hands," she demanded.

"Madam, please," he uttered, croaking out the words.

"Do not defy me, Butler. Remove your hands this instant."

Helplessly, his hands fell to his sides, revealing a quivering thickness that writhed like a large snake.

She glanced at his erection and smiled, a crooked twist in one corner of her mouth. "You're pathetic and you have absolutely no discipline. A good trainer must be able to control his lust, anger, jealousy, and his desperate yearning for love." She turned up her nose and spat out the word *love* and as if it were a disgusting disease.

"Madam, I become weak in your presence. Your beauty and power render me—"

"Excuses, excuses, I've heard it all before. Now shut your mouth and crawl to me, you sniveling fool."

"As you wish." The butler lowered himself to his hands and knees and carefully crawled toward his wife. It was embarrassing for the twins to see him being treated like a common pleasure-slave but the treat that awaited him was well worth the humiliation.

Madam leaned back in the high back chair. The way she tilted her chin and tossed her head was regal and commanding like a queen. Slowly, she parted her silken robe, welcoming the butler's face between her thighs.

CHAPTER 8

There was a tinkling sound of gently splashing water as Madam Midnight rose from her mint-scented bath. Like magic her handmaiden, Lyza, appeared in the enormous, ultra-chic room holding out an oversized luxurious towel. Lyza, with her glorious caramel skin, sensual pouting lips, and long ringlets of chestnut-colored hair had been with Madam for only ten months, yet had become proficient in anticipating her mistress's needs as if she'd been catering to her whims for many years.

Unlike the other maids who wore drab one-piece shapeless uniforms, Lyza wore a sexy maid costume that consisted of a skimpy top, short skirt, frilly apron, fishnet stockings, and removable garter.

With careful movements, she wrapped the towel around Madam, gently dabbing her damp skin. "Your Vera Wang was delivered an hour ago," Lyza said softly. "The train of the gown is a lot longer and heavier than I'd realized and I won't be able to handle it by myself. I have Brynne and Marnie, the trainees from the United Kingdom, on standby to accompany us to the Secret Sunset Gala and help carry the train of your dress."

"Hmm, I'm not sure about that," Madam uttered, peering upward, deep in thought.

"If you prefer having the twins escort you to the gala, I'll summon them from the stables and make sure they clean up and dress appropriately," Lyza added quickly.

"No, those two trainees will be fine if I decide I actually want to attend Colden's tawdry little affair."

Lyza wrinkled her brow. "I thought you were looking forward to Master Colden's Secret Sunset Gala. You've been talking about it for weeks."

"I've been attending Colden's various dinner parties and other events for years. And frankly, I doubt if he'll dazzle me with anything I haven't already seen or experienced. It would be a pity to waste couture fashion on a dull, unimaginative party. Through my association with Countess Hedvig, I've been invited to a very special festivity at the Royal House of Norway…" Madam paused and waited for Lyza's reaction.

"The Royal House of Norway?" Lyza squealed with an appropriate degree of joy.

Convinced that she would secure an invitation to an evening gathering, Madam did not feel that she was lying or even stretching the truth. "My custom designed Vera Wang, which took six months to create, is much too magnificent to be wasted on a little shindig hosted by Colden."

"Should I remove the gown from your bedchamber and put it in storage?"

"Yes. If I decide to attend Colden's dreary get-together, I'll wear the ivory and gold Dior gown. It doesn't have a train requiring me to suffer the company of those vile scullery maids. But then again…maybe I'll take Brynne to the gala with me. That dimwitted girl broke my Chinese vase and hasn't been sufficiently punished.

"Colden has been dying to get his sadistic hands on her. Perhaps tonight I'll grant him a half-hour flogging session with Brynne."

"As you wish, Madam. I'll let Brynne know that she is to accompany you to the gala. Do you want her to dress in her regular uniform or should she wear something special?"

"Her regular drab uniform will be perfect. But I want her to be bare-assed—not a stich of underwear."

"Absolutely, Madam. Although they're crude and ignorant, the trainees know better than to cover their intimate parts," Lyza assured her mistress.

"Brynne doesn't know how to dust an exquisite vase without shattering it to smithereens, so I can't assume she has any information in her thick head."

"I could pack your personal riding crop or one of your favorite paddles should Madam choose to demonstrate her displeasure with Brynne in front of the guests at the gala," Lyza suggested as she delicately dried Madam's perfectly sculpted breasts.

"No, that won't be necessary. I have something more diabolical in mind."

Colden's annual gala wasn't the monotonous affair that Madam had presumed it would be. Upon entering the mansion that Colden had leased for the evening, she was immediately impressed by the glamor of the event. In a ballroom illuminated only by twinkling candlelight, naked men and women sprayed with silver body paint served libations carried on a silver tray held high in the air. Naked silver-painted contortionists hung from the ceiling like human chandeliers. The ambiance was hauntingly beautiful, yet decadent at the same time.

"Good evening, Madam Midnight, and welcome to the Secret Sunset Gala," Colden greeted and then respectfully kissed her hand. "I'm sure you'll enjoy all of the festivities I've planned for the evening." He waved a hand around the vast ballroom where invited guests were dressed in formal evening attire while the servers and other willing pleasure-slaves were naked—some wearing body paint and others adorned only with sleek silver collars around their necks.

"If you see anything that interests you, simply let me know. The owners in attendance would be honored for you to use their pleasure-slaves in any way you see fit," Colden offered. "My guests would also be exceedingly grateful if you would inspect their property and perhaps consider them for admittance to your fine training program."

"Did you invite me here for business or pleasure, Colden?" Madam asked tersely.

"Both," Colden replied, wearing a roguish smile.

"Well, you should know that I never mix the two—it's vulgar. If anyone is interested in enrolling their pleasure-slave in my program, they'll have to go through the proper channels."

With her mouth turned down in haughty disapproval, Madam observed the guests. "My fee has quadrupled since I trained that famous actress who was sold at auction. I highly doubt if any of your guests could afford the services I offer. At present, most of my clients have made the *Forbes* 500 list. Those who aren't business tycoons are titled nobility from around the globe. They're people with deep pockets and a voracious desire to be worshipped by their pleasure-slaves twenty-four-seven," Madam said pointedly.

Although they considered themselves the crème de la crème, most of Colden's acquaintances were upper middle class—college deans, lawyers, dentists, and small business owners—who earned a couple hundred thousand or less per year. They were weekend pleasure seekers. Working stiffs who dabbled in bondage and discipline as a hobby. For them, wielding a whip was nothing more than weekend folly.

For Madam and her select clientele of the superrich, enjoying the pleasures of erotic servitude was a lifestyle, not a favorite pastime.

She found the pseudo dominants and dominatrices to be beneath contempt. If she could choose who to discipline this evening, it wouldn't be a pleasure-slave. She'd punish one of the so-called masters and mistresses and bring them down a peg by scolding them and spanking them soundly in front of their human property.

Madam smiled as she imagined enjoying the evening's five-course meal while one of the pretentious dominants, stripped of their fashionable evening attire, was ordered to sit naked at her feet while being fed crumbs from her plate. Now that would be entertainment!

Although Lyza and Brynne flanked Madam, the two women were appallingly ill-matched. Lyza's brown eyes were alit with eagerness as she stood ready for service. Tall, sleek, and resembling a bronze-skinned goddess, she was completely naked except for a silver collar and a silver hoop that pierced her clit. Her makeup was flawless and her curly hair was straightened and upswept into a stylish bun.

Brynne, on the other hand, devoid of makeup, looked drab and her hair hung limp and plain. Garbed in her dismal-gray maid's uniform, she lacked luster and stood out like a sore thumb among the beautifully attired guests and the silver-painted pleasure-slaves.

Colden regarded Brynne with a scowl and then shifted his gaze back to Madam. "Would you like one of the attendants to get her undressed and spray-painted or did you bring her here to scrub the floors?" he asked snippily.

With a glint of mischief in her eyes, Madam glanced briefly at Brynne. "I brought her here for after-dinner entertainment. I've been made aware that she has quite an aptitude for pain, and so I decided your little soiree would be the perfect platform to showcase her amazing endurance."

"Interesting," Colden said.

"I've arranged for a prop to be delivered, but it won't get here until around ten. So, in the meantime, she can make herself useful by being on bathroom duty."

Colden raised a brow. "Bathroom duty?"

"Yes, since the clumsy twit can't be trusted around anything of value, I've decided that during the gala she'll assist your guests with their most intimate needs in the bathroom."

"I love the idea, Madam. You're so clever. One never knows what's going on inside that devious mind of yours."

Madam rolled her eyes and sighed at the way Colden was so blatantly sucking up to her. He didn't typically hand out compliments so freely, but after learning of her success with training and selling the A-list actress, he'd been trying to finagle his way into the world of international underground auction sales. But it wasn't going to happen. On a local level, Colden was a respected real estate developer, but when compared to the power players with whom Madam conducted business, he was nothing more than a two-bit hustler.

"Assign the girl to one of the bathrooms located in a discreet area…such as the basement, and then alert only your VIP guests to use the bathroom where she'll be working. Let them know that her services include a lot more than handing out warm towels," Madam said with a wink.

"Fantastic. I love the idea and only wish I'd thought of it." Colden beckoned Brynne to follow him and when she took a few shaky steps forward, he shook his head and glared at her. "Did I give you permission to walk? On your hands and knees, you insolent girl."

Brynne shot a panicked look at Madam.

"Do as you're told," Madam said with an edge to her voice.

Obediently and with practiced grace, Brynne lowered herself to the floor.

A sprinkling of nearby guests stopped conversing and their eyes became focused on Brynne. Shame-faced, Brynne crawled toward Colden.

Instead of leading the way, Colden positioned himself behind Brynne and swatted her ass heavy-handedly as he pointed the way to the stairs that spiraled down to her work station in the basement.

CHAPTER 9

Four more weeks of this hell and I'll be back with Ian, sleeping on the floor beside his bed, Brynne reminded herself. She closed her eyes briefly and imagined him smiling and pleased with her and calling her his sexy cum-slut. *Sexy cum-slut* was such a sweet term of endearment and she yearned to hear Ian whispering tenderly in her ear.

Yanked from the sweet reverie, Brynne's eyes popped open when a snooty beauty queen type wearing a diamond encrusted tiara pranced into the bathroom. She was tall and willowy with an elegantly structured face and long blonde hair. With her evening gown gathered around her waist the beauty queen squatted over the toilet and ordered Brynne to remove her tampon. The sight of blood made Brynne nauseous but she dared not refuse. Averting her gaze, she extracted the tampon and quickly tossed the gross object into the toilet bowl.

"Are you kidding me? Tampons aren't biodegradable. I can't believe you're seriously trying to ruin the environment," the beauty queen complained with her ice-blue eyes bugged out.

"Sorry," Brynne responded with an expression of remorse.

"Don't be sorry. Get it out of the commode and throw it in the waste bin where it belongs. Honestly, some people have no couth!"

Willing herself not to vomit, Brynne fished the used tampon out of the water and averted her eyes as she wrapped it in a paper towel and properly disposed of it. Next the insufferable woman demanded that she wipe her pussy and kiss it before inserting a fresh tampon.

Brynne got through the bizarre request by fantasizing of the day she was reunited with her one true love and master, Ian Pepperidge. She lived and breathed to please him and had cried hysterically when he insisted upon sending her to the United States for enhanced training.

"It's for the good of our relationship," Ian had rationalized. "I've taught you everything I know, but this woman who's known as Madam Midnight can take you to the next level." Wiping the tears from Brynne's cheek, Ian had continued. "Don't you want to please me, Brynne?"

"I want to please you in every way, but why must we be separated? Why can't I be trained here in Edinburgh or better yet, why can't I relocate to London? We could spend more time together if you allowed me to move closer to you."

"Hush. Your impertinence is exactly why you have to be trained by a master of the craft. You talk back and…"

"But—"

"Silence!" Ian had held up a hand. "Go get my flogger. Maybe a few stripes across your ass will humble you."

It was a fond memory. Spankings at Ian's hand or with a device were always welcomed. Besides, he never really hurt her. He dispensed love taps that prompted her nipples to harden and her cunt to grow moist, and then he took her from the back, yanking her hair as his cock glided in and out of her.

The beauty queen left the bathroom, allowing Brynne a few minutes to devote her thoughts to her one true love and master. *Oh, Ian, I miss you so much but I'll see this through and make you proud of me. You'll delight in my cock-sucking skills and you'll marvel at how much better I am at eating pussy. When you bring home one of your grand lady friends, I won't show a trace of jealousy. When she spreads her legs for me, I'll lap up her juices with an eagerness that will astound you. Oh, Ian, my love. I miss you so much, there's a pain in my chest as I feel my heart splintering.*

Her eyes brimming with tears, Brynne jerked her head toward the door when it opened. She quickly wiped her eyes and produced a weary smile for a considerably sized and appallingly unattractive man who entered the bathroom. The blimp of a man had a big belly that strained the buttons of his tuxedo. His handlebar mustache was startling both for its bulk and its scruffy appearance. The hair on his head was badly thinned, and what was left was peppered liberally with wayward strands of gray.

"I'm at your service, sir," Brynne said timidly, her long lashes lowered in humility.

"Hold my dick while I pee." His voice was a rough baritone that demanded she follow his order without delay.

"It is my honor to hold your dick while you pee, sir," she said, mouthing the words that were expected of a dutiful pleasure-slave.

The big man grunted in satisfaction as he stuck his hammy hand inside his pants and whipped out his cock. Brynne grasped it delicately between her fingers, and when it twitched and lengthened, she gave it a tighter clutch in her fisted hand. Aiming the head of his dick toward the toilet bowl, she said in a soft voice, "If it pleases you, sir, I would be happy to suck your cock after you pee."

"Sure, why not?" he replied nonchalantly.

Hopefully, the man whose dick she was holding would let Madam know that Brynne had taken the initiative and had offered him her mouth. If she could get into Madam's good graces, then perhaps the icy, intimidating woman would send Ian a favorable report regarding her progress.

Thoughts of Ian caused her pussy to quiver and overflow with steaming juices, and while in the midst of sucking the disgusting man's dick, it was on the tip of her tongue to propose that he use her cunt as a cum receptacle, but urgent raps on the bathroom door prompted her to withhold the offer.

"Geez, will you hurry the hell up in there?" yelled a shrill female voice.

"Hold your horses," the man choked out, gripping the sides of Brynne's head as he thrust desperately into her wet mouth.

After having the butler's ginormous dick rammed down her throat, the big, mustachioed man's medium-sized cock was easy to handle. Her tongue had been snaking up and down his hard length in a slow, lurid dance but now she quickened the pace, slurping with her lips and applying suction to the head.

He gasped and grunted. "Mmm. Yeah, suck it, you filthy, piss-house whore."

To be so completely degraded aroused her enormously and she moaned low in her throat. She needed to cum so badly, she squeezed her thighs together tightly as she attempted to apply friction to her clit. She let his dick slide out of her mouth.

"How dare you stop sucking," he bellowed, indignation booming in his voice.

"You can fuck me if you'd like, sir," she moaned, yearning for the awful-looking man to fuck her senselessly. At that moment, she wanted his cock as desperately as she craved the hard length of her handsome one true love and master. Writhing in sexual agony, she ignored the sharp and repetitive knocks on the door. "Please fuck my cunt, sir."

The great big blob of a man gawked at her with fire in his eyes. "You are out of line. You're not here to receive pleasure, only to give it. Now finish blowing me before I decide to put on my studded glove and discipline you for your boldness."

Her ass was still fiery and sore from the spanking she'd received from the butler, and she doubted she could take any more physical abuse. "I'm sorry, sir," she murmured quickly and commenced to sucking him off.

His massive body shook violently as he flooded her mouth. His cum didn't have the creamy consistency of Ian's nor the pleasant taste. Being so close to the toilet, she was tempted to spit it out, but she thought better of it when she looked up at him and noticed that beneath his scraggly mustache, his lips were drawn into a tight, grim line.

Fearing his studded glove, she forced herself to swallow.

Instead of withdrawing his dick from between her lips, the big man began undulating, trying to work himself up for another round of getting his dick sucked. But when the impatient woman on the other side of the door began pounding on it, stating that a line had formed and then began threatening to tell the host of the gala that the bathroom attendant was shirking her responsibilities, Brynne begged the man to please allow her to cater to the needs of others.

With a strained smile she promised to blow him again after the line of guests had shortened.

Muttering in dissatisfaction, he stuffed his dick back in his pants and stomped out of the bathroom.

The loud-mouth woman raced toward the toilet, practically tripping over the hem of her mauve-colored gown. She wasn't exactly ugly, but her bony, mean face, slightly crooked nose, and pointy chin made her far from attractive. Despite her haste to get to the toilet, she managed to grab Brynne by the arm, her nails digging into her skin. "Make yourself useful and hold up my gown for me."

Brynne hoisted up the gown while the woman flopped down on the seat. With a sigh, she released a powerful jet of urine. "All that champagne wreaks havoc on the bladder," she said, producing a smile that looked anything but friendly.

After a few moments, she cut off her pee stream and fixed her gaze on Brynne. "Insert four fingers up my twat."

"Pardon me, ma'am?"

"Are you deaf? Stick four fingers up my twat, right now!"

Hastily, Brynne obliged the woman by shoving four fingers up her pissy cunt, and to Brynne's surprise the bony-faced woman began peeing again into Brynne's cupped palm. It started out as a trickle and then turned into a full-on gush like a spigot turned on full force. Playing water sports was not something she was accustomed to, and Brynne was surprised the warm jet stream pooling in her palm and trickling through her fingers felt so sensual.

She wondered how Ian would feel about peeing in her hand when she returned home. It would be a wonderful way for him to reward her for her good behavior or to show how much he cared. She'd have to figure out a way to bring up the subject without offending him.

"Go wash your hands and then come back and dry off my pussy," the woman ordered.

Brynne washed and dried her hands thoroughly and then reached for the roll of toilet paper.

"No tissue," the woman snapped, giving Brynne a penetrating look. "I'd rather you use your tongue."

"Excuse me?" Brynne said in a faltering voice, her arm suspended in midair.

The woman gave her a look that said she would not repeat herself.

Fighting back anxiety, Brynne slowly lowered her arm. Piss tasting was not something Ian had ever requested of her. She wondered if he would approve of her getting involved with something that was so utterly taboo.

Not wanting to receive an unfavorable report from Madam, Brynne lowered herself to her knees, squatting between the woman's gaped thighs. Timidly, she slid her tongue against the woman's dampened clit. The salty-champagne taste on her tongue had an odd appeal, prompting her to lick greedily between the woman's folds and then stabbing her tongue as deeply into her cunt as she possibly could.

CHAPTER 10

The décor of the formal dining hall was reminiscent of Victorian-era elegance with flowery wallpaper, clusters of lavishly set tables, drapery made of rich brocade fabric, elaborate crystal chandeliers, and Oriental rugs over polished hardwood flooring. Museum-quality oil paintings hung in gilded frames on the walls, and there was a marble fireplace with a huge mirror above the mantle set in an antique silver frame.

Madam was impressed with the opulence of the room but doubted if the meal would meet her standards. Colden always insisted upon having Melanee, his pet pleasure-slave, prepare the meals for all his social events. Having Melanee attempt to create high-end cuisine was such a ludicrous idea being that the girl was a baker by profession and should have stuck to rolling out dough and frosting cupcakes.

Colden and Madam shared a table and their pleasure-slaves sat on the floor at their feet. Lyza, looking elegant even while assuming a submissive posture, sat at Madam's feet. Two of Colden's pleasure-slaves, Ebony and Tonga, sat on either side of him: Ebony, a Nubian female was a dark-skinned beauty with almond-shaped eyes and full, sensual lips. Tonga, a brawny male whose arms and chest were covered in tribal tattoos, hailed from The Pacific Islands.

Colden affectionately rustled the curls on Tonga's head with his left hand and ran the fingers of his right hand through Ebony's shoulder-length cornrows. Then, turning his attention to Madam, Colden said, "Tonight's cuisine is guaranteed to please your refined palate."

"I don't have high expectations, Colden. I'll consider myself fortunate if the food is at least palatable."

Showing appreciation for Madam's dry humor, Colden chuckled.

Naked male and female servers glided into the dining hall carrying wine while others carried steaming covered dishes. Both the wine and the starter course were delivered to the guests who were seated at various tables.

The pert-breasted woman who appeared at Madam and Colden's table gracefully placed the first course in front of them. The server ignored the pleasure-slaves who sat as still as statues at their masters' feet, treating them as if they were invisible and not offering them as much as a sip of water.

Expecting to loathe everything on the menu, Madam's lips were pursed in disapproval before the dishes had even been uncovered.

"Oysters and Pearls," the server announced theatrically as she lifted the lid. She then explained that the dish consisted of a resplendent sabayon of pearl tapioca combined with Island Creek oysters and a generous clump of white sturgeon caviar.

The food had arrived in an exquisite red bowl made of the finest porcelain and Madam was impressed by the fanciful presentation as well as the captivating aroma. She sampled a forkful and was astonished by the intriguing burst of flavor that was like a symphony in her mouth, and was so delectable, Madam blissfully closed her eyes.

The creamy and rich sabayon laid the foundation for the dish and the tapioca supported this richness with its silky texture. The perfectly cooked oysters had a wonderful sweetness while the caviar provided the right balance of saltiness.

"I see the chef has started the evening on a high note," Colden said, pleased with Madam's reaction to the cuisine.

Chewing contentedly, Madam nodded, swallowed, and then said, "Aside from the magnificent appearance, taste, and texture, the inventiveness of this dish is pure genius. It's unlike anything Melanee has ever created."

"No, no, Melanee didn't prepare the cuisine," Colden corrected. "She's taken on the role of pastry chef and is working her magic on the bread and the desserts. Our guest chef this evening is Nico Bradford."

Madam shook her head. "The name doesn't ring a bell."

"He's an emerging new chef, very talented. Nico's a graduate of the Culinary Institute of America, and has worked in a number of restaurants on both coasts. He's been exposed to some of the finest dining establishments in the country."

"Sounds like you have a hard-on for the chef," Madam said wryly.

"Our relationship is strictly business."

"Is he a part of the fetish community?"

"Not that I'm aware of."

"How'd you convince this illustrious chef to cook at such a decadent event as this?"

"I offered him an obscene amount of money."

"Well, that explains it. Money talks," Madam replied.

"Yes, it does," Colden agreed. "Now, sit back, Madam. I want you to enjoy every bite as you journey into the culinary world of Nico Bradford."

Judging by the satisfied murmurs throughout the room, the other guests were equally enthralled with Chef Nico's first offering. Then the bread cart arrived and sounds of heightened excitement ensued.

The cart was brimming with endless selections of fresh artisan breads. There was every imaginable variety of doughy goodness. While other diners were going overboard, filling their plates with four and five different types of bread, Madam, while tempted to overindulge, limited herself to only one roll.

She broke off a piece of the roll and fed it to Lyza, who somehow managed to maintain her charm and dignity even while eating crumbs from her mistress's hand.

Madam then pinched off a small piece of the fluffy roll and popped it into her mouth. Eyeing Colden closely, she said, "Melanee's a talented baker and I'm glad you've finally come to realize where her strength lies. The way you've forced her unimaginative menus on your guests over the years has been completely torturous."

Colden chuckled. "You're exaggerating, Madam. Obviously, Melanee's food can't compare to Chef Nico's, but I think she possesses above average culinary skills."

Madam made a scoffing sound. "You're delusional, Colden. Anyway, back to the guest chef this evening... I hope this Nico fellow isn't a one-trick pony. I'd be surprised if the remaining courses can compete with the first," Madam said snippily.

And indeed, she was surprised when the second course was served. Placed before her was a delightful delicacy: fried frogs' legs, made into lollipops on a long stick of bone and served with a tangy parsley sauce. It was pure heaven on a plate and every bite was a revelation.

After she finished the lollipop frogs' legs, the servers immediately appeared and placed before her a napkin-covered bowl of rosemary and lemon-scented water for rinsing her fingers. It was a very nice touch, she noted.

Chef Nico cooked like an abstract painter. His dishes pulled together a full palette of concentrated flavors and unexpected textures. Visually, the third course, which consisted of artichoke and black truffle soup, looked like modern art in a bowl. It came with mushroom brioche and black truffle butter. The luxurious black truffle butter on the mushroom brioche was to die for. Enchanted by the experience of Chef Nico's food, Madam was nearly swooning.

Next on the menu was Muscovy duck that had been glazed with lavender honey until it was a golden brown. According to the server, the chef then dusted the poultry with star anise to give it an exotic Asian flavor. Again, the presentation was whimsical and artsy. Amazingly, the duck course was even more delicious than the first three. She found herself startled by the excellence of the chef's ingredients and his talent for unlocking all they had to offer, and with every exquisite bite, she experienced deeply layered flavors that incited her to curl her toes and moan.

The chef engaged the diners with an orchestrated progression of divine dishes that showcased his amazing cooking skills. In Chef Nico's hands, the simplest of foods had been turned into a gourmet event. His food was unlike anything Madam had ever tasted.

The servers brought out the entrée, Black Angus tenderloin that was pooled in rich Bordelaise and crumbled with bits of bone marrow, along with a medley of crisp vegetables and wild rice. Madam smacked her lips as she took a bite of the juicy steak. A taste of the farm fresh vegetables and wild rice incited her to tap her foot as if overwhelmed by spirituality.

She laughed gaily throughout the course, taking generous sips of wine. It was a meal that went right to the heart. The food was sensual. It was sexual foreplay. It was a sweet, lingering kiss. By the time servers removed the plates and cleared away the crumbs from the table in preparation for the dessert course, Madam felt as if she were on the brink of a soul-shattering orgasm.

The dessert carts were being wheeled out, and there was a chorus of excited murmurs from the other guests, but Madam had no interest in Melanee's cakes and pies. She placed a hand upon her chest and spoke breathlessly to Colden. "I simply must meet the chef!"

"It'll be my pleasure to make the introduction. I told him that you were my honored guest this evening and I'm sure he'll be delighted to make your acquaintance." Colden adjusted his tie and stood. He grabbed two strawberry tarts from the dessert cart and handed one to Ebony and the other to Tonga before striding to the kitchen.

She checked her reflection in her compact, reapplied lipstick, and made sure there was no food on her teeth. Suddenly there was a burst of applause and her gaze jerked to the sound of the commotion. Her heart gave a fast thud when she saw Chef Nico standing in the archway of the dining hall, a faint smile tugging at the corner of his mouth as he bowed his head in acknowledgment of the applause.

He was tall. She guessed his height to be roughly six-feet-four and his weight to be somewhere around one hundred and ninety pounds to two hundred. He was rock-solid with broad shoulders. Big and strong and incredibly masculine. She could tell that beneath his chef's jacket he had a killer body. He was handsome in a rugged, unruly way, and his complexion was the color of rich, dark earth. His gleaming white teeth and cocky smile were hard to resist and Madam was instantly charmed by him.

Even though they were separated by several yards and clusters of dining tables, Madam felt an intense connection to him. The room temperature seemed to increase due to the smoldering heat emanating between her and the chef. Her already pounding heart picked up speed when she watched him making strides toward her.

Surprisingly, he was even more attractive than she'd realized when she saw him up close.

"It's an honor, Madam Midnight," Nico said in a warm tenor,

oozing with sex. He was cool and suave, seeming to be totally at ease in the unconventional dining room where masters and mistresses were surrounded by naked pleasure-slaves. Of course, he'd been interacting with the naked servers throughout the evening, and perhaps those exchanges had prepared him for this moment, Madam ruminated.

"The food was quite good. I enjoyed every course," she said coolly, her even tone and stoic expression never betraying her true feelings. It would have been unbecoming of a woman of her stature to admit that the chef had provided her with an unforgettable gastronomic experience, and that the mere memories of the delectable flavor profiles caused her mouth to water and her breath to quicken. She gave no outward signs that having the sexy chef standing so close to her had started a heat burning in her loins that was spreading throughout her body like wildfire. She desperately wanted Lyza to fan her, but clenched her teeth, biting back the command.

"It was a pleasure meeting you, Chef Nico," she said, abruptly dismissing him from her presence. But he wasn't intimidated and didn't skulk away. He stood there for a few moments, boldly running his gaze over her. Though she was aware that her adrenaline had spiked, Madam didn't realize she was perspiring until she felt the moisture on her fingertips when she swiped at a bead of sweat that trickled down the back of her neck.

"Again, it was a pleasure meeting you," Nico said smoothly before pivoting away from her.

Madam restrained herself from turning in her chair and watching the chef saunter across the room. She felt a bit woozy, but tried to collect herself while wondering why in the world the chef was having such a profound effect on her. She interacted with handsome men all the time, particularly in the film industry, and she'd never had a reaction like this.

"The entire evening has been a huge success. Do you agree, Madam?" Colden asked, breaking into her thoughts.

Madam agreed with a slight dip of her head. Bringing herself back into the moment, she looked around and noted that the pulse of the evening had reached its frenzy and the guests seemed to be getting louder and drunker by the minute.

Desiring to be intoxicated, also, she turned her wineglass up to her lips and drained it. "More wine." She held out her glass and Colden immediately beckoned the server to bring a full bottle to the table.

CHAPTER 11

After the initial rush of guests had utilized Brynne's services in the bathroom, she was left with idle time while they dined. She occupied herself by tidying up the bathroom. She wiped down the sink, commode, shower stall, and bathtub several times with an anti-bacterial spray. She also attended to her personal hygiene and fussed with her hair. After a long stretch of time had elapsed without any guests entering the bathroom, her thoughts inevitably turned to Ian and the wonderful times they'd shared.

Brynne fondly recalled times when he'd been able to get away and spend long weekends with her in Edinburgh, Scotland. Although the flight to Edinburgh from London was only an hour and twenty minutes, there were many weekends when Ian simply couldn't get away. Family and business commitments could be such a nuisance at times. In his absence Ian always kept in touch via Skype, phone calls, emails, or texts.

I want you to finger fuck your twat, now, he once texted while she was in the midst of conducting a late-night walking tour where she, costumed in a hooded monk's cloak, led tourists by candlelight through the so-called haunted Blair Street underground vaults. While delivering her memorized spiel in an eerie, ghostlike voice, her tone became breathy and high-pitched as her hand worked busily beneath the monk's cloak.

It was a good thing her job as a tour guide required her to dress in monk's garb. Otherwise she had no idea how she would have been able to hide her hand and follow Ian's instructions without being fired for lewd behavior.

She'd taken a leave of absence from work in order to get the training she needed to better serve Ian. It was her greatest hope that she would return to Edinburgh with such impressive skills that Ian would want to be with her on a permanent basis. His wife could never please him the way Brynne could.

A wistful smile came to Brynne's lips as she recalled Ian saying she was the perfect woman for him. But that smile vanished when the host of the gala sauntered into bathroom.

"Bathroom duty is over. My attendants will prepare you for your next punishment," Colden said brusquely.

"Yes, Master Colden," she said with her eyes directed to the floor.

Colden left and two naked, silver-painted female pleasure-slaves entered the bathroom and filled the bathtub with warm soapy water. Without speaking a word, the taller of the two women motioned for Brynne to get undressed, and then she tossed Brynne's shabby maid's uniform into the trash receptacle. Both women pointed toward the tub.

Following their silent instructions, Brynne bathed, washed her hair, and toweled herself dry. Afterward the pair of mutes rubbed her down with oil until she glistened from head to toe.

Part of her was looking forward to the next phase of her punishment. The more punishment she endured the better trained she'd be. Still, part of her was scared to death of what Madam had in store for her. The fear of the unknown gave her goosebumps.

Her mind reeled with possibilities as she was escorted from the bathroom, and along the hall of the basement. Brynne was led to an even lower level: the dungeon. She was ushered through darkened corridors with crude stone walls, passing rooms with sturdy wooden doors that muffled the screams within.

She wanted to be brave for Ian but her steps began to falter. As if expecting her to try to bolt, the women flanked her, clutching her arms and practically dragging Brynne to the far end of the hall. They paused outside a room with a massive set of double doors with a knocker that was fashioned to resemble some sort of demonic creature.

She imagined a crowd of masters with their trousers open in the front and a throng of mistresses with their gowns gathered around their waists, their sex organs throbbing and hungry with desire. She'd be ordered to satisfy every one of them, offering all three orifices for their pleasure. The idea was both intoxicating and terrifying.

She hoped Madam would film her being gangbanged. It was the kind of thing that Ian would enjoy watching while he stroked himself to orgasm. It was the perfect erotic vignette for them to watch together once they were reunited.

"How many people are in there? Do you know what they're going to do to me?" Brynne asked in a voice that shook with fear and excitement.

Remaining silent, the pleasure-slaves ignored her queries. The taller one—the alpha woman of the two—raised the demonic-looking knocker and banged it against the door.

"Enter," said a male voice that unmistakably belonged to Master Colden. Although Brynne feared him, she looked forward to doing all sorts of dirty things to him. Ian had never seen her blow a black man and she was positive that a video recording of her giving head to Master Colden would keep Ian sufficiently entertained until she returned to him.

The taller pleasure-slave pushed open the double doors.

As many scenarios as Brynne had imagined, the scene before her had not been one of them.

Masters and mistresses sipped wine from crystal goblets. Like house pets, the pleasure-slaves were on their hands and knees beside their owners, lapping wine from bowls set on the floor. The masters and mistresses applauded when Brynne crossed the threshold.

The expansive room was equipped with intimidating fetish furniture and all sorts of cruel-looking devices: a spanking bench, a bondage bed, a steel cage, shackles, floggers, whips, and nipple clamps. Out of all the frightening equipment, it was the apparatus in the center of the room that caused Brynne's heartbeat to quicken.

It was a steel rotating bondage wheel that was complete with handgrips, footplates, padded leather ankle straps, three arm straps, and a padded leather chest harness. Like the Wheel of Fortune at a casino, at the outer edges of the rotating wheel in specific positions were images of various torture devices: a flogger, a slapper, a dragon tail whip, a gargantuan dildo, a set of nipple pincers, and a rattan cane.

It was apparent that once securely strapped in position, the victim could be rotated through 360 degrees and locked in any one of six positions with a long lever, and she would be punished according to the image depicted by the pointer when the wheel stopped spinning.

Brynne stole a glance at Master Colden and noticed him studying her closely as he stood near the lever, his fingers dancing over the knob, obviously anxious to give her a spin on the wheel.

The fear of the ominous wheel caused her heartbeat to quicken while at the same time a dull ache pulsed within her cunt.

"Strap her in," Madam instructed.

Brynne's two silent captures tugged her forward and she didn't resist. Obediently, she allowed them to blindfold her and stick a ball gag in her mouth before hoisting her onto the bondage wheel, her four limbs strapped down securely. Breasts pressed against the padding, Brynne was bound to the menacing device with her oil-shined, bare ass facing the crowd.

"Apparently her ass has already been given a good whacking," said a male voice that Brynne didn't recognize.

"Yes, that does appear to be the case," said Madam's distinctive voice. "No one at House of Stevens has laid a hand on her, so I suppose one of the guests must have become upset with the way she performed her bathroom duties."

With a ball gag in her mouth, Brynne couldn't correct Madam and let her know that the welts across her ass were the handiwork of her deranged butler.

"Welcome to the dungeon. I promised you an evening of arousing entertainment and with the generosity of my dear friend, the esteemed Madam Midnight, I assure you I won't disappoint," Colden said in an affected voice similar to a circus ringmaster. "Some of our guests have chosen to chastise their submissives in private rooms down here in the dungeon, but for those of us who have gathered here for the group flogging session, let us raise our glasses in cheer. Hear, hear!"

The crowd of spectators repeated the cheer and Brynne wondered if her fellow pleasure-slaves were allowed to join in the merriment. Were they allowed to raise their gazes toward the spectacle in the middle of the room or were their eyes still downcast as they continued to slurp from their bowls?

"Are you ready for an activity that is guaranteed to arouse and amaze?" he shouted in a showman's voice.

Brynne gulped.

"Ready!" the crowd exploded.

"Then, let the games begin!" Master Colden pulled the lever and the wheel turned with enormous speed.

Even though Brynne was fastened securely to the wheel, the sensation of spinning frenziedly in midair was terrifying. She squeezed her eyes together and gritted her teeth, silently praying that Master Colden hadn't sabotaged the restraints, setting her up to be ejected from the wheel. She didn't put it past him to consider it enormously entertaining for her body to catapult from the device and end up smashed to a bloody pulp against a stone wall.

She could only hope that Madam had informed Master Colden that she was the prized possession of a distinguished international financier. Holding her breath, Brynne tightly clutched the hand grip, trying to convince herself that she would be all right. Madam wouldn't allow her to be seriously injured. After all, Ian Pepperidge would not be pleased if his beloved pleasure-slave was not returned to him in one piece.

Finally the wheel began to slow down. Exhaling in relief, she willed herself to relax and try to calm down. She'd survived. She was safe.

The wheel came to a complete stop and a single female voice yelled, "I won! I won!"

Apparently Master Colden and Madam had accepted wagers. A lucky guest had won the opportunity to use a fetish device on her. Blindfolded with her back turned to everyone, Brynne had no idea where the arrow had landed. In light of the fact that her cunt was particularly juicy after enduring that fear-inspiring spin on the wheel, she mentally crossed her fingers, hoping the arrow had stopped on the giant dildo.

No such luck. The fluttery strands of what felt like soft suede ribbons caressing her buttocks told her the arrow had stopped at the flogger. The lucky winner dragged the soft straps of the flogger across her ass, tantalizing her or perhaps she was taunting her. It depended on how one viewed being flogged. Ian often used a soft suede flogger as a warmup tool. Although the device gave a loud thwack, it wasn't hardcore at all. It delivered a sensation that was more like a massage or a soft sting.

Eyes closed behind the blindfold, Brynne moaned inaudibly as she enjoyed the pleasurable stings. But after five minutes or so, she was wrenched from her euphoric state as the wheel began spinning again. Butterflies fluttered wildly in her stomach as the wheel picked up speed. It seemed to zoom around even faster than before. Panicked and lightheaded, she clamped her fists around the hand grips.

"Let me off. Let me off," she pleaded incoherently, her speech unintelligible due to the gag ball. The fear of being hurled through the air was unbearable this time. Zooming around on the wheel was insane. It was more frightening than sitting in the first car of one of those extreme thrill coaster rides. A violent death seemed imminent and she'd rather be thrashed with a bullwhip than be spun around for another second.

Finally, the wheel stopped. Master Colden was talking in an excited tone and the guests seemed livelier than ever, but Brynne, feeling both nauseous and dizzy had no interest in where the arrow had landed.

As it turned out, this time she was punished with a rattan cane. She recognized the sound of the sharp whoosh through the air and the meaty smack of the thin wood. Though searing pain radiated from her ass and her thighs, she preferred the cane to the torturous wheel. After numerous spins and a thrashing with every device pictured on the wheel, Brynne was barely conscious, and thus derived no satisfaction when the enormous dildo was eventually inserted into her cunt.

Unshackled and her blindfold removed, she was taken down from the wheel and carried off to a room in the dungeon where she was carefully placed inside a cage. She was so dizzy and her vision so terribly blurry, she couldn't discern if she'd been transported by the two mute pleasure-slaves or two entirely different ones.

The closing metal door and the clang of the lock jostled her out of the mental fog she was in. Feeling acutely claustrophobic she clutched the bars of the cage. "Would you leave the door unlocked… please? I won't try to leave," she said faintly.

"We have to follow orders," said a male voice.

Brynne stared in the direction of the voice, trying to make out the man's features. With her world still spinning violently, all she could see was a blur of silver body paint and dark hair. His partner who'd helped take her off the loathsome wheel was also out of focus—a silver distortion with startling blue eyes.

"We'll bring you food and drink in a little while, but don't attempt to eat if you don't think you can keep it down," said blue eyes in a voice tinged with compassion.

She nodded glumly, and reminded herself that she had to make Ian proud.

CHAPTER 12

Brynne was left alone in the cage, naked and without so much as a pile of rags to lie upon. Physically bruised and her spirit broken, she sobbed quietly. She'd feel comforted if only she had something of Ian's to cuddle with: a used bath towel, a soiled T-shirt with dampened armpits, a pair of nylon sport shorts that had been tossed in the hamper after a workout, a pair of worn briefs that held the heavy scent of masculine groin. She'd be grateful to have anything with her true love and master's wonderful scent.

At home, there were times when he'd tested her endurance and devotion by leaving her bound by the wrists to a bar inside a closet. Falling asleep on her feet, surrounded by his clothing and other belongings made those bondage sessions bearable. But now, when she needed him the most, she had nothing of his.

With buttocks too sore to sit on, she lay on her side, and was too weak and dispirited to prop herself up or show any outward interest when she heard the rolling wheels of a cart and the rattle of covered dishes as the two pleasure-slaves returned to the dungeon with food.

Brynne ignored the two tin bowls and metal dish that were pushed inside the cage.

"You must eat," said one of the men.

"I don't have an appetite," she responded and gave a desolate whimper.

"Madam Midnight has instructed us to film you while you enjoy your meal. The film will be for your master's enjoyment."

"I don't belong to Master Colden," Brynne said wearily.

"It's not for Master Colden," said the other pleasure-slave. "I overheard Madam Midnight say that she needed to send some footage of you in-training to your owner who lives in the United Kingdom."

Brynne perked up instantly. She turned and gazed at the men excitedly. "Are you serious? Does Madam really plan to send footage to Ian?"

They nodded and for the first time Brynne could see them in full focus. Both men were muscular and handsome, though one had a mature, angular face with a strong jawline and the other had cherubic, more youthful facial features.

The mature-looking man held up a camera. "It's time to eat. You have to hurry. We don't want to get in trouble for spending too much time away from our masters."

Brynn crawled over to a bowl and lapped up a plain broth soup. When she finished, she gobbled up chunks of bland chicken and beef from the saucer. Realizing that Ian would see her and would be judging her level of training, she became enlivened and began biting into the chunks of unseasoned meat like a ravenous puppy. Finally, she slurped water from a bowl, turning her body around in a way that allowed the camera to capture the slashes and welts on her ass.

After the filming was completed, the men removed the empty bowls and saucer from the cage and returned them to the wheeled cart.

"In a few moments guests will be streaming in and out of this here, so we're going to have to lock you in or risk severe punishment," said the baby-faced pleasure-slave.

"It's okay. I understand." Knowing Ian would be watching her on tape and no doubt missing her as much as she missed him was empowering, enabling Brynne to deal with the claustrophobia. And there was something else. The lack of control—the complete act of submission was stimulating.

The men said their goodbyes and left her in alone in the dungeon, locked in a cage.

But she wasn't alone for very long. Within minutes of their departure, three drunken men wearing tuxedos came up to the cage and pointed and laughed at Brynne as she cowered in a corner of the confined space.

One of the men, a jowly man with an abundance of pure white hair and a blotchy face that was flushed from too much alcohol, lay down on the floor and scooted up to the cage. His buddies laughed boisterously when he drunkenly fumbled with his fly and then poked his cock between the bars.

"Don't be shy. Get over here and suck this cock like a good little slut-slave."

The man's voice was gravelly and mean. Afraid of him, she did as she was told, pressing her face against the bars and opening her mouth. The incredible humiliation of it all caused her to visibly shudder.

"You like this dick, don't you, slut?" he asked in a voice filled with disdain.

His inquiry elicited raucous laughter from his friends.

"Answer me, you little bitch. Tell me how much you like this sweet meat?"

Hearing the aggression in his tone thrilled her, prompting her to blurt out an answer. "Your sweet meat is delicious. I love it, sir," Brynne responded quickly. But her words came out garbled due to having a cock in her mouth, and this incited the men who were waiting their turn to again erupt in hilarity.

"Get ready because I'm gonna slam this dick all the way down your throat," the man said in a slurred voice. He stuck his hands between the bars and held her head firmly in place, thrusting into her mouth hard and fast. "Here it comes, here it comes," he announced with a violent tremor.

Brynne stretched her lips open as wide as possible, accepting the deluge of hot cum that flooded her mouth.

"If you don't swallow every drop, I'm dragging you back to that wheel to teach you a lesson," the drunken man threatened.

The mere mention of the wheel persuaded Brynne to not only gulp down his thick ejaculation, but to also lick his dick clean, and then thank him for the privilege.

As each man came forward, he undid his pants in front of the cage and thrust his penis into her mouth. Brynne sucked one dick after another. Plunging into her mouth were dicks of various size that ranged in color from opaque white to dark brown. The huge cocks were forced deep into her throat, and having grown accustomed to the butler's huge dick, she was able to control her gagging reflexes, allowing the hefty-sized dicks to glide easily down her throat. And as her mouth and throat became coated with cum from multiple men, there was enough lubrication to assist with the extra-large dicks.

During her time spent with Ian, she'd succumbed to numerous perverted requests that had caused her great shame, but never had she felt quite as dirty and sullied as she did now. Her face flushed as she envisioned Ian's reaction when she admitted to sucking countless cocks while locked in a cage.

He'd undoubtedly be upset that she'd been subjected to such inhumane treatment. Then he'd press her for details, his own dick lengthening and hardening as she confessed to ingesting large quantities of anonymous cum. Then he would smile and affectionately call her a nasty little slut before taking her over his knee and giving her a sensual paddling.

While fantasizing about Ian, Brynne became so unbearably aroused, she increased the suction she applied to the cocks of the nameless, tuxedo-clad men, all the while fighting the urge to press her juice-sodden cunt against the bars in hopes that one of the men would take pity on her and fill her pussy with a big, beefy dick.

"I need to be fucked," she said, her words distorted by the big dick that was stuffed down her throat. "Will somebody, *anybody*, please fuck me?" she beseeched the group of men, but her muddled words fell on deaf ears.

In a state of sexual distress she continued to suck and swallow until at last, the gala came to an end. After the last group of men had departed the dungeon, Brynne heard footsteps padding toward the cage and the voice of Madam's personal maid, Lyza, calling her name.

"Are you okay?" Lyza asked as she unlocked the cage.

Shaking her head and whimpering, Brynne crawled out and then collapsed on her side.

"Poor thing," Lyza cooed, stroking Brynne's hair. "I'm going to get you cleaned up right away. Otherwise you'll have to ride home in the trunk of the car if Madam detects even the slightest unpleasant scent coming from you. And you do smell rather ripe, Brynne."

"I know," Brynne said, humiliation reddening her face.

"Are you able to walk up the stairs to one of the bathrooms?"

"I think so," Brynne said in a hoarse whisper.

"Good. We have to hurry before Madam realizes I've been gone for longer than the time it takes to fetch you. She's rather tipsy at the moment, but she's been known to sober up at the blink of an eye."

Brynne stiffly rose to her feet. Bent over and shuffling along, she and Lyza headed for the winding corridor of the darkened dungeon.

"If luck is on our side, Madam will drink herself into a stupor. Or perhaps she'll end up in the kitchen, enjoying a nightcap."

Brynne's eyebrows shot up. "What?"

"Madam has her eye on the chef," Lyza said in a confidential tone. "Lately, she's been complaining about Azalea's cooking and it would be an extreme upgrade to replace her with a handsome and talented chef. But he's an accomplished man and seems quite self-assured, so I'm not sure if she'll be able to wrangle him and bring him into the fold."

Lyza and Brynne slipped into a remote bathroom in the dungeon, and Lyza quickly turned on the faucets in the bathtub.

"Wait!" Brynne said desperately.

"What's wrong?"

"I have a need," Brynne said, her hand brushing across her cunt.

"No one relieved you?" Lyza asked incredulously.

Brynne dropped her head pitifully. "Yes, with an oversized dildo, but I was too dizzy to enjoy it. Now I'm in an awful state."

"That's such a pity. I can use a finger on you if you'd like."

"I need something much bigger and harder. I hate to ask…the last thing I'd want to do is get you in trouble with Madam, but could you please go get that humongous dildo that's down the hall in the room with the fetish wheel?"

"We don't have time for that."

"Please, Lyza. I desperately need an orgasm. If I don't fuck something I'm going to lose my mind."

Lyza nodded in understanding. "All right, Brynne, I'm willing to take a risk. If Madam gets upset with me the worst that will happen is a light paddling. She says my ass is too lovely to bear welts and bruises."

Lyza whisked out of the bathroom, on her way to fetch the dildo. Having a little free time, Brynne decided to freshen up. She stood on a large fluffy rug in front of the sink, scrubbing her tongue with a wash cloth and gargling with mint-scented soapy water to get rid of the bitter taste of cum.

Shifting from foot to foot, she anxiously waited for Lyza to return. It seemed that a lengthy amount of time had passed, and Brynne thought it best to go ahead and bathe now or risk Madam's wrath. The moment she stuck her toe in the bathwater, Lyza returned to the bathroom with a stocky male pleasure-slave in tow.

"You're in luck, Brynne," Lyza said with a sneaky grin. "This is Tonga. He belongs to Master Colden. Both Master Colden and Madam are preoccupied in the kitchen with the pastry chef and Master Colden's other girl, Ebony."

Brynne's eyes wandered to the ink that circled the large bicep of Tonga's right arm. His left arm was covered with black tribal designs that traveled from his shoulder and down to his wrist—as if he were wearing a long, intricately designed sleeve. The shaft of his large pulsing dick was inked with vibrant colors and the head and his scrotum were completely covered with body jewelry.

Brynne licked her lips. "Tonga," she said dreamily, reaching out to him and watching in amazement as his cock grew even bigger.

Tonga didn't speak English, but he knew what Brynne wanted. Taking her hand, he bent her over the sink and then crouched between her legs, sniffing her ass and licking into it for a few moments before grabbing her hips and pressing the metal covered head of his dick against her pussy.

Her pussy did not show the least bit of resistance. The soft folds parted on their own accord, allowing his dick to slide right in. Responding to the raw pleasure of having a dick inside her, Brynne let out a sigh, and her pussy walls clenched and tightened around the thick shaft that stabbed in and out of her. Tonga's grunts and Brynne's loud moans echoed in the bathroom. Brynne was thoroughly immersed in the pleasure that Tonga was giving, and for the first time since her arrival in America, her mind didn't wander to thoughts of Ian.

"I'll be back in ten minutes," Lyza said, closing the door behind her.

With Tonga grunting and plowing into her mightily, it didn't take a full ten minutes for Brynne to shed tears of sheer joy as her body convulsed violently.

CHAPTER 13

Still slightly inebriated, Madam was slouched in the back of the limo during the ride home. Lyza and Brynne sat beside her. Lyza wore only a silver collar while Brynne was dressed in her wrinkled maid's uniform that she'd retrieved from the trash receptacle.

Feeling sticky and uncomfortable, Madam fussed with her gown. Beneath the fabric, she could feel traces of cake frosting that Melanee and Ebony had neglected to lick from her rigid nipples, her shaved pussy, and her tight asshole. Of course, it would be a privilege for her to allow Lyza or Brynne to lick-clean the residual crusted frosting, but Madam had no intention of enduring the sensation of yet another moist tongue.

A hard dick was what she desired.

Nico is probably hung like a horse, she thought with a faint smile. Envisioning Nico's big dick, she squeezed her thighs together, trying to pacify her throbbing clit.

At home, the Nordic twins were at her beck and call, but they were too pretty and not manly enough to suit her needs tonight. Perhaps she'd summon Hugo from the stables. Then again, maybe not. No amount of bathing could wash away the stench of horse shit that seemed to cling to him. She considered giving Colden a call to request that he deliver Tonga to her. But she decided against the idea. Those piercings on the head of his dick made her cringe and the weird black ink that decorated his body caused him to look downright dirty.

She wanted the chef and she wanted him badly. Her body ached for him and no other dick would do until she'd had her fill of Nico.

Raindrops began to fall, splashing against the windshield. The limo driver turned on the wipers and cautiously lowered his speed as he navigated traffic. Up until now, she hadn't bothered to give him as much as a glance, but was now interested in what he had to offer. It wasn't possible that he could compare to Nico, but as long as he had a dick, he'd have to do until she could make arrangements with the hot chef.

The limo traveled along the driveway that led to her palatial home and no sooner had the vehicle glided to stop when she noticed the butler rushing out of the house carrying an oversized umbrella, prepared to protect Madam from the elements. No doubt, he would use the opportunity to slip an arm around her waist as he escorted her inside. The man was so pathetically transparent, always looking for an excuse to touch her.

As the butler approached with the umbrella, the driver got out and opened Madam's door.

"Escort the girls inside and come back for me in twenty minutes."

"Yes, Madam." The butler gave a quick head nod and then hurried to the opposite side of the limousine.

"Driver, get in the back with me. There's a matter we need to discuss," Madam said.

"Is something wrong?" the driver asked, raindrops pelting him, wetting his clothes as well as the thick lenses of his glasses.

He didn't have much going for him in the looks department. He was awkwardly gangly with spindly arms and legs, but hopefully he was packing something worthwhile in his pants.

Madam scooted over, making room for the driver, who wore a confused expression as he slid in the back beside her.

"Was I driving too fast, ma'am?"

"No, your driving was superb, which is why I want to reward you," she said, clutching his lapels and pulling him on top of her. She hitched up her gown and added, "Consider this a tip for excellent service."

For the past few mornings, the butler had ordered Marnie, Brynne, Christoff, Arnoldus, and several other pleasure-slaves to trot like ponies around the grounds of the estate for two solid hours—even in the pouring rain. Afterward, the two maids were placed on laundry duty.

Marnie was responsible for tackling the numerous loads of dirty laundry accumulated by the entire household, while Brynne was in charge of ironing Madam's luxurious linen and hand washing and steaming out the wrinkles in her delicate intimate apparel.

"Doing laundry or even scrubbing floors is a piece of cake compared to pony-trotting," Marnie remarked.

"God, I hate pony-trotting," Brynne replied bitterly. "I wonder why Mr. Hardwicke makes us gallop like horses around the grounds of the estate."

Imitating the butler's stance when he oversaw their morning exercises, Marnie stood with her shoulders squared and her back erect. Mimicking him, she clapped her hands together. "I want your backs erect with lots of high-stepping. Pleasure-slaves must trot like proud ponies—not like you're hobbling your way to the glue factory."

Brynne grimaced. "Mr. Hardwicke is a spiteful man. What does trotting like a proud pony have to do with pleasure-slave training?

I can't think of any purpose for such an awful form of exercise other than to make our lives here as miserable as possible."

"Well, at least you got away from him the other night. It would have been wonderful if Madam had taken me along with her to the Secret Sunset Gala. I bet you had a fine time, didn't you, Brynne?" Marnie asked.

"I wasn't invited to have fun. It was a form of punishment for breaking Madam's vase. Between you and me, I believe Mr. Hardwicke wanted the vase to break," Brynne confided.

"Everyone knows he worships Madam, so why would he want to destroy something of great value to her?"

Brynne shrugged. "My instincts tell me that he set me up for failure when he insisted that I wipe it down with a cloth instead of using the feather duster."

Marnie shook her head as she took a load of laundry out of the dryer. "I'm sorry that happened to you, Brynne. Let's change the subject to something more pleasant. Tell me about the gala. I don't understand how it's considered a punishment to spend an evening with handsome masters and beautiful mistresses all decked out in their finery. There was good food and an open bar, which is nothing to complain about in my opinion. I'd give anything for an umbrella-topped cocktail."

"I was fed scraps from the kitchen. No cocktails. I had to slurp bitter wine from a bowl while locked in a cage on my hands and knees. I don't even want to think about the dreadful fetish wheel that I was strapped to and spun around on until I nearly vomited."

"Sounds wonderfully kinky," Marnie said with a sneaky smile.

"Actually, it was rather kinky," Brynne admitted with a quick grin. "So many spankings with a variety of devices and the sweet humiliation of being caged like an animal. By the end of the evening, I was losing my mind with desire, but Madam had forbidden anyone from alleviating my sexual tension."

"What did you do? Did you get yourself off?"

"I didn't have to. Thank goodness, Lyza took pity on me."

"What did she do…strap on a dildo?"

"Neither. While Madam and Master Colden were being serviced by a couple of pleasure-slaves, Lyza spirited away one of Master Colden's new pets—a Samoan lad named Tonga—who had the most interesting-looking cock I've ever seen. The sheer length of it was outrageous. His cock was completely covered with tattoos and the enormous head had numerous piercings. Tonga's really hot. He's medium height, solidly built, and strong as a bull. He fucked my brains out, Marnie. I never thought any man could make me cum as hard as Ian does. But Tonga made me cum so hard, I shed tears."

"You actually cried?"

"I did. And now I can't get him out of my mind."

"But I thought you were insanely in love with Ian."

"I am! But I'm in lust with Tonga. And I've got to figure out a way to be with him again before Ian comes to collect me."

"When this training course is over, my master won't be coming to collect me," Marnie said casually as she dipped a pair of Madam's panties into lilac-scented water and swished them around.

"Why not?"

"Our arrangement is completely different from what you have with Ian. He gambles heavily, and he auctions me off for months at a time in order to pay off his debt. But this time he needs a lot more money, so he's going to let the highest bidder have me for six months."

Brynne frowned. "That's dreadful."

"It's kind of exciting because you never know what kind of master you're going to get. Some are monstrous while others are very kind. I'll be back on the auction block when I've completed training here, and I hope I find someone like Ian who's wealthy and handsome and totally in love with me."

"I don't understand why you stay with a master who can't afford to take care of you."

"We're a good match because I'm a complete masochist. I love pain and humiliation and my master is wonderfully sadistic."

"Yeah, I get that. Ian isn't physically cruel to me but he likes to taunt me by calling me low-class and making me lick the pussies of his socialite girlfriends."

"I thought Ian was a married man."

"He is. But he has women on the side. He makes me tongue all his mistresses and sometimes he tells me to dress up like a maid and serve him and his whore breakfast in bed. It's utterly humiliating. I hate it but I get so aroused by being treated like crap."

"Yeah, me, too. It's such a rush," Marnie said, nodding in agreement.

Marnie put on a pair of rubber gloves before picking up a pile of Hugo's smelly socks, undergarments, and stained work uniforms. "Can you keep a secret, Brynne?"

"Sure. What is it?"

"As you know, Madam hasn't been feeling well, and Mr. Hardwicke has been making all the decisions regarding the pleasure-slaves. He spoke to me about elevating my position."

Brynne looked at Marnie curiously.

"He wants me to take on some of Lyza's duties."

"He wants you to work directly with Madam?"

"Yes."

"Are you nervous?"

"Very much. If I accept the positon, I run the risk of frequent whippings."

"I don't understand," Brynne said, her eyebrows scrunched together.

"Lyza will train me and Mr. Hardwicke will monitor how well

I perform my duties. If my behavior is not impeccable…if I make the slightest mistake while serving Madam, Mr. Hardwicke will punish me severely."

"Don't do it, Marnie. Mr. Hardwicke is a devious man, and he's most likely setting you up for failure. My bottom has already made acquaintance with his leather strap and I can tell you from first-hand experience that his punishments are brutal."

"If I don't accept the position I won't get the experience I need, and I'll never be sold to a wealthy man at auction."

"If you don't get sold, you'll return to your true master. Wouldn't you prefer that?"

"You don't know my master. He can be so heartless, sometimes he's terrifying. If he doesn't get the money he's expecting, he'll be furious and there's no telling what he'll do to me."

"He wouldn't maim or seriously injure you, would he?" Brynne asked.

"His heart is set on the sale, and if he's disappointed, it's entirely possible that he'll hurt me really badly."

"How badly?" Brynne inquired, grimacing.

"God only knows," Marnie said grimly. "That's why I have to get Madam's certification and make it to the auction block."

CHAPTER 14

It was another dreary, rainy day, and the weather matched Madam's mood.

She'd been melancholy for over a week now and she couldn't seem to snap out of it. Nico, with his rugged good looks and devil-may-care attitude, had made quite an impression on her. Still, it was utterly ridiculous to yearn for someone she barely knew. Colden would have a hearty laugh at her expense if he had an inkling that Madam was pining away for the hot-looking chef he'd introduced her to.

She was in such a state of depression, she didn't have the energy to give a single lesson in submissive training. The twins had a desperate drive to be perfect for her, yet she had no interest in challenging them. Countess Hedvig had become quite the pest, phoning Madam at all hours of the day and night, questioning her about the progress of the twins. Madam had grown so weary of the countess's relentless inquiries, she now refused to take the woman's calls.

She'd given the butler permission to conduct the training sessions for all the pleasure-slaves except Lyza and she'd authorized him to mete out punishment whenever necessary.

As she reclined on her chaise lounge, staring blankly out the window, there were two sharp raps on the door, and it was difficult to muster the strength to say, "Come in."

Dressed in his customary vest, white gloves, tie, and tails, the butler entered Madam's private rooms with Marnie at his side pushing a little cart. Instead of her usual dowdy uniform, Marnie was dressed in a short, frilly maid's outfit with thigh-high nylons, a variation of the sexy uniforms that Lyza tended to wear.

Madam gave Marnie a quick glance but her eyes registered neither interest nor appreciation.

"Pour Madam's tea in the manner you were taught," the butler instructed.

He clapped his hands together and on cue, Marnie reached for the teapot and gracefully picked it up. She began pouring, but her hand began to shake so badly, droplets of tea spilled down the side of the teapot.

"You clumsy idiot," the butler uttered in disgust, taking the teapot from Marnie's trembling hand and pouring Madam's tea himself.

"Please accept my apology for being so clumsy, Madam," she said with her head hung in shame.

The butler carefully placed a biscuit on an elegant saucer and served it to Madam. Then he looked at Marnie with narrowed eyes. "You have earned a session with the flogger." He grabbed a fistful of hair and dragged her toward him.

"Ow!" Marnie cried, reflexively pulling away.

He jerked harder on her hair and again she cried out in pain.

With his free hand he smacked her across the mouth. "Back talk will not be tolerated."

Marnie flinched and gasped at the shock of the impact and stared at the butler with eyes bulging in astonishment.

"Do not let me see such exaggerated reactions from you ever again. You must learn to accept discipline without as much as a flutter of your lashes."

"Yes, sir. I'll do better."

Pleased with himself, the butler glanced at Madam, hoping that his severe method of disciplining the young apprentice had ignited a spark of excitement in Madam's eyes.

Disinterested, Madam gave him a blank look and then returned her gaze to the window.

"Leave us," he said to Marnie, waving her away.

Eager to leave, Marnie hurried toward the set of double doors.

"Wait!"

Marnie froze.

The butler pulled out his pocket watch and noted the time. "Report to my room for your flogging session in precisely one hour."

"I'll be punctual, sir."

"My new flogger is made of a thicker grade of leather than my former device. Sometimes unruly trainees need to be spanked with something specially designed to expunge every last speck of disobedience out of them. Something that will snap obstinate pleasure-slaves quickly back into shape."

"But I wasn't being obstinate or disobedient, sir. I—"

"Silence! Your backtalk has earned you ten extra lashes. Now, go. Get out of my sight."

"Yes, sir." Marnie curtsied and she managed to lift the corner of her mouth in an uneasy smile before hastily departing Madam's chambers.

Again the butler cast a searching glance at his wife, hoping to see a look of approval on her face. He was, after all, transforming the entire lot of Madam's trainees to exhibit impeccable behavior. Now that he was wielding the whip with Madam's full knowledge and blessings, he would not tolerate even the most minuscule imperfection.

"I've been training a few of the apprentices to trot around the grounds like ponies—"

"I'm not interested, Butler." Madam spoke in an emotionless monotone.

"What's wrong, Madam?" he asked with tenderness. "I don't believe I've ever seen you quite like this. You've always derived sadistic pleasure in dispensing punishment, but you no longer seem to care. Might I remind you that you've been paid handsomely to train this pack of dullards and you put your professional integrity at risk if the apprentices aren't returned to their owners with brand new skill sets that showcase their eagerness to please."

"I know," she said softly. "I've been considering returning the fees I collected."

"Excuse my impertinence, Madam, but I don't think that's a wise decision."

"Why isn't it?"

"In my opinion, if you fail to turn out expertly-trained pleasure-slaves, not only will your business suffer, but you'll also lose the respect of the fetish community—respect that you've worked so hard to earn."

"I don't care."

"Of course you do." He knelt down on one knee before her and clasped her hand in his gloved hand. "Tell me what's wrong? It's causing me great pain to see you in such despair."

"I don't know what's wrong. Lately, I've been feeling despondent—in a constant state of tearfulness, and I can't shake the mood."

Taking advantage of Madam's weakened condition, the butler took the liberty of removing a glove and softly caressed the top of her hand. Being so physically close to his wife was a bit overwhelming, and for a few moments he said nothing as he inhaled her perfume and silently basked in her magnificent aura.

When his sneaky fingers glided up to her wrist and began stroking her flesh, Madam looked down at his hand disdainfully. "Have you lost your mind, Butler? How dare you touch me without permission?"

He stared at his hand as if he had no idea how it had found its way to Madam's velvety skin. "My apologies. I only wanted to comfort you." He replaced his glove and stood up, shoulders erect, hands folded together as if to restrain them from any inappropriate activity.

"Can I be frank with you, Jamison?" Madam said, softening her tone.

"Of course."

"I met an amazing chef at the Secret Sunset Gala. He prepared all manners of culinary delights—the food was unlike anything I've ever tasted. I love Azalea like a sister, but honestly, her food is awful. The chef I met learned his craft at the Culinary Institute of America and for the past few years has trained in Michelin-star restaurants under the tutelage of world renowned chefs.

"His name is Nico Bradford and his focus is on combining the freshest ingredients and cutting edge techniques to create high-end, designer cuisine."

"You seem to know his full resume."

Madam chose to ignore the butler's sarcasm. "I deserve to have a man like that working in my kitchen, and cooking exclusively for me. It infuriates me to think of him delighting the taste buds of anyone else."

"Could it be that your desire for this chef is the reason for your unexplained depression?"

"It's possible. I haven't been the same since the evening of the gala. I want him so badly, Jamison. I won't be happy until I possess him completely. I feel humiliated that he hasn't contacted me to offer himself—mind, body, and soul."

"Either he's a fool or he's too intimated to attempt to seek out the attention of such an accomplished woman as you. All you have to do is contact the man and offer him the opportunity to be your personal chef as well as the coveted position of being one of your prized pleasure-slaves."

"It would be magnificent to have such a rugged, manly-man being in service to me."

Madam's remark was a personal dig at the butler—an affront to his manhood—but he didn't flinch. He indulged her ego and poured on the praises as he always did. "Don't worry, you'll get your way. With your charm and beauty, how could the chef deny you? There isn't a man or woman on earth who isn't enchanted by you. It's not as if we're talking about the prime minister of a country, a general of an army, or anyone of any importance. We're talking about a common chef. Convincing him to give up his freedom and become human chattel should be child's play for a renowned dominatrix such as you."

Madam considered the butler's comments and then said, "I fear this particular chef is far too high-minded to accept a life of servitude."

"I can't imagine why he wouldn't want to become your personal property unless he has pleasure-slaves of his own. Actually, that shouldn't be an excuse. Even the most tyrannical masters have been known to switch to a submissive role when coerced by someone as strong-willed as you, Madam. "

"That's the problem, Jamison."

"I don't understand."

"According to Colden, Chef Nico isn't into the fetish lifestyle at all."

"That's preposterous. No one in the vanilla life would agree to work at a hardcore fetish event like the Secret Sunset Gala."

"He's open-minded and non-judgmental, I suppose," Madam

said with a shrug. "And it didn't hurt that Colden offered him an indecent amount of cash."

"You're a very wealthy woman, why don't you triple what Colden paid him—make him an offer he can't refuse."

"I'm not interested in making him an offer for only one night. I want him to willingly submit to me on a permanent basis. Like every other man whom I've charmed, he should be begging to kiss my shoe. But so many days have elapsed, I'm afraid the chef wasn't captivated by me. Perhaps I'm not as captivating as I once was."

"Nonsense. He's somewhere at this very moment trying to muster the courage to ask if you'd allow him to kneel at your feet."

Madam gave a quick smile. "You may be right, Jamison. I should put him out of his misery and let him know that he's more than welcome to be my personal chef and pleasure-slave."

"You must take baby steps, Madam," the butler advised. "Don't make the offer too hastily. I suggest you hire him for a particular occasion, and then gradually incorporate him into the household. I'm excited for you, and relieved that we'll soon be rid of Azalea and her crew of ghastly cooks."

"You know I have a special connection with Azalea and it won't be easy letting her go, but I'll lighten the blow with a handsome severance package once Nico is on board. Or maybe she could work as his sous chef."

"Frankly, you've never opened up to me about your connection with Azalea. It's a mystery to me. All I know is that you feel obligated to the crude woman for some unknown reason. She has absolutely no business cooking in your kitchen. She'd be much more suited slinging hash in a diner somewhere."

A look of intense sorrow filled Madam's eyes. "Let's not talk about my connection with Azalea right now—it saddens me."

"I'm sorry to have upset you, Madam. Let's change the subject."

Madam nodded solemnly.

"If you're not ready to take over the reins of running House of Stevens, I'm more than happy to continue acting on your behalf. I've been holding down the fort to the best of my ability, but my methods of handling your unruly charges can't compare to your unique skills in training pleasure-slaves in specific areas of behavior.

"At present, I'm teaching Marnie how to conduct herself appropriately when offering her rump to be smacked by aristocrats. Sadly, I lack your savoir-faire and creativity, but my training methods will have to do until you're feeling up to par."

"It's true that you're nothing more than a lowly butler with no idea of what it takes to be a true master," Madam said with reestablished pomposity.

Stung by Madam's harsh words, the butler flinched.

"I'll get back to the business of running House of Stevens after I've settled the matter of the chef. I need you to help me come up with an idea of an important occasion that would require the service of a chef."

"Your birthday is coming up in a few months," the butler reminded her.

Madam shot him a look of fury. "I don't acknowledge birthdays, and you very well know that, Butler."

"My apologies, Madam." The butler stroked his chin and looked toward the ceiling, thoughtfully. "I've got an idea."

"Yes?"

"Why don't you invite a select group of masters and mistresses to spend an afternoon at House of Stevens and allow them to see with their own eyes how magnificently well-trained your apprentices are. The chef can dazzle them with his fine cuisine and I have quite a few ideas along the lines of entertainment."

Still smarting from the mention of her upcoming birthday, Madam wore a sour expression as she listened to the butler's ideas, but after hearing him out, she couldn't suppress a smile.

"That's a splendid idea, Jamison," she exclaimed. Then suddenly, her smile faded.

"What's wrong?"

"I totally dread having to contact Colden for the chef's personal information. I don't want him to have the satisfaction of knowing I'm the least bit interested in Nico."

"Why not? You and Colden are good friends."

"We're associates."

"Don't worry, leave everything to me. I'll get the chef's information online, and I'll make the arrangements with him, urging him, of course, to be discreet. Additionally, I'll organize the special event, and all you have to do from now until then is luxuriate, look beautiful, and concentrate on feeling better."

"I'm starting to feel better already, Jamison," Madam said brightly.

"By the way, Countess Hedvig has been calling the landline every hour, inquiring about the twins. I must admit I haven't spent too much time with those boys, simply because I can't understand a word they say, and I have no patience for communicating with hand gestures," the butler said with his mouth turned down.

"The countess is such a bore. If she didn't have connections with the royal family of Norway, I wouldn't give her the time of day."

"I wish I could brush her off as easily as you do, but I feel obligated to put her mind at ease when she frets about Christoff and Arnoldus. That woman desperately needs to brush up on her language skills, however. Her English is atrocious, and I can barely make out a word she's saying whenever she manages to hold me captive over the phone."

"Her broken English doesn't bother me since I rarely listen to her prattle on and on. Sometimes I set the phone down and walk out of the room while she's talking, and when I return she's still yakking away," Madam said with laughter.

The sound of Madam's laughter warmed the butler's heart.

It was the lengthiest and most intimate conversation that he and Madam had shared in years, and he felt more like a beloved spouse and a cherished confidante than a mere servant. The butler believed that he and his wife had finally reached a point in their relationship where they would treat each other with tenderness and mutual respect. If he played his cards right, it wouldn't be long before he consummated his thirteen-year marriage and moved his few belongings into Madam's private quarters. Perhaps, behind closed doors, she'd even allow him to call her by her given name. And if he approached the subject with careful consideration, maybe, she'd consider finally taking his last name.

House of Hardwicke had a nice ring to it.

CHAPTER 15

Marnie wore her dark hair in a high ponytail, going for a look of sweet innocence. Wearing a contrite expression, she made her way to the attic. Climbing the stairs, she worked up a batch of fake tears along with a trembling bottom lip. In reality, she had no fear at all. The butler's leather strap couldn't possibly compare to the sadistic punishments that her master had doled out, but it would be worth the effort if she could gain the butler's sympathy and get the colloquial slap on the wrist.

She gave a soft, timid knock on the attic door. When no one answered, she called out in a quavering voice, "Mr. Hardwicke. Are you there, sir? It's Marnie…I've come for my punishment."

Still no answer. As she was about to turn and leave, she heard footsteps bounding up the attic stairs. To her surprise, the butler appeared on the landing and he was carrying a bucket of ice with a pair of tongs protruding from the top. Maybe she'd get that fancy cocktail she'd been craving since arriving in America. Back in Ireland, Master always took her out to the pub after a chastisement. Often, it was difficult to sit on the barstool with a sore bum, but a stiff drink had a way of numbing the pain.

She lowered her head in humility, but the butler didn't acknowledge her at all. He strode past her as if she were invisible, pulled a set of keys from his pocket and opened the door. He returned the keys to his pocket and startled Marnie by taking hold of her hair and roughly yanking her into his dismal room.

Resisting being dragged any further into the room, Marnie dug her heels into the floor when she noticed the implements of torture that the butler had laid out with precision and care on top of the dresser.

The butler released her hair and set the bucket of ice on the dresser beside the ominous devices, and then regarded Marnie with a dark look that was utterly frightening.

"I'm really sorry about the tea. I was a bit nervous, and my hand was unsteady, sir."

"I told you there'd be painful consequences for your mistakes."

"But…but I only spilled one little drop," Marnie protested, eyeing the foreboding, medieval-looking implements that were lined up on the dresser.

"Shh." The butler held a finger up to his lips. "I told you you'd be disciplined whenever you make a mistake. Now, stop talking and listen. I'm going to hurt you," he said in a soft tone that was almost kindly. "The things I'm going to do to you will hurt a lot. You'll be in agony, and you'll beg me to stop. But over time you'll learn to appreciate the time and effort I've devoted to your training."

The butler locked the door and Marnie's eyes darted to the solitary window that was so high up, it practically reached the ceiling. There was no escaping this room.

He clutched her by the chin, forcing her to look at him. "Remove your clothes and present yourself properly."

"Yes, sir." Slowly and gracefully, Marnie removed the skimpy maid's uniform, and then rolled down the stockings. She placed her neatly folded clothing on the seat of a wooden chair. Very carefully, she positioned her pumps on the floor beneath the chair.

"May I kneel for you, Mr. Hardwicke, sir?" Marnie asked, hoping to please him by showing enthusiasm.

Without warning, he grabbed her by the throat and applied pressure. "Don't call me Mr. Hardwicke and don't refer to me as sir. When you're in this room, you will call me, master."

"Yes, master." She croaked out the words.

He released her neck and stood back, observing her with satisfaction as she tried to catch her breath.

"Are you a good kisser, Marnie?"

"What?" Marnie was baffled. The butler didn't seem to be the romantic type.

"Never answer a question with another question. Are you a good kisser?" He raised his hand in a threatening manner.

"Yes, master," she blurted. "I am a very good kisser." She added a flirty smile, hoping to persuade him to go easy on her.

"In that case you may kneel before me and kiss my shoe."

"Yes, master." She bent daintily and lowered herself to the floor until her butt touched her heels. Then she continued the downward movement seamlessly until her forehead touched the floor.

"Kiss it," he said, inching his right shoe forward.

She placed a soft kiss on the shiny black shoe, and was careful not to leave the faintest smudge from her lips.

"Impressive," he said.

"Thank you, master."

"Now, position yourself properly."

Charmingly, Marnie rose up to her knees, keeping her eyes focused downward, her lips puckered and ready to kiss his other shoe.

The butler took steps to the dresser where his instruments were set out.

Stealing a glance, Marnie's panicked eyes followed him and watched as he retrieved a pair of wrist restraints.

"Head up," he said, clapping his hands together. She lifted her chin and when their eyes met, he pointed to a particularly darkened corner of the dim attic.

Marnie pushed up slightly, preparing to rise to her feet, but the butler placed the sole of his shoe on her shoulder. "Did I give you permission to stand?"

She shook her head vigorously. "No, master, you didn't and I apologize for not waiting for your command."

He let out a cruel laugh. "That's another strike against you; now crawl over there."

She crawled in the direction he'd indicated, making sure not to go to fast or too slow. She tried her best to crawl with controlled movements that were graceful and sensual.

"Now stand."

She obeyed, and was once again careful to present fluid movements.

Stealing glances, she observed her surroundings. Her lashes fluttered rapidly when she noticed a hook jutting out of the wall.

"You won't be needing use of your hands," the butler said, grasping her wrists and placing leather restraints on them. He then raised her arms, attaching the chain that dangled from the cuff to the hook that was slightly above her head—not high enough to force her to stand on the tip of her toes, but high enough to make her uncomfortable.

A naked captive, Marnie's eyes filled with fear as the butler turned and paced toward the instruments again. Curious to know what was going to happen next, she craned her neck and stretched her eyes open wide, but was unable to discern which device he'd selected.

He returned and stood in front of her, ominously towering over her in the shadowy room. He looked at her for a long moment without saying a word and she found the silence to be more oppressive than the fiery sting of the dragon tail whip that her master used on her back in Ireland.

The silence continued for far too long and the suspense was agonizing. So agonizing she wished the butler would hurry up and deliver the intended punishment so that it could be done and over with.

"Spread your legs," he finally said, breaking the silence.

She wondered what sort of cruel object the butler would stick inside her. And though fear caused her heart to beat rapidly, she didn't dare refuse his command. Standing with her legs wide apart, she held her breath as she anticipated the excruciating sensation of an enormous object being forcibly inserted into her vagina.

The butler bent down to crotch level and used his gloved fingers to stretch open her cunt. Marnie took a deep, shuddering breath as her pussy grew moist, a reaction she was ashamed of. Bracing herself for a dreadful vaginal intrusion, she closed her eyes and clenched her teeth; all the while her rebellious pussy dripped in slutty anticipation.

But she wasn't penetrated with a foreign object. What was done to her was far, far worse. She yelped in pain when he clamped an object that was terribly sharp onto her clit.

"Oh, my God. Take it off, master, please!" With her wrists restrained, all Marnie could do was twist and whimper like a wounded animal.

The butler chuckled as he made another short trek over to his collection of medieval torture devices. He picked up something metallic and slowly, menacingly headed back to the torture corner.

When Marnie realized he was holding a pair of crude metal clamps, she winced and tried to shrink away from him.

"There's nowhere to run, my girl, so stand still and let's get on with testing your tolerance for pain. My collection was purchased piece-by-piece from fetish-connoisseurs all over the world. These ancient beauties came from China, and I was told that during war times, enemies eagerly spilled secrets once these mean, little clamps were attached to their nipples."

"Master, I promise to be more careful. I'll never spill Madam's tea again. Not ever!"

"Hush, hush." He softly patted her lips. "Take some deep breaths to prepare yourself."

Marnie quickly gulped in a burst of air and blew it out, rapidly repeating the process as if coping with contractions during labor. She emitted an ear-splitting shriek when both clamps bit into her nipples so deeply that two crimson trails trickled down her torso.

"Take them off, take them off. Master, please, please, please," she begged. Wild-eyed, she swung her head from side to side, her long raven hair whipping through the air. Bucking her body, she attempted to jerk free from the wrist restraints.

Crazed from the pain, tears streaked her cheeks as she begged for mercy. Ignoring her pleas, the butler turned away from her and once again proceeded to the dresser and picked up the tongs from the ice bucket. Whistling a sinister melody, he shoved the tongs inside the bucket, crunching through chunks of ice.

She couldn't begin to imagine what his next plan was, but when he removed the clamp from her clit and soothingly ran the ice cube over her swollen genitalia, she uttered repeated words of thanks, practically delirious with joy that the punishment was over.

But it was hard to enjoy the healing ministrations when her boobs felt like they were on fire. "Master, would you be kind enough to remove the nipple clamps?" she asked in the sweetest voice she could manage while under such extreme duress.

"You empty-headed, little twit," he seethed. "I told you not to make any recommendations to me. Now, spread your legs wider."

Whimpering and trembling, Marnie complied. He shoved the chilling ice cube along with the clawed tong inside her cunt as deeply as they would go.

Her upper body stiffened and her mouth stretched open as she emitted a long, croaking gasp.

Reverting to a more tender approach, he glided the ice and tong in and out, using twisting motions. "Does it feel good?"

Teeth chattering, she nodded, but her expression was one of misery.

"Show me how good it feels. If you don't fuck this ice cube right, I'm going to heat up the tongs and introduce you to a different type of temperature play? So, tell me, Marnie, do you want to play with fire?"

"No, master, I don't want to play with fire," she said with conviction and commenced to swiveling her hips around, humping hard, and accepting the thrusts of the tong as if the horrible chilled metal were a meaty, erect dick.

CHAPTER 16

After lunch, Brynne, Marnie, Christoff, and Arnoldus were pulled from their household chores and summoned to the stables by the butler. They'd already run around the grounds at dawn, galloping like fools merely to satisfy the butler's sadistic streak. It was baffling why he'd called them back to the dreaded stables at this hour of the day when the temperature had risen to eighty degrees.

Standing in a cluster, the four pleasure-slaves looked at each other questioningly. Marnie and Brynne wondered aloud why they had been summoned by the butler, while Christoff and Arnoldus spoke in Norwegian, shrugging their shoulders and making other gestures that indicated they had no idea why they'd been called outside. The twins with their sensitive pale skin were quickly turning red, roasting under the scorching heat of the sun.

Finally, the butler strolled out of one of the two stables. He was puffing on a cigar, which was something Brynne had never seen him do inside the house. She supposed Madam didn't approve of the smell. Hugo was at the butler's side, clutching a menacing riding crop.

Though there were a few blades of grass stuck to the butler's high-gloss boots, as usual, he was immaculate in his customary formal attire.

Hugo, on the other hand looked as scruffy as ever with mud-stained boots and dusty coveralls. But as disheveled as he was, Hugo, heavily tanned with straggly sun bleached hair that he continually pushed out of his eyes was a handsome lad with striking features and hazel eyes.

The butler motioned for Brynne, Marnie, and the twins to join him where he stood, beneath the shade of an apple tree. Grateful to get out of the heat, the four of them hurried over.

"I won't keep you in suspense; I'm going to get right to the point of why I called you out here today. You four have exhibited the best posture and fastest speed during our early morning pony-trotting exercises and you've been selected to compete in a very important horse race that will take place in three weeks. That's a short amount of time to get you properly trained to race, but I have faith that Hugo, an experienced horse trainer, is up to the challenge." The butler clapped Hugo on the back.

"But I've never ridden a horse before, sir," Marnie said worriedly.

"Me either," Brynne concurred.

The twins looked at each other quizzically.

"You're not here to learn how to ride." The butler laughed heartily. Hugo cut his eyes at the four pleasure-slaves and then sheepishly dropped his gaze.

"None of you will be riding horses during the race—you *are* the horses."

"What do you mean, sir?" Brynne asked.

"What I mean is that your identities have officially changed. Brynne and Marnie are now ponygirls and the twins are ponyboys. You'll no longer reside in the house doing chores or attending to Madam's needs. We can't have horses indoors clunking around and stinking up the place, now can we?"

Bafflement furrowed the brows of the group of four, and there were murmurs of discontent.

"Silence!" the butler shouted. "There won't be a discussion about my decision. Henceforth, you will no longer regard yourselves as people. I want you to get it through your thick skulls that you are horses, and all your behaviors, mannerisms, and even the sounds that you make will emulate horses. But not just any kind of horse. Think of yourselves as the best of the best—proud thoroughbreds. Hugo will be your trainer and he will provide me with a daily report of how well you're all adjusting to your new lives. If I receive an unfavorable report on any of you, you can be certain that you'll be horsewhipped."

Brynne cringed at the idea of being horsewhipped.

"Do we understand one another?" the butler inquired.

"Yes, sir," Brynne and Marnie responded quickly.

The twins, having no idea what the butler had said mimicked Brynne and Marnie and said, "Yes, sir," with a charming accent.

"There'll be no more talking, ponies," the butler said, wagging a finger. "Being a good ponygirl and ponyboy doesn't require language. It doesn't matter anymore that the twins don't speak English. There'll be severe consequences if they're heard speaking their own language or attempting English. I expect you all to become quick studies in the language of horses."

After completing his spiel, the butler stepped away from the apple tree, striding over the grassy field, and then taking the smooth path that led to the main house with all its many comforts.

"Listen up," Hugo said after the butler was no longer in sight. "Since we all realize that horses don't talk, I want one of you to tell me how horses communicate."

"They whinny, neigh, squeal, snort, and nicker," Marnie quickly responded.

A shadow fell over Hugo's handsome face and swift as lightning, he cracked Brynne across her rump with the riding crop. "Horses don't talk, Marnie. I want you to throw your head up and answer the question the way a horse would."

At first, Marnie looked at Hugo in disbelief, but when she noticed his mouth tighten in irritation, she responded by raising her head up and doing her best version of a neighing horse.

Considering her bizarre display comical, Christoff and Arnoldus burst into laughter, which earned them each a sharp crack across their backs.

"I take horse training very seriously and by the day of the race, I expect all of y'all to be running like prize-winning thoroughbreds."

Taking on a more jovial expression, Hugo said in his Southern drawl, "Can't nobody say I don't love horses. I done spent the majority of the day moving all the regular horses into the second stable, and then cleaning it up spic and span for you racing ponies." He pointed to the stable on the left. "Like Mr. Hardwicke said, that's where you'll be housed from now on."

Brynne cut an eye at Marnie and frowned. Fearing the riding crop, Marnie looked away from Brynne, keeping her gaze fixed on Hugo's face.

"Now I want y'all to take a good look at this here apple tree because it's gonna make up the bulk of your meals. Horses don't eat hot dogs or burgers or whatnot, and they dang sure don't eat potato chips and other kinds of snacks. While y'all are training with me, you're gonna eat what horses eat. You're gonna dress like horses, and most importantly, you're gonna run in the proper form of a thoroughbred."

Brynne listened to Hugo in disbelief, feeling a powerful urge to escape the House of Stevens. But how would Ian react if she returned home without receiving a certificate from Madam Midnight? Ian's friends in high places had gotten Brynne bumped up on the long list of pleasure-slave applicants, and Ian would be upset if his friends' efforts had been in vain.

Perhaps Ian will understand when I explain how bizarre the training has been. It's actually beyond bizarre, making me wonder what planet I've landed on. Everyone here is crazy. Hugo, Madam, Mr. Hardwicke—everyone! Ian did not send me here to be turned into a pony by a freakin' redneck, stable boy. Nor did he expect most of my training to be at the hands of a lunatic butler. Ian paid a handsome sum for me to get Madam's personal attention; he wanted me to learn at the feet of a world-renowned dominatrix. Yet, in the weeks that I've been here, Madam hasn't given me any instruction at all. If I'm to remain sane, I simply must get a message to my beloved and inform him of what's going on. I have to beg him to—

The sound of Hugo's voice interrupted Brynne's musings. "In the stable, each of you has an individual stall, and that's where you'll spend your time when you're not training. Inside your stall is where you'll eat, sleep, and have your grooming done. With that said, let's go. Today we're going to get you fitted in your boots and let you practice running around with hooves."

"Oh, my God," Brynne muttered under her breath as she and the others fell into an orderly line and followed Hugo to the stable. Their high-stepping march with knees parallel to the waist, feet landing with heels first, and heads held high was indicative of the rigid training they'd received thus far. Not one pair of eyes wavered. As if wearing blinders, they all stared straight ahead as they marched to their new home.

Brynne feared there'd be the stench of horse feces and a mess of hay strewn about, but to her relief the stable was immaculately clean, smelling of new leather, lemon oil, and the lingering scent of the butler's fine cigar.

"Get into your stalls, and strip down," Hugo ordered.

Hesitantly Brynne ambled inside. The clang of the stall's gate banging shut echoed with a terrible finality.

Inside her cramped new home were a pile of saddle blankets for bedding and a neat bale of hay that could be used as a table or a nightstand. In a corner of the stall, Brynne noticed a pair of thigh-high leather boots that laced up the front and had rows of silver buckles running up the sides. The foot portion of the boot was oddly shaped—thick-soled and clunky with no heel—and looked exactly like horse hooves.

"Those boots aren't for decoration, so after you peel off those clothes, hurry up and put 'em on," Hugo instructed as he paced through the stable.

Brynn undressed and tucked her folded uniform in a corner on the floor of the stall. Sitting on the bale of hay, she forced her feet into the awkwardly shaped hoof-boots and could hear the others rustling around in their stalls struggling with the odd footwear. She found it difficult to walk in the boots. Without a proper heel to the shoe, she had to walk on the balls of her feet. It was extremely uncomfortable but she managed to hobble to the gate of her stall.

Standing there, only her neck and head was visible over the gate. Like horses, Brynne and the others stretched their necks, their gazes swiveling as they took in their environment. Brynne glanced at Marnie who was in the stall next to hers, and saw humiliation in her friend's eyes. Brynne made a sad face that told Marnie that she was equally humiliated.

The twins wore angry expressions. They backed away from the gate and began pacing, obviously upset about their predicament.

Hugo walked up to each stall, passing out rubber bands, hair brushes, and sunscreen. "I want y'all to pull your hair up in a pony-tail, and that goes for the ponyboys as well as the ponygirls. Use that sunscreen to protect your skin while you're out in the sun."

Although the twins couldn't understand Hugo's words, they did exactly as Brynne and Marnie, fashioning their white-blond hair into short ponytails and then slathering on sunscreen.

Hugo came into Brynne's stall, took the sunscreen from her hands and told her to turn around. He covered her back, her ass, and the backs of her legs with it. And even though his hands were calloused and rough, his touch felt surprising soothing.

"My money's on you, Brynne. I think you'll win the race for sure," he said softly, fondling the back of her neck and stroking her hair. He opened her stall and led her out by her ponytail. "Come on, girl. Trot on over to the corral and practice walking in those boots. Be mindful of your form," he added, tapping her shoulder with the end of the riding crop.

Brynne's steps were unsteady, and Marnie soon caught up with her as Brynne cautiously hobbled across the field.

"It's not so bad pretending to be a horse," Marnie remarked. "Hugo seems to be a decent chap. He's strict, but not cruel like Mr. Hardwicke."

Marnie had told Brynne about the heinous actions committed against her by the sadistic butler, and how her ass still bore the stripes from his cane. Feeling bad about what had happened to her, Brynne looked at Marnie with compassion and patted her arm.

"Don't feel sorry for me, Brynne. I've already moved past what Mr. Hardwicke did," Marnie said casually. "Since I wasn't graceful enough to continue training as a personal attendant to Madam, I hope I can succeed as a sexy ponygirl."

Brynne wrinkled her nose. "What's sexy about being a ponygirl? Seems ridiculous to me. It's the kind of nonsense that only Mr. Hardwicke would cook up in order to humiliate us. I can't imagine a wealthy master being enticed by something as bizarre as a ponygirl."

Marnie sighed. "You may have a point, but I've got to get auctioned off or my master will do far worse things to me than Mr. Hardwicke did."

"Oh, Marnie. You have to get away from that man."

"I know I should." Marnie brooded for a few moments, her look of misery deepening, and then her mood turned suddenly cheerful. "I've been wondering what an exotic beauty like Lyza saw in a grungy stable hand, but after being around Hugo for a while, I can see why she's attracted to him—he's hot! And he has a sensual side."

"Oh, yeah?"

"Uh-huh. Inside my stall, the way he brushed my hair and helped me into my boots was sort of romantic. My whole body tingled when he smoothed sunscreen all over my skin."

Brynne looked at Marnie as if she were crazy. "I agree he has a nice touch, but that doesn't mean it is okay for him to treat us like we're actually horses."

"He's only following Mr. Hardwicke's orders. Let's not be hypocrites, Brynne. We're all here for the same reason, to learn how to become perfect pleasure-slaves. We all consented to be taken to the limits of our endurance—and that's exactly what's happening to us now."

"I suppose," Brynne said resignedly.

Marnie flashed a quick smile. "Hugo promised to give me a good rubdown if I maintain good form while he's taking me through my paces."

Brynne simply shrugged. She couldn't accept being a ponygirl as easily as Marnie had warmed up to the idea.

CHAPTER 17

Walking in the uncomfortable boots was nearly impossible. Holding on to each other, Brynne and Marnie hobbled, stumbled, and limped their way to the horse enclosure.

Remarkably, Christoff and Arnoldus weren't having any trouble wearing the hooved boots. Brynne's mouth fell open in surprise when the twins trotted past her and Marnie and easily made their way into the corral. Once inside the fenced area, they ran around with their hooves clomping loudly. Enjoying the freedom of the outdoors, the boys threw their heads back and neighed happily.

"Looks like they're adjusting," Brynne remarked.

"Yes, and we'd better figure out a way to make the adjustment, also." She looked over her shoulder and said, "Here comes, Hugo. We'd better stop chatting and concentrate on learning how to trot in these damned boots before he gives us a bad report."

Inside the corral, the twins ran around like they'd been wearing hoof-boots for years. Hugo sat on the top of the fence, drinking water from a squirt bottle and eating an apple while he kept an eye on his four charges.

"Whoa, girl," he called out to Marnie, who had started a wobbly trot around the corral. "Pace yourself and get used to wearing hooves. If you were to fall and hurt yourself, my ass would be on the line. Mr. Hardwicke wouldn't take kindly to one of you horses getting injured before the race."

Hugo hopped off the fence and entered the corral, taking Marnie by the ponytail and leading her off to the side. With a finger he pried open her mouth and gave her a couple of squirts of water. He rubbed her ass fondly and then struck her softly with the crop. "Go on, girl, step lively—but not too fast."

Still hobbling along and holding on to the fence as she lazily circled the corral, Brynne observed Hugo's gentle treatment of Marnie and felt a stab of envy. It surprised her to realize she desired individualized attention from him. She wanted to feel his strokes and caresses and she wanted him to brush her hair. If it took behaving like a horse to get some special treatment, then so be it.

Feeling competitive, Brynne set her mind on maintaining her balance. With her head held high and body erect, she stepped high, bringing her knees up the way she'd been taught. She caught Hugo's attention by neighing loudly with each proud, marching step.

"Whoo-hoo!" Hugo cried out. "Way to go, Brynne. You're looking good, girl. Like a true thoroughbred."

Feeling proud, Brynne neighed again and the twins responded by whinnying as they galloped around the corral.

After a couple of hours of trotting and running in the hot sun, their bodies were grimy, covered in perspiration, grass, and dust.

Hugo led them back to the stables, but before taking them inside their stalls, he hosed them down, and one-by-one, and he gave each of them a brisk rubdown with a towel.

Inside the stall, Brynne was grateful for the cool water that Hugo poured inside a metal bowl. Realizing what was expected of her, she got down on all fours and lapped the water greedily.

"Hey, you were really were thirsty, weren't you, girl?" Hugo said with affection. He knelt down and patted the top of Brynne's head, then ran his finger through her ponytail. He ran his hand all over her body, squeezing her breasts, rubbing her back, and fondling her buttocks and her cunt. It was obvious from the way he touched her that Brynne had done a good job of trotting in the corral.

She continued lapping water from the bowl while Hugo petted her; his coarse hands felt like a loofah on her soft skin. When he ran a finger along the crack of her ass, she trembled with pleasure. He parted her cheeks and pushed the tip of his finger inside her butt hole.

"You're pretty tight in there, girl. I'm gonna have to open you up a little more, but don't worry, I'll be gentle."

She wanted to tell him how much she looked forward to him opening up her ass, but deprived of speech all she could do was snort and nicker like a horse. It was the happiest she'd been since arriving at the House of Stevens. Trying to escape was no longer in her mind. There was no fight left in her. Although she'd never protested when Ian had insisted on using her body in various ways, she now realized that she'd never totally relinquished her person-hood. But taking on the identity of a ponygirl was the closest she'd ever come to completely relinquishing control. She was intoxicated by the thrill of being reduced to the status of a nonperson.

"I'll be back with your dinner in a little while," Hugo said softly, patting Brynne's ass before exiting the stall.

She was ravenous and so she whinnied in appreciation of the meal Hugo had promised. Her stablemates, hearing her horse sound, neighed and whinnied in response.

Hugo returned with a large stainless steel bowl filled with a creamy combination of chopped apples, kernels of corn, mushed-up oats, beet pulp, and baby spinach. The bowl of goulash was sweetened with raw honey. Brynne stuck her face in the bowl. Using only her mouth—no hands—she ate the surprisingly delicious meal and then licked the bowl until it was spotless.

"Good girl." Hugo patted her on the head and rubbed her face. "I'll be back after I check on the others," he said softly.

Brynne nodded but was careful to imitate the way a horse moved its head up and down, and nickered to convey happiness. She curled up on her pile of straw and waited for Hugo to return.

Being enclosed with her stablemates was quiet and serene. She enjoyed hearing the soft sounds emanating from each stall that Hugo visited. Judging by the soft moans emanating from Marnie's stall, Brynne figured she was getting that special rubdown that Hugo had promised her. When Hugo left Marnie's stall, Brynne listened to the sound of one of the twins grunting and breathing harshly.

Finally, she heard audible sucking sounds and the other twin was squealing softly. The sucking stopped momentarily and there was the low rumbling sound of Hugo's voice. She couldn't make out everything he said to the twin, but she clearly heard him say, "You ran like a champion today, and that's why you're getting your dick sucked."

Brynne slid a finger in her pussy, and moved it to the dick-sucking rhythm that echoed throughout the stable.

With her finger embedded in her pussy, Brynne drifted off to sleep. She didn't hear him enter her stall and shed his clothes, but she felt his hard naked body when he snuggled up behind her, his groin grinding into her ass.

"Wake up, girl," he said, softly smacking her ass. "Wake up, horsey," he whispered affectionately, tugging her arm until she pulled herself up on all fours.

Hugo mounted her from behind and the moment his cock entered her wet cunt, Brynne bucked wildly. She threw her head up high and whinnied with pleasure as he pushed his cock in increments, deeply inside her cunt.

"You're my best ponybitch, aintcha?"

Oh, yes!

"Seeing your pretty ass strutting around the corral with your big tits bouncing up and down made my dick as hard as concrete."

A mixture of sweat and body heat seemed to cause steam to seep from Brynne's pores. Overcome with passion, she made throaty inhuman sounds. Spreading her legs as wide as possible, she encouraged Hugo to ram her pussy. The fierce desire to be filled with every inch of his dick caused her to rotate her hips wildly as she panted and neighed. It was as close to the edge of madness as she'd ever come.

"Whoa, girl," he whispered, pulling her ponytail until she stopped thrusting and gyrating. "I'm gonna bust a big nut before I'm ready to if you don't calm yourself down. You hear me, girl?"

She bobbed her head up and down. Fighting the urge to continue thrusting, she willed her limbs to become taut and rigid and her hips to cease swiveling.

"Good girl. Now, keep still while I do all the work. I'm gonna fuck that pony pussy until it bleeds, you hear me?"

She nodded.

"And every time I see your ass strutting around like a thoroughbred with perfect form, I'm gonna bring you back to your stall and tear that cunt up."

Brynne let out a grunt and Hugo yanked her hair hard, letting her know that he expected her to stand still, take the dick, and shut up.

He stabbed into her pussy, splashing about the syrupy juices that leaked out and trickled down her thighs. Being forced to remain still while being exquisitely fucked was a wonderfully sweet torture. And when he reached a hand beneath her and pinched her engorged clit, Brynne's knees gave out. Flat on her belly, feeling paralyzed, she groaned as if in pain while incredible jolts of intense pleasure rocketed through her body.

The unexpected creak of the main door to the stable suddenly opening startled both Brynne and Hugo. Mid-stroke, Hugo froze. "Oh, shit," he said, pulling out of Brynne and grabbing for his coveralls.

"Hugo! What the hell is wrong with you? Have you lost your fucking mind?" Lyza shouted in a high-pitched, incredulous tone.

Although Brynne was relieved that she and Hugo had been caught by Lyza instead of the butler, she was nevertheless terrified by the fiery gleam in Lyza's eyes. Brynne scampered to a corner of the stall and wrapped her arms around herself protectively.

"What are you doing in here?" Hugo asked Lyza as he hurriedly dressed.

"Why the hell are *you* in here? I can't believe what I saw." Lyza shook her head incredulously. "Are you such a pervert that you couldn't resist sticking your dick inside a goddamn ponygirl?" Infuriated, Lyza began to pound on Hugo's arms and his chest.

To restrain her, he grabbed her, locking her inside his muscular arms. Lyza stomped on the floor of the stall, and then attempted to kick Brynne, but Brynne quickly scooted out of the way.

"As nice as I've been to you, Brynne, this is how you repay me? You have no sense of loyalty—no decency whatsoever. You're going to be sorry for this," Lyza shouted before turning her fury on Hugo, kicking backward, and jabbing the heel of her stiletto into his shins.

Hugo yelped in pain and released Lyza.

Fleeing the stable, Lyza shouted over her shoulder, "I'm going to have a talk with Mr. Hardwicke right now!"

"Oh, fuck," Hugo uttered and ran after Lyza.

Cowering in a corner, Brynne dared not even imagine the hellish fate that awaited her once the butler found out about her and Hugo.

CHAPTER 18

Early the next morning before the sun had even come up, Brynne and her stablemates were awakened by Hugo, who brought fresh water and a breakfast of mushed grains, berries, and apple chunks.

Brynne yearned to speak to him. To ask him whether or not he'd been successful in calming Lyza down. But having no idea if the butler was lurking nearby, she didn't dare risk uttering a single word. She felt awful for betraying Lyza, but her fear of being punished by the butler was much stronger than any sense of guilt.

While eating breakfast, she heard Hugo tell Marnie good morning and she also heard him making friendly comments to the boys. But he had no kind words for Brynne. In fact, he seemed to be going out of his way to avoid her—hanging out in the other stalls, refilling water bowls and giving out second helpings of barley and oats.

After licking her bowl clean, she looked over the gate of her stall and watched solemnly as Hugo lined up her stablemates and led them outside. She heard him mention that he was taking them to the portable restrooms and afterward would hose them down. Brynne was confused as to why she was being left behind.

Alone in her stall, her imagination ran wild. Maybe the butler was on his way to the stable, intent on horsewhipping her while the others were occupied with the morning routine. With her eyes fixed on the main door, she feared that at any moment the enraged butler would burst inside the stable, wielding a riding crop or cracking a whip.

It seemed that a lengthy amount of time had elapsed when Hugo finally returned Marnie and the twins to their stalls. Going stir crazy, Brynne was eager to get out into the open air and was also desperate to be alone with Hugo. She had to know whether or not Lyza had exposed them, and planned to take the risk and verbally question Hugo.

Hugo gripped her ponytail and led her outside, and though he seemed to be jerking her hair a little harder than necessary, she derived joy in walking freely without the discomfort of hoof-boots. As she and Hugo made the short journey to the restrooms behind the stables, Brynne basked in the simple pleasure of feeling blades of grass between her toes and dandelions beneath her bare feet.

"Make sure you empty your bowels," Hugo instructed without meeting her eyes.

Before entering the portable restroom, she gazed in his eyes, hoping to see at least a glimmer of the delight that had been there as recent as last night. But Hugo, with his hands stuffed in his pockets, stared down at the ground, refusing to meet her gaze.

"Go on in there and do your business. When you come out, I'll hose you down."

She opened her mouth to speak, but Hugo shook his head and held a finger to his lips, warning her to keep quiet.

She nodded and went inside.

When she came out of the restroom, to her surprise Hugo had a long brown box tucked under his arm, the kind that typically contained long stem roses. It was a sweet way to put her mind at ease and let her know that he cared.

He placed the box on a tree stump and gently took her by the arm and began spraying her with water. In a bucket there was a rag and a bar of soap, which he used to thoroughly clean her, and then he toweled her dry.

"Bend over." There was no emotion in his tone, yet the box of flowers on the tree stump was proof that she had won at least a piece of his heart.

Behind the stable they were hidden from prying eyes. Assuming he wanted anal sex, Brynne who was extremely flexible, bent low enough to grasp her ankles. She bit down on her lip, bracing herself for the discomfort of his thick cock forcing its way inside her tight asshole.

He retrieved something from his pocket and said, "I'm sorry about this, Brynne. It shouldn't be too painful if I give you a good lube-job, first."

If Brynne were allowed to speak she would have told Hugo there was no need for an apology. It wasn't as if she was an anal-sex virgin. But with Ian's cock being the size of her little finger, her ass had never been stretched completely open.

This would be her first time getting a full-sized dick up her ass, so she supposed in a sense, she was an anal virgin. Nevertheless, Brynne was willing to endure the pain simply to share an intimate moment with Hugo.

Using his index finger, he polished her anus with a lubricant, slipping in the tip of his finger to test her readiness.

"You're tight," he commented with a sigh.

She clasped her ankles even tighter, and wiggled her ass invitingly. Unable to verbalize her feelings, it was the only way to let him know that she wasn't afraid and that she was ready to be penetrated. But Hugo was taking forever. He stepped back and then walked over to the tree trunk. It was an odd time for him to give her the flowers, but then again, everything about her life as a ponygirl was odd.

While waiting to be presented with the flowers, Brynne pictured them on display in her stall and wondered how on earth she'd explain them to Lyza if she paid another unexpected late-night visit to the stable.

With her head turned in his direction she observed him opening the box. At first glance, she thought her eyes were deceiving her when instead of presenting her with a dozen roses, Hugo walked toward her carrying a long swatch of brown hair.

She released her ankles and stood up straight. Her astonished eyes bulging at the sight of the long, coarse horsehair that was attached to a monstrous-looking butt plug with a spiraled shaft that was deeply ridged.

"Lyza says you have to wear this here tail all day long."

Brynne recoiled in horror.

"If you don't cooperate with her demands, she's gonna let Mr. Hardwicke know about us."

Brynne sighed in resignation.

"I'm really sorry I got you in this mess. I should have had more self-control, but you looked so pretty trotting around the corral, I let my urges get the best of me."

The remorseful sound of Hugo's voice coupled with the troubled look in his eyes tugged at Brynne's heartstrings. She wanted to take him in her arms and comfort him and assure him that she was on his side and that everything would be okay. But denied the privilege of speech, the only way to convey her sentiments was to bend over and spread her butt cheeks, welcomingly.

At the sight of the stretched and lubricated fleshy pinkness inside Brynne's ass, Hugo let out a grunt that held a primal sound that came from deep within his throat. "I gotta fuck that ass before I put the tail in," he mumbled, unzipping his coveralls.

Goosebumps formed on her arms. Both her mouth and her cunt

began to water the moment she felt the lump of hardness rubbing against her flesh, bobbing up and down with desire and smearing pre-cum along the crack of her ass.

"I shouldn't be doing this, but I just can't help myself," he said, his voice sounding tortured. The intrusion of his dick in her ass caused her to stiffen at first. But his sensual strokes relaxed her and soon she was enjoying the invasion. He started off fucking her ass slowly while standing upright, but they quickly toppled to the ground when he picked up the momentum.

On her hands and knees, she steadied herself by clutching handfuls of weeds and grass and digging her toes into the ground. With her butt poked out, her thighs widened, she communicated her desire for Hugo to fuck her ass without restraint.

With hot hands, Hugo pried her cheeks farther apart and slowly eased the enlarged cap of his dick inside her. There was no pain, only pleasure as he forcibly plunged himself deeply inside. Thrusting, he balanced himself with one hand planted on the ground and used the other to fondle her plump breasts.

"Damn, you're a sexy, fat-tittied, ponybitch," Hugo muttered as he drove inside her ass savagely.

CHAPTER 19

Minus the white gloves, which he'd carefully placed next to a collection of identical pairs inside the middle bureau drawer, the butler exited his room at precisely six in the morning. He was pleased by the ease and speed in which he was able to lock the door behind him. Until a few days ago, he hadn't realized how cumbersome and weighty those vexing white gloves had been. And the symbolism behind them was appalling. When the help wore white gloves, the persons being served were assured that the silver wouldn't be smudged by oily fingertips or tainted by an unclean hand.

White gloves had gone out of fashion eons ago and servants in private homes no longer wore them, but Madam was not aware of that. How could anyone so woefully ignorant and with such a glaring lack of social graces possibly be aware of the trends among the wealthy elite? Madam and her acquaintances exemplified the vile pretentiousness and vulgarity of the nouveau riche. As far as the butler was concerned, there was only one kind of aristocrat: someone who inherited a good name, influence, and wealth. The pretenders, like Madam, had no family lineage to speak of. He considered those types of people beneath contempt. They were bottom feeders who could afford to pay a small fortune for expensive designer gowns to attend charity balls and other social events, but also had to spend a great deal of money on a publicist who made sure the media would attach the word "socialite" to their meaningless names.

The butler was a rare breed. He was a genuine black, blue blood, a descendant of freed slaves who possessed a six-hundred acre plantation with slaves of their own. Truly elite, the butler had come from a life of privilege. He was a member of African-American aristocracy, and his family's name had once been listed in the Social Register. Sadly, his family's fortune had been watered down over generations, but the Hardwicke name still held clout when he'd first met Quintoria Stevens. But due to her greed and conniving nature, the last of his money had been squandered, and his good name was now mud.

In her current fragile state, he doubted Madam would even notice that his hands were bare (the better to fondle her when she required comforting).

Like a snake shedding its skin, the butler intended to slowly but surely peel away the outerwear that was associated with being a butler. First the gloves and then he'd get rid of the vest and tie. It was only a matter of time before he discarded the entire uniform. As the rightful king of the castle, he planned to spend most of his time lounging in a smoking jacket of the finest quality, puffing away on a Cuban cigar while sipping sherry.

The longer Chef Nico was kept at bay, the weaker Madam became. Every day she inquired as to whether or not the butler had connected with the chef and every day, he said, "Not yet, Madam. I'm still working on it."

Her shoulders would sag in disappointment before turning to the window and staring out vacantly. For the past thirteen years, she'd grown accustomed to merely snapping her fingers to get her way. Easy living had turned her soft, and Madam had apparently forgotten how to scuffle and fight for what she wanted.

She was wilting and wasting away before his very eyes. Day after day, she sat staring out the window, or lay curled beneath her silken coverlet, refusing to get dressed or to even eat. She declined to speak to her numerous business associates, and they had started to buzz with concern over the security of the monetary investments they'd sank into her various enterprises.

Never, ever had the butler seen the iron-willed, indomitable Quintoria Stevens at such a low point in her life…and by gosh, he liked it!

Whistling as he bounded down the attic stairs, he roused the female pleasure-slaves from their comfortable sleep by pressing a feature on his phone, which produced the booming sound effect of a traffic accident followed by a blaring siren and multiple car horns.

The women's comical responses never ceased to entertain him. Some woke up with a yelp while others sprang upright with their eyes bulging in shock. And then there were those scant few who gave theatrically dramatic performances with heaving breaths and hands clutching desperately at their chests as if in the throes of massive heart attacks.

"Rise and shine," he said calmly in the midst of all the commotion he'd caused.

Gathering their wits, the women followed his command and immediately began making their beds. After the beds were made, they were programmed to walk to the communal showers, single file, and perfectly silent.

Besides the butler, the twins, and Hugo, there were no other men residing on the property. With the twins out of the house and now sleeping in the stable, there was no one else to jolt into wakefulness.

Feeling sprightly and self-confident, the butler walked with a jaunty step as he headed down the hall and around the corner that led to the back stairs that would take him to the kitchen.

To his surprise, Azalea and her helpers were actually working. They were busily mixing and stirring and lifting the lids of pots to check whatever was cooking on top of the stove. Though the aromas were unfamiliar and not particularly pleasant, the butler's stomach rumbled, announcing his appetite.

"I'm ready for breakfast," he said in an unusually cheery tone.

"I'll start your French omelet in a few minutes, Mr. Hardwicke," said Darcie as she lifted the lid from a steaming pan and stirred the contents.

The butler made a great show of pulling out his pocket watch, raising a brow as he noted the time. His cheerful mood was over. There was a tightening in his face and then the corners of his mouth began a downward turn as he gave Darcie a look of reproach. "Why is my breakfast being delayed? As you all well know, I eat at the same time every day, without exception. I'm a busy man with many responsibilities, and my workload doesn't allow for numerous breaks like some of you are able to enjoy."

"Calm down, Jamison, and climb on down from your high horse for a minute," Azalea said, breaking protocol by calling him by his first name.

He made a sound of indignation before pulling out a chair and taking a seat at the kitchen table.

Edwina, the nicest of the two kitchen helpers, immediately mollified the butler by setting a hot cup of cocoa in front of him. "It's exactly the way you like it, sir. I didn't use cocoa power; I made it with hand-chopped Belgium chocolate."

"Thank you, Edwina. At least someone around here gives me the respect I deserve."

Azalea sucked her teeth. "It's not about you, Jamison. I'm worried about Quinnie…uh, I mean Madam. She hasn't been eating lately, and she needs something on her stomach. It's not good for her to be depressed for a long stretch of time. It would be God-awful if she ever returned to that dark place she's gone to before."

What dark place? It wasn't the first time Azalea had alluded to Madam's tenuous grip on sanity. She never came right out and said exactly what was on her mind; she always spoke about it in a cryptic way.

"I decided to whip together one of her favorite meals," Azalea said.

"Whatever you're cooking smells awful, and I doubt if Madam will go near it," he said with his nose turned up.

"Instead of making her one of those gourmet meals she usually eats, I decided to fix her a big ol' plate of chicken livers, hearts, and gizzards with onions, tomatoes, and plenty of my secret seasoning," Azalea said with a wink.

"Sounds ghastly, and Madam will no doubt retch when she tastes it."

"I'll have you know, this meal is something Quinnie and I used to eat when we were teenagers. It'll spark good old memories and snap her out of whatever is wrong with her."

"Those old memories of her impoverished youth will most likely fill her with horror."

"Life wasn't easy back then, but it wasn't all bad, either," Azalea commented.

"If you say so," the butler said, idly turning the pages of the newspaper. "Still, I'm not serving her that concoction of chicken feet and livers. It sounds barbaric," he said, shaking his head in disapproval.

"Chicken gizzards, hearts, and livers," Azalea corrected.

"Whoever has the misfortune of delivering that plate of slop to

Madam will most likely end up wearing it," he said with a wicked smile.

Darcie set the French omelet in front of the butler, and she and Edwina exchanged a worried look.

The butler cut into the omelet and smiled. "It's cooked perfectly, Darcie. But please remember to have my breakfast prepared on time tomorrow."

"I will, Mr. Hardwicke," Darcie responded.

"For a man who's nothing more than another staff member, you sure are picky," said Azalea. She looked at him closely and drew her brows together. "I knew something was off about you this morning. Where are your gloves?" Azalea asked, eyeballing the butler's bare hands. "Look at those hands; they sure are soft. Looks like you've never put in a hard day's worth of work in your life, Jamison," Azalea teased.

"Mr. Hardwicke," he reminded her, his lips drawn together in displeasure. The butler despised being made fun of, and one way or another Azalea would pay for taunting him. He could bet she wouldn't be laughing when she found herself collecting unemployment. The coarse woman was no more a chef than he was, but her adolescent ties to Madam had kept her gainfully employed for the past thirteen years. But if he had his way, Azalea wouldn't be around much longer.

Maybe he should give some more thought to getting in touch with Chef Nico. Seeing Azalea's reaction to being given her walking papers would be worth the irritation of enduring the presence of another man in the house.

The butler cut another piece of omelet and closed his eyes as he chewed. He washed it down with Edwina's delicious cocoa.

It was time to get to work, and so he pushed his plate away and stood. "By the way, Azalea. When you make your shopping list for the week, be sure to add a barrel of pink lady apples."

"What do you need all those apples for?"

"For Madam's horses, of course."

"That apple tree over by the stables provides enough apples for those horses to eat."

"We have four new ponies."

"I didn't know that."

"There's a lot you don't know. The ponies arrived a few days ago—not that it's any of your business."

Azalea glared at the butler and tightly folded her arms.

"Also, add to the list a sack of oats, gallon tubs of flax seeds, bean sprouts, arugula, and peanut butter. Oh, and we need a couple jugs of honey and molasses delivered to the stables."

"Now I've heard it all—honey and molasses for horses," Azalea said with a tsk. "Cash is tight for a lot of folks due to the state of the economy, but yet you want to waste good money feeding those dang horses a bunch of expensive flax seeds and arugula and whatnot."

"Madam wants her horses to be given the very best of care," the butler said.

"Madam doesn't even visits the stables, and she stopped riding those horses a long time ago."

"I have a feeling the new ponies are going to be just the trick to get her out of the doldrums," he said with a knowing look.

"We'll see," Azalea said doubtfully.

We shall see, indeed. Having a skilled chef in her kitchen instead of someone who should be flipping burgers will undoubtedly lift Madam's spirit.

CHAPTER 20

The butler hung up the phone. He'd successfully appeased the primary investor in Madam's latest film production. It was only nine-thirty a.m. and he'd already accomplished what amounted to a full day's work. He'd overseen the delivery and setup of new office furniture for a space on the main floor that he'd designated as his official office. He'd given a sound spanking to a new apprentice for having the gall to carelessly leave a streak on the outside of a pan she was responsible for scrubbing to a brilliant shine.

He'd devoted a huge amount of time on the phone with Countess Hedvig, assuring the bothersome noblewoman that her Christoff and Arnoldus were getting individualized training that would set them apart from any other pleasure-slaves in all of Scandinavia. Although she was impatient for their return, the butler convinced her that the twins would derive extraordinary benefits if they were allowed to stay on at House of Stevens for an additional week of intense training.

He had similar conversations with Brynne's and Marnie's owners. Brynne's owner was an agreeable chap, but the butler had to offer Marnie's bad-tempered master a considerable amount of money to get him to agree to postpone Marnie's auction sale until after the date of the pony race. He didn't actually tell any of the owners that their pleasure-slaves were busy learning all things equine.

They'd find out soon enough that their human chattel preferred the taste of oats to a juicy steak.

Yes, he'd accomplished a great deal today, but most importantly, the butler had tracked down Chef Nico, and he'd done it without having to endure a conversation with Madam's insufferable friend, Colden. Overly inquisitive, Colden would have badgered the butler endlessly to find out the reason Madam wanted Chef Nico's information.

Locating Nico Bradford hadn't been difficult at all. He did a search of Michelin-starred restaurants in the United States and then narrowed the search to restaurants on the east coast, and by a process of elimination he found Nico, guest-cheffing in a restaurant in Vermont. According to the website it was a quaint, homespun place, off the beaten path, tucked away in a wooded paradise, well concealed from the crowds.

During their phone conversation, Nico hadn't been enthused at all about the prospect of preparing cuisine for Madam's big event. He'd asked if the event was another of those freaky gatherings where half the people were walking around naked. The butler assured the chef that the guests would be fully clad and the food servers would also be appropriately covered. He told him that only the four people providing entertainment would be baring any skin. He further placated the narrow-minded chef by guaranteeing that he would be ensconced inside the kitchen, never having to set eyes on the nude entertainment that would take place outside on the grounds of the estate.

Still, Nico was reluctant to commit, making one excuse after another: He had a two-week commitment in upstate New York after he finished his stint in Vermont. He didn't like one-day bookings, and complained that his cooking suffered when he had only a day to purchase ingredients and to prep the food.

After a large amount of cajoling and major ass-kissing on the butler's part, along with the offer of an outrageous sum of money, the chef finally agreed to cook for Madam's event.

It seemed that as soon as the butler had let out a breath of relief, the chef informed him that he wouldn't be available until a week after the date the butler had selected for the pony race.

That's when the butler had to place phone calls to Brynne's, Marnie's, and the twins' owners and rearrange their departure from House of Stevens to coincide with the chef's availability. It was a nuisance, but the end result would be well worth it: Madam would be ecstatic and Azalea would be finally terminated from the positon she never deserved.

The butler set a new date for Madam's event and Nico agreed to arrive four days in advance to become acquainted with the kitchen, shop at local farmers' markets, and prep the food.

The butler checked his pocket watch. Nine-forty. Time to deliver the good news to Madam.

He knocked on her door and Lyza told him to enter. As usual, Madam sat listlessly by the window with Lyza at her side fussing with her hair. Throughout Madam's convalescence, Lyza had nursed her tenderly, applying cool compresses to her forehead, and keeping the curtains pulled shut when the sunlight invaded the room and disturbed Madam's afternoon nap.

"Would you excuse us, Lyza? I'd like to speak with Madam alone," the butler said.

Lyza glanced at her mistress and Madam gave a nod so slight it was almost imperceptible.

Alone with Madam, the butler got down on one knee, taking one of her hands in his. The contact of skin on skin was so intimate and sensual, his dick responded by throbbing beneath his zipper. Dizzy with lust, it took a few moments for him to collect himself.

"Madam, I have very good news for you."

She gazed at him, the vacant look that had been in her eyes was replaced with a light of hope.

"I've located Chef Nico and he agreed to cook for your upcoming event."

Madam blinked. "Really?" she asked with the faintest of smiles.

"Yes. I gave him full range on creating the menu for your grand event."

She furrowed her brows. "What grand event?"

"Don't you remember, my dear?" The butler stroked the top of her hand, his fingertips rubbing soothingly past her wrist and up her arm. "You and I agreed I would organize a special event to serve as a ruse to get the elusive chef here at House of Stevens."

"Oh, yes, I recall now. What did Nico say? Was he excited about cooking for me?"

"He was absolutely delighted, and extremely apologetic that he couldn't commit to the original date I proposed. I moved some things around, including the date of Marnie's auction sale, and now we're all set to host the most creative and entertaining event of the year."

Madam gave a full smile as she patted her husband's face. "Good job, Jamison. I knew I could count on you." She slid her hand downward from his cheek to his lips, allowing him to cover the palm of her hand with kisses.

For the butler, kissing his wife's palm was a sexual experience and he groaned loudly, the croaking sound of a man in agony. His breathing became hard and jagged, passionate and crude words pouring out of him as if he were in the throes of hot sex. "Oh, how I love you, Madam. You treat me like scum, but I allow it. There's nothing I wouldn't do for you," he declared, stabbing his tongue between her fingers, bobbing his head up and down as he simulated a dick slicing through pussy folds.

He came up for air, taking a rousing deep breath and then continued his ardent pronouncement of love and loyalty. "I worship the ground you walk on. No one is more devoted to you than me. To prevent even a speck of dust from ever touching your precious feet, I would lay my body on the ground and let you use me as your personal carpet," he said with fervor and began running his broad nose up and down her arm, deeply inhaling her scent—sniffing her like a bloodhound.

"Oh, the scent of your perfume makes me higher than any drug. The smell of your panties worn after an hour of horseback riding or after a Pilates class drives me insane."

Madam gaped at the butler. "You steal my panties?"

"No, no. I borrow them from the hamper. I, uh, I always put them back."

Realizing he'd divulged too much information, he stopped talking and devoted himself to licking her palm. Slurping on her flesh as if trying to physically consume a portion of her very being.

"That's enough, Jamison," she said tersely, disengaging her hand from his. With a look of disgust, she wiped her tongue-moistened hand on the shoulder of his jacket. "I can never be nice to you; you always take advantage of my good will."

"I'm sorry, Madam. I lost my head."

"I've heard enough. Please, shut up."

He immediately fell silent.

"You're a loathsome, despicable creature. Now, stand up and have some dignity about yourself," she said, gazing at him with utter contempt.

He pushed to his feet, straightening his clothing as he did so. "I realize I'm not worthy of you, Madam—"

She gestured impatiently. "For God's sake, will you shut your mouth? How many times do I have to hear about your pathetic devotion? When will you get it through your head that you sicken me? Now, keep your emotions to yourself and bring me up to speed on important matters. I also want to know every detail regarding the event you've been planning."

Although he was crushed by the cruelty of her words, he pulled himself together and began by telling her that he'd transformed one of the spare rooms into an office for himself, explaining that he needed a private place to conduct business on her behalf. He also informed her that he had to placate Marnie's owner with a MoneyGram, and that he'd taken the money from the household-expenses account.

"That's fine, Butler. Now tell me about all about the event."

He took a deep breath and launched into a lengthy account of how, with Hugo's help, he had successfully trained the twins, Marnie, and Brynne to behave like horses.

"The title of the event is Madam Midnight's Equestrian Festival. It will be spectacular, with competitions in both jumping and racing. The guests and the judges will include Madam's clandestine inner circles from both overseas and here in the States.

"I don't get it. An equestrian theme with pleasure-slaves pretending to be horses sounds rather foolish. I don't think my esteemed acquaintances would be entertained by something so ridiculous."

"It's not ridiculous at all, and I assure you that the fetish community will be regaled by the event."

"My good name would be ruined if this event fails to wow my guests."

"Your guests will inundate you with requests to pony-train their pleasure-slaves. I predict that you'll have to build several new stables to accommodate all the new ponies that will train at House of Stevens."

Madam peered out the window thoughtfully and then gazed at

the butler. "So, you have assigned Marnie, Brynne, and the twins to sleep on beds of straw in the horse stalls?"

"Yes, Madam."

"And you say they're eating oats and barley?"

He nodded. "Along with other important nutrients, of course."

"And they're no longer verbalizing, only communicating with horse-like sounds?"

"Yes, Madam. I'm sure it's hard to envision, but please trust that they have fully embraced the equine lifestyle. When you've recovered fully, I suggest you make a visit to the stables and see the wonder of it all with your own eyes."

At ten o'clock sharp, there was a sharp rap on the door and Lyza entered. "The kitchen girl has arrived with your breakfast tray. If Madam doesn't have an appetite, I'll send the tray back to kitchen."

"No, no. Don't send it back. I'm suddenly famished."

Worriedly, the butler watched Edwina wheel in the breakfast cart. He shook his head as he imagined Madam's reaction to the plate full of the foul-smelling slop that Azalea had whipped together. In a matter of seconds, Madam would go from zero to one hundred, her good mood replaced by a whirlwind of fury that could quite possibly be directed at him.

Edwina lifted the silver lid and announced in a shaky voice, "Sautéed chicken livers, hearts, and gizzards served on a bed of wild rice with a fried egg."

All smiles, Madam leaned forward and peered at the concoction. "Oh, my goodness, I haven't had this meal in such a long time." She inhaled deeply, and said, "The aroma brings back so many wonderful memories."

What wonderful memories? The butler was astounded by Madam's response. Apparently, she had selective recall. Years ago, during a bout of binge drinking, Azalea had slipped up and divulged that

Madam's childhood had been so deplorable, that she'd suffered some sort of mental collapse. He hadn't gotten the whole story, but he'd stored away the little information he had, thinking it might be useful one day.

Madam dug into the concoction. "Mmm," she murmured and smiled at Edwina. "Tell Azalea that she and her kitchen staff can expect to see a big raise in your next paycheck."

CHAPTER 21

Brynne envied the ease with which her stablemates trotted and ran inside the corral. She had barely gotten used to wearing the hoof-boots and now there was the added complication of having a butt plug jutting out of her ass and itchy horsehair tickling the back of her thighs, making it difficult for her to maintain proper form.

In his usual perch atop the fence, Hugo gave out squirts of water when his four naked charges were thirsty. When they grew hungry, he provided slices of apples and scoops of raw nuts, which he fed them from his grimy cupped hand. He generously doled out words of praise and encouragement in equal amounts to all four of them and would affectionately scratch Marnie and the twins behind the ears.

Whenever Brynne stopped in front of Hugo, opening her mouth for water or to be fed, he used those private moments to tell her how sexy she looked with her new tail. He'd lightly tap her bouncy breasts with the riding crop, giving her shivers. After affectionately swatting her on the ass, he'd send her back to the pack to continue trotting in an endless circle.

The monotony of the training regimen didn't bother her at all. She enjoyed walking around in the open air with the sensation of the warm sun kissing her naked skin. Best of all, she enjoyed fucking Hugo outdoors behind the stables, their entangled bodies hidden by tall weeds and bushes.

It had been four days since Lyza had caught Brynne and Hugo together in her stall, yet Brynne no longer felt fearful. Life at the stables was so peaceful, giving her such a sense of wellbeing, she had come to the conclusion that Lyza was content with the knowledge that Brynne was being forced to wear the humiliating horsetail.

At first Brynne was terribly embarrassed to have taken on another equine characteristic, but after a few days, she had gradually started to feel sexy with the bristly tail protruding from her ass. Though Hugo no longer lingered in her stall at night, he made up for his absence by showering her with attention first thing every morning.

Their morning routine consisted of Hugo leading her to the toilet after the others had gone, and then soaping and hosing her afterward. He'd talk sweetly to her, telling her how well she'd been doing with her posture and her trotting, every word of praise causing her to swell with pride. Then he'd satisfy her cunt before fucking her ass, which he rammed forcefully, making sure it became loose enough for him to glide the butt plug in with ease.

When he removed the plug in the evening after exercises had been completed, there was a noticeably thick, meaty lump in his pants. Most nights, he had to rush out of Brynne's stall before he became completely aroused and overcome by lust.

No longer did the fear of being horsewhipped by Mr. Hardwicke loom like a dark cloud. Brynne was well cared for by Hugo and she was certain she would miss him terribly when she inevitably returned to Scotland.

Lunch was always followed by an afternoon nap, and Brynne found it difficult to sleep comfortably with the butt plug and tail. She tossed and turned on the straw, and finally gave up on the idea of sleeping and simply lay on her side trying to sort through her feelings and thoughts. She missed Ian terribly and longed for the comforts and conveniences his wealth provided. But she clearly had a strong sexual attraction for Hugo. Being his ponybitch had awakened something inside her that she would never experience again once she left House of Stevens.

She wondered how she would explain her desire to be treated like a pony to Ian. Hopefully he'd be understanding and help her locate a stable that housed people with equine fetishes. She wouldn't expect to be treated like a pony every day, but it would be nice to trot around in the open air and get fucked in both holes by a scruffy stable hand at least one weekend out of a month.

Dreamily, she closed her eyes, her hand meandering downward. Since becoming a ponygirl, she hadn't been allowed to shave her pussy. Her pubic hair had grown as long and wild as an animal's. Hugo often petted the thick thatch of hair that covered Brynne's pussy.

Stroking her cunt hair and toggling her clit, she fantasized about the upcoming race. It would be nice to win but she doubted that she'd be competition for Arnoldus or his brother. The twins had amazingly strong legs and were fast. The brothers had adjusted quicker than she had to being ponies.

At the sound of the cast iron bell, which Hugo rang to rouse them from their naps, Brynne got up and climbed into her tall boots. She readjusted the ponytail on the top of her head and brushed it and she also brushed the thatch of tangled pubes that concealed her pussy lips. She reached behind her and finger combed the horsetail. Ready to give Arnoldus and Christoff some unexpected competition, she stretched and jogged in placed and then strutted up to the gate, impatient for Hugo to lead her back to the corral.

The look of surprise on the twins' faces when Brynne trotted past them was priceless. Every day Brynne's legs had grown stronger and her stamina had improved drastically, leading her to believe that it was entirely possible to win the pending race. And if she won, perhaps Ian would be encouraged to continue her race-training.

With four pairs of hooves clumping loudly, no one heard the Escalade approaching until it glided to a stop on the grass next to the corral. Hugo immediately hopped off the fence, rushed toward the SUV, and opened the passenger's door.

Brynne nearly toppled off her feet when Madam emerged from the Escalade. From the driver's side, Lyza stepped out, carrying a frilly umbrella, which she held over Madam's head. Careful to keep Madam protected from the sun, Lyza kept in step with her mistress as Madam sauntered toward the corral.

Madam dazzled in an off shoulder, black and white striped top and tight white pants that were tucked inside black, Balenciaga riding boots, affirming her status as a fashion icon.

Mindful of demonstrating good pony behavior, Brynne and Marnie continued trotting at a regular pace, maintaining good posture.

But catching sight of Madam triggered something in Christoff and Arnoldus and the twins began to run amok, tossing their heads back and neighing at ear-splitting volumes. Seemingly rabid with lust, they took galloping leaps in the air and kicked at the fence in an attempt to be near Madam.

Hugo had no choice but to subdue the boys with harsh cracks from the riding crop. Finally, Madam ordered him to lasso them both and drag them back to the stable.

"Lock them in their stalls," she called out to Hugo.

Brynne had enraged Madam when she broke her vase, and today was an opportunity to make up for her past mistake. Aware that Madam was an experienced horse woman, Brynne pranced about, showing off her perfect posture and form in an effort to win the approval of the mistress of the house.

Eyes directed straight ahead, she performed a high-stepped trot and then broke into a gallop. Feeling good about herself, she threw her head back and whinnied for Madam's benefit. It was Brynne's way of saying, *Good afternoon, Madam. I'm going to make you proud of me when I win the upcoming race.*

With her eyes staring straight ahead, Brynne hadn't realized that Lyza had been beckoning her until she yelled her name. Brynne galloped over, breathing hard, snorting and nickering.

"This is absolutely remarkable," Madam commented with a pleasant lilt in her voice. "I honestly have never seen anything like it. Human ponies," she said, shaking her head in astonishment. "Butler has certainly outdone himself by coming up with the idea of a competition between ponyboys and ponygirls." She stroked the hair on Brynne's head and said, "Turn around."

Brynne turned, displaying her butt-plug tail. Madam fondled Brynne's pert ass and then toggled the butt plug. "It's nice and secure," she commented as she ran her fingers through the horse-hair. "This tail is truly ingenious."

"Putting a tail on Brynne was my idea," Lyza piped in.

"Great. So, why aren't the other ponies wearing tails?"

"Oh, um…I figured I'd test it out on Brynne, first. You know, to see if it would stay put while she's running."

"It obviously stays put and it looks very attractive. I want all the ponies to have tails. Take care of that immediately," Madam added.

"Yes, Madam. I'll see to it right away," Lyza answered.

Madam returned her attention to Brynne. "You're a beautiful horse," she said, stroking her from the side of her face and down to the forest of ringlets that hung between her thighs.

"I can tell you've been training very hard, Brynne. Your calves and thighs are toned and strong." She knelt down and ran her palm over Brynne's quads. "This is the kind of effort I've been waiting for you to put forth, and I must say that I couldn't be more pleased."

In her wildest dreams, Brynne hadn't expected this amount of praise coming directly from Madam's lips. And all the petting and stroking from Madam's hand was beginning to start a brush fire beneath the thicket of pussy hair.

Brynne threw her head back and neighed in happiness and gratitude.

"Oh, my goodness, she sounds exactly like a little pony," Madam said, laughing delightedly.

Happier than she'd been in a very long time, Brynne cut an eye at Lyza and gave her a sweet smile that she hoped conveyed her desire to bury the hatchet and resume the friendship they once shared. But Lyza did not return Brynne's smile. She narrowed her eyes in such a threatening manner, Brynne shrank back and buried her face in Madam's bosom.

"Oh, you sweet little pony. You dear, dear, sweet pony," Madam crooned, smoothing her hand over the side of Brynne's face.

Fuming, Lyza inhaled and exhaled audibly.

Madam took Brynne by her ponytail. "Come on, girl," she murmured. "Let's get you back to your stall."

Before walking Brynne across the field, Madam turned to Lyza. "Use your fingers to size up Marnie's anus. Make sure you get her a horsetail that has a secure fit."

"Yes, Madam," Lyza said grudgingly. The scowl on her face spoke volumes, and it was obvious that when she'd gotten behind the wheel of Madam's luxurious Escalade, she hadn't expected to be ordered to stick her manicured fingers up the ass of a ponygirl.

En route to the stable, Madam smiled gaily as she caressed Brynne's shoulders and arms, speaking to her in lilting tones. "You know, Brynne, I've loved horses since I was a little girl. The first thing I purchased after I became wealthy was this mansion, and it was the stables that helped make up my mind about buying it. I can't express the amount of pleasure I derived from filling those stables with different breeds of horses. I don't ride as frequently as I used to. I suppose the thrill has worn off. However, after observing you trotting with your firm ass poked out proudly and that sexy tail swinging behind you, my passion for riding has been reignited. You and your stablemates are the rarest breed of horse that I could have ever hoped to find. And I'm going to make sure that all of you get the best care possible. You are a show horse, Brynne, and I'm going to make sure you have the finest equipment money can buy."

Brynne wanted to say, *Thank you*, but whinnied instead.

Much taller than Brynne, Madam had to bend over to give Brynne a kiss on the cheek. She squeezed and rubbed Brynne's boobs fondly, and then took a tighter hold of her ponytail before running her the rest of the way to the stable.

CHAPTER 22

Three days later, Brynne and her stablemates were loaded into the open cargo area of Hugo's pickup truck. They were being driven to the track for the first time, and Brynne was eager to get out in the open space and show off her speed and stamina.

Marnie and the twins swished the horsetails back and forth, testing the fit. Marnie's tail was a beautiful raven color that perfectly matched the hair on her head. Although luxurious and flowing, the tails the twins wore were a darker shade of blond than their natural hair color.

Christoff, who was Brynne's biggest competition, couldn't seem to get the hang of running with a butt plug, and he made exasperated snorting sounds as the truck bumped over pebbles and gravel during the half-mile ride along the northern perimeter of the property.

Hugo pulled to a stop at the track, and Brynne was happy to see Madam's SUV parked on the gravel beside the track.

A vision of loveliness, Madam stepped out of the vehicle wearing a short flowing skirt, a skimpy crop top, a wide-brimmed straw hat, and cowgirl boots. Brynne couldn't contain a loud neigh, her way of saying, *Hello, Madam. You look fetching today.* The twins and Marnie joined in the greeting, neighing and whinnying and clumping around in the back of the truck.

More eager than ever to show off her skills, Brynne rushed ahead of the others, jumping out of the truck the moment Hugo walked to the rear and let down the tailgate.

Happy to see Brynne, Madam sprinted toward her with Lyza trailing behind her, burdened with a large box in her arms.

"Hello, girl. How's my favorite ponygirl?" Madam patted Brynne on the cheek and squeezed her luscious breasts. "I have a surprise for you today." She turned and motioned for Lyza to hurry up.

Moving as quickly as possible, Lyza huffed and puffed while carrying a heavy box. Winded, she let out a deep breath and plopped the box on the ground when she reached the spot where Madam and Brynne were standing.

Smiling, Madam reached inside the box and pulled out a leather harness. "This is yours. It's part of your racing outfit, and I want you to get used to wearing it."

Though Brynne preferred the freedom of running naked and unrestricted, the harness was nothing more than leather straps and buckles. Brynne felt cared for and quite special as Madam and Lyza fussed over her, hooking and buckling the harness onto her body. Next, Lyza pulled a snug-fitting bridle over her head.

"Look at my sexy pony," Madam said, beaming at Brynne.

Brynne smiled back but her smile froze when Lyza grabbed a horse's bit from the box and jammed it between Brynne's teeth and then fastened it to the bridle, making it impossible for her to spit out the long rubber-coated bar. Now she could barely neigh with any real volume. Noticing Madam's brown eyes sparkling with approval, Brynne instantly decided the uncomfortable bit and bridle was another ponygirl element that she'd simply have to get used to.

"I no longer have to guide you by pulling your hair," Madam informed her. She attached a set of reigns to the metal rings on the ends of the bit. "Are you ready, girl?"

Brynne answered yes by stamping her right foot on the ground, exactly the way Hugo had taught her.

"Good girl." Clutching the reins tightly in both hands, she urged Brynne forward with a gentle tug. Brynne high-stepped in the direction of the track and ever so often, Madam would yank on the reins merely to demonstrate who was in control.

"While the others are getting dressed in their horse gear, I want you to practice running with proper form. Don't you dare disappoint me or I'll have no choice but to spank you."

Responding accordingly, Brynne stamped her left foot. *I won't disappoint you.*

Madam released the reins. "Go," she ordered, smacking Brynne fondly on the ass. She watched Brynne run for a little while, and then decided to observe her from the comfort of her air-conditioned SUV.

Christoff, Marnie, and Arnoldus joined Brynne on the track, but the restrictions of the leather harnesses along with the discomfort of their new tails prohibited them from keeping up with Brynne's fast pace. Ahead, she noticed that a sharp turn was coming up. Mindful of the requirements of a show pony, Brynne concentrated on the perfection of her form as much as speed as she galloped along, taking the difficult turn.

Though she was well ahead of the others, she could hear the sharp strikes of Hugo's riding crop as he ran alongside her lagging stablemates, urging them to pick it up and to improve their posture.

An hour or so later, practice was over and they were all loaded back onto the truck. Brynne was so exhausted her chest heaved up and down. Her back, her legs, and her heavy breasts glistened with perspiration. It was a great relief when Hugo wiped her down with a towel, paying particular attention to her sweaty boobs.

The ride back to the stables was pleasant with cool air blowing on her body, but more than anything Brynne yearned to quench her thirst with cool water and to gorge on several bowls of oat-mush, spinach, and barley.

In her stall, Brynne tried to wait patiently for Hugo to feed her, but she was growing irritable. She snorted. She paced for a while. She stamped her hoof-boots and still no food or water. At last, the familiar creek of the stable door sounded, but it wasn't Hugo who opened the gate and entered her stall.

It was Madam! Glorious Madam. A beauteous sight to behold.

Brynne stood up straight, arms behind her back, tits pointed outward.

"You did a good job out on the track today. Come over here, girl, and let's get you out of that gear," Madam said, wearing a smile.

Brynne half-danced, half-trotted over to Madam, ignoring her hunger pangs. Madam removed the bit from Brynne's mouth, and then worked on undoing the straps and buckles of the harness. "I want you to keep the hoof-boots on for a few more hours. Not only because you look sexy wearing them, but I also want you to start feeling as if the hooves are an extension of your body—like your tail."

Agreeing with Madam, Brynne stomped her right hoof.

The stable door squeaked as Hugo came inside. He entered Brynne's stall carrying a bucket of chow in one hand and a bucket of water in the other.

"Fill both her bowls to capacity," Madam instructed Hugo as he scooped out mush with a ladle and plopped it into the bowl.

Smelling the pleasant aroma of the grain, greens, raw honey, and fruit mixture had Brynne trotting around in a delirious circle. When Hugo filled the other bowl with water, Brynne dropped down to her hands and knees and lapped it up in record time.

"She's really thirsty; give her some more," Madam said, and Hugo complied. Again, Brynne greedily slurped the cool water, splashing it about as she satisfied her thirst.

After Hugo moved on to the next stall, where Marnie was waiting, Madam gazed at Brynne and said, "Alone at last with my ponygirl." She pulled the bowl of chow away from Brynne's hungry mouth and held it possessively as she took a seat on the haystack.

Wondering what she'd done to displease Madam, Brynne's happy expression changed to one of confusion.

"It's okay, girl. Come over here, so I can feed you."

Relieved, Brynne scampered like a frisky puppy over to Madam and rose up on her haunches. With the bowl in her lap, Madam scooped out a clump of the mush-mixture and fed Brynne from her hand. Famished, Brynne bit into the chow, chewing rapidly, and then licking bits of slop from between Madam's fingers and cleaning out the palm of her hand.

Madam couldn't seem to scoop up the clumps of chow quickly enough. Brynne went after the food, ravenously attacking it, slurping on Madam's fingers and swishing her tongue up and down her hand.

"You're eating too fast. You have to slow down before you make yourself sick," she said sternly.

Heeding the warning, Brynne paced herself, chewing slowly and leisurely licking Madam's fingers. Surrendering to Madam was a divine experience and it was no wonder that people from around the world were willing to pay excessive amounts of money to worship at her feet. The woman was a goddess as far as Brynne was concerned.

After Brynne had eaten the last morsel of food, Madam placed the bowl on the ground beside the haystack.

"I said you did a good job today, but actually you were better than good. You were magnificent. And for all your hard work, you deserve a special treat," Madam said as she slowly and enticingly lifted her skirt, revealing a smooth-shaven pussy that was the color of dark molasses.

"Down, girl." Madam grabbed Brynne by her ponytail and forced her head between her smooth thighs. "I want you to eat this pussy to your heart's content."

The extreme honor of dining between Madam's legs sent quivers up Brynne's spine. It took all of her willpower not to pounce on Madam's cunt with the same fervor in which she'd attacked her food. Exercising self-restraint, she timidly licked into Madam's folds using only the tip of her tongue.

Madam sucked in a deep breath as Brynne delved deeper, probing her beautiful mistress's dewy insides with another inch of warm tongue. Madam arched her back, grinding the baby soft flesh of her bare cunt against Brynne's lips. While administering to Madam's needs, Brynne felt her nipples growing hard and she could only hope she didn't insult her dear mistress when she brushed her rigid nipples back and forth against Madam's soft skin.

Reaching downward, Madam groped Brynne's hefty breasts, pinching and twisting the jutting nipple, all the while frenziedly circling her hip. Brynne slowed Madam's movements by capturing her taut clit between her lips and then lashing it mercilessly with her tongue. She alternated, going from tongue lashes to clit-sucking until a thick spurt of nectar seeped from Madam's slit.

Madam's breaths came in short gasps and Brynne dutifully kept her face buried in her mistress's pussy until Madam tugged her ponytail and said, "That's enough. Up, girl."

CHAPTER 23

Brynne's morning grooming session with Hugo was interrupted when the butler showed up at the stables. Total panic seized Brynne's entire being. Seeing him walking across the field sent waves of fear buzzing through her. The hunched tension of his shoulders suggested that he intended to discipline her.

Cold dread gripped her. Afraid of being horsewhipped, her first instinct was to run. Her second instinct was to cower behind Hugo. But Hugo, who'd been hosing her down, left her naked and unprotected as he stepped forward, extending his hand to the butler in greeting.

"Good morning, Hugo. I'd like to have a word with Brynne. I'll finish hosing her while you attend to the others."

Looking at Hugo with terror in her eyes, Brynne silently pleaded for him not to leave her alone with the sadistic butler. Following the butler's orders, Hugo readily handed him the hose and jogged toward the main door of the stable.

The butler held the hose and Brynne braced herself for some form of water torture. She was taken off guard when he gently soaped her back and buttocks and then hosed away the suds.

"I believe I've been unkind to you, Brynne, and I'd like to apologize."

Startled, she stared at him, expecting his hands to rise up and strike her or to form into a claw and pinch her nipples painfully.

"You've made Madam very happy with your equine skills. You've become her pride and joy."

Embarrassed by the praise, she could feel her face flushing bright red.

"No need to be self-conscious, my dear. Whatever you've been doing to make Madam happy, I want you to keep it up. Behave with even more horse-like traits."

Brynn frowned, wondering what more she could do to improve upon her equine behaviors.

Noticing Brynne's puzzled expression, the butler said, "For example, when you're between her legs showing your gratitude, I want you to use your teeth a little. I want you to bite her clit. Give it a hard nip. I'm certain that's what a real horse would do. The more horse characteristics you exhibit, the happier Madam becomes. Happy wife, happy life…I'm sure you've heard the expression." He laughed and the sound was completely sinister.

The butler began soaping Brynne's anus, moving his finger around the hole sensually. Then he commenced to unzipping his pants. "I hear your horsetail fits you amazingly well. Madam says it's the perfect fit. The sight of it jutting proudly out of your ass arouses her and drives her wild." He paused and looked at Brynne and there was no mistaking the look of pure hatred in his eyes.

He laughed his mirthless laugh again. "I think it's time to take you up a size. What do you think, Brynne?"

Of course she couldn't respond with words. All she could do was shake her head, but her silent protest didn't stop the butler from forcing his mammoth cock into her asshole without lubrication. Brynne shrieked and Hugo came running, but when he realized that the butler was pleasuring himself by butt-fucking Brynne, the stable hand was powerless to do anything except back away.

Brynne watched with envy as Christoff and Arnoldus jumped the hurdles effortlessly. For Brynne, jumping hurdles didn't come as easily as running. Despite her best effort, she couldn't get a clean jump. She continuously knocked over sticks, and kept tripping and falling. Even Marnie was able to jump over the obstacles far better than Brynne.

She blamed her bad performance on her wobbly horsetail. The pain in her ass from the butler's big cock had yet to subside. That discomfort along with having to focus on keeping her butt muscles clenched around the loose butt plug was distracting. Until her anus healed, Brynne would not be able to put forth the necessary effort to ensure a good performance on the track.

As much as she wanted to see Madam today, as much as she yearned to smell her scent, Brynne dreaded the mistress showing up at the course and discovering that her favorite ponygirl was horrendously bad at jumping hurdles.

Imagining the shame of it, Brynne tried harder, leaping as high in the air as her legs would allow, but she failed to jump with accuracy. Determinedly, she ran full speed toward the hurdle and tripped, landing on her butt. She winced when she heard the crack of her horsetail breaking off the end of the plug.

Hugo helped her to her feet and then picked up her tail. "I can probably fix it with some Krazy Glue when we get back to the stables," he said somberly.

She stamped her right foot.

"Come here, girl; bend over so I can check on something."

Obeying, Brynne bent over and Hugo slid out the unstable butt plug and gingerly stuck a finger into her anus. She flinched and whinnied.

"Sorry, girl. I had to check to see if I need to resize your tail." He peered at the damaged tail. "Until we can get you a new one,

I'll have to glue this tail onto a larger butt plug. Looks like Mr. Hardwicke stretched you out real good. Your asshole's twice its normal size."

For the duration of practice, she berated herself for her lack of jumping ability and felt terribly inadequate without her tail. When Hugo called an end to practice, Brynne was the first to gallop toward the pickup truck.

Standing near the tailgate, waiting for Hugo to open it, Brynne's heart thumped in surprise when she saw Madam's Escalade pulling up. She had mixed emotions. A part of her was thrilled to look upon the glorious mistress, but another part dreaded seeing the disappointment in Madam's eyes when Hugo made her aware of Brynne's unsatisfactory performance today.

It wasn't until Lyza got out that Brynne realized the passenger's seat was empty. As much as she wanted to be stroked on the head by Madam's hand, and as much as she wanted to spend hours grazing between Madam's legs, she was relieved that the mistress of the house had not shown up at the track today.

"How'd they do today?" Lyza asked.

"Pretty good for their first day of jumping," Hugo replied. "The twins were phenomenal."

"What about Marnie and Brynne?"

Hugo shrugged. "Marnie did okay. Brynne needs a lot more practice."

Lyza cut an eye at Brynne and sneered. "Where's her tail?"

"Broke it during a fall, but I can fix it back at the stables."

"Don't bother. Madam would be horrified if she saw her favorite ponygirl wearing a makeshift tail. I'll order her a new one online and get next day delivery," Lyza said. Then she regarded Brynne with a loathing that made Brynne's stomach churn. Lyza's eyes were ice-cold and Brynne flinched beneath their glare.

"Hugo, why don't you take the others back while I work with Brynne for another hour or so," Lyza suggested. "If her jumps aren't accurate, Madam will be sorely disappointed."

"Okay, but don't work her too hard. She has to rest her muscles and she's gonna get real hungry soon…it's getting close to supper-time."

"Don't worry. I'll take good care of her and I'll make sure she gets back in time for supper."

Suspicious of Lyza's intentions, Brynne yearned to gallop behind Hugo's truck as she watched it drive away.

Lyza retrieved a riding crop from the back of the SUV and shook it threateningly at Brynne. "You are going to jump those damned hurdles and you better not miss any of them."

Holding her by her ponytail, Lyza walked Brynne halfway around the track and then cracked her with the crop and shouted, "Take the next jump!"

Brynne's body screamed in protest. She'd put in so much effort today, and she was so fatigued, she could barely move a muscle. But she pushed herself past her limit and followed Lyza's command. Telling herself she was doing it for Madam, she leapt high in the air and made the jump! Grinning, she neighed in celebration.

Thwack! Another crack of the riding crop. This time it landed across her shoulder, a searing sting that nearly took her breath away. "Pay attention to what you're doing. There's no time for self-congratulation," Lyza chastised.

Lyza ran beside Brynne around the course, striking her with the riding crop every step of the way and giving her a particularly harsh whack right before it was time for her to jump each hurdle. The method worked. At last Brynne was able to perform like the show pony Madam expected her to be.

"Good girl, good girl. No wonder Madam adores you. You're

such a hard worker. Let's do the whole course again. Run! Faster! Knees up, as you're nearing the hurdle."

Brynne jumped again and made it and Lyza sang her praises.

The compliments and kudos from Lyza motivated Brynne to keep moving despite the exhaustion pouring over her.

"Whoa, girl. That's enough for today," Lyza finally said. She gave Brynne a pat on the head and then brought the tip of the riding crop to her breasts, poking them. "Madam is crazy about your big boobs. She says she loves the way they bounce up and down when you're running like a stallion." The tone of Lyza's voice did not betray her emotions, yet Brynne was leery of her and braced herself to be hit, pinched, or probed with an uncomfortable object.

Smirking, Lyza pointed the riding crop at Brynne's lips. "I've been told that your lips are magical. Madam says they pleasure her better than mine do. What's the secret to having such a gifted mouth? Perhaps you can work some tongue-sorcery on my cunt."

Relieved that she wasn't going to be beaten, Brynne eagerly sank to her knees, licking Lyza's crotch as she waited for her to pull down her pants.

"I bet you haven't had an orgasm since the day I caught you fucking Hugo. He's too afraid of my wrath to ever touch you like that again, and Madam…well, she's all about herself. She never gives pleasure; she only takes. Taking all that into account, I'm sure you must be feeling terrible deprived."

Despite her secret sex sessions with Hugo, Brynne could never get enough good dick. She stamped her right foot, agreeing that she felt sexually deprived. Brynne wondered if Lyza had Tonga stored in the back of the SUV. Her pussy muscles clenched involuntarily as she imagined Tonga's chunky, tattooed dick with the countless piercings on the head.

Then again, if Tonga wasn't around, it was entirely possible that

Lyza had a strap-on inside her handbag. Beautiful Lyza could be mean as hell at times, but her fiery temperament only added to her sensuality. Brynne pictured Lyza strutting around with a big cock that she demanded Brynne to suck and the imagery caused Brynne to nearly collapse with desire.

"I know you need a good, hard fuck, Brynne, and I'm going to make it happen for you," Lyza promised.

With a glint in her eyes, Lyza stuck out her sturdy boot. "I want you to fuck yourself on my boot. I want you to get off like the nasty animal that you are. Come on, ponyslut. Get on this boot and fuck it the same way you fucked my man."

The desire to obey was incomprehensively strong, stirring powerful sexual sensations. Whimpering with lust, she squatted low and slowly grinded her wet cunt against the finely stitched riding boot, gradually working herself up to such a frenzy, she trembled, squirmed, and moaned.

Like a dog in heat, Brynne shamelessly humped leather until her creamy juices spurted out, and puddled at the toe of Lyza's high-quality riding boot.

CHAPTER 24

The doorbell rang insistently; it was an irritating sound. The butler was in his office in front of the computer, occupied with creating a guest list for the Equestrian Festival. He didn't have the time to play butler today and so he ignored the bell and continued working. His fingers were hovered over the keyboard when the bell chimed again. Whoever was on the other side of the door wouldn't take a hint and go away. With an impatient sigh, he pushed back his chair, stood up, and stalked out of his office, making a mental note to assign one of the pleasure-slaves the task of answering the door from now on.

Angrily dashing across the marbled floor and past the potted plants and polished granite columns in the foyer, he was of a mind to thoroughly tongue-lash whoever was on the other side of the door. After all, he wasn't expecting any deliveries and no invitations had been extended to anyone. It was rude to simply show up and intrude upon others.

He swung open the door and for a moment stared without comprehension at the tall, broad-shouldered man who stood on the doorstep, smiling confidently.

The butler looked him over with disdain. The vile man had a pair of Tom Ford aviators pushed back on his head. He wore cargo shorts and tasteless footwear—a pair of ostentatious sneakers that were gapped open and their strings untied. Slung casually over his shoulder was a black gator backpack and a matching duffle bag was clutched in his hand. The man had all the glitz and vulgarity of a Hollywood actor, and the butler was beside himself with outrage.

How dare an actor, no doubt looking for a part in one of Madam's films, have the audacity to show up on her doorstep with packed bags as if he'd been invited to move in?

The butler opened his mouth to unleash his fury when the man extended his hand and said, "I'm Nico Bradford, and you must be Mr. Hardwicke. How are you? I had a cancellation, and decided to come through earlier than planned. Get a feel for the kitchen and take my time visiting some of the local farmers' markets. I also thought it would be a good idea for the lady of the house to sample a few of my dishes, and perhaps collaborate on the menu."

Who the hell do you think you are, showing up here unannounced and dressed like a common thug? Get away, you piece of gutter trash. I will not allow the likes of you to get anywhere near my wife.

Before the butler could express his sentiments, he heard the purposeful clicks of Madam's footsteps approaching.

"What's going on, Butler? The nonstop ringing of the bell has given me a splitting headache. Do I have to start answering the door myself? Are you too busy to do your main job now that you've been allowed to take on a little more responsibility?"

"My apologies, Madam," the butler said with contrition. He hadn't mentioned being a butler when he'd made the arrangements with Nico over the phone. He'd introduced himself as Madam's advisor, and now the brash young chef knew the truth.

Eyes lowered in embarrassment, he pulled the door open and stepped back, giving Madam a full view of the chef framed in the doorway, smiling with the confidence of a man who was presenting himself as a gift.

"Nico! Oh, my God, Nico, you're here!" Without a hint of dignity, without a trace of the regal bearing she usually possessed, Madam raced toward the chef and flung her arms around his neck.

Seeming somewhat confused by her overly familiar welcome, Nico embraced her briefly and then took a step back. "I hope my early arrival doesn't upset the rhythm of your household."

"Not at all." She waved an elegant arm. "Come in, come in. Welcome to my home."

"Your home is lovely," Nico said, looking around the grandeur of the foyer.

She gazed at him for a long moment, taking in the sight of him. "You look so different without your chef's jacket—so trendy and even more attractive than I recall. Come in, let me show you around. *Mi casa es su casa*, and I hope you'll be happy here."

Nico had a surprised look on his face. "Really?"

"Yes, really," she said eagerly.

"Don't get me wrong. I'm happy to be doing business with you but you didn't seem very impressed with my food at the event, and I'm curious as to why you want me to cook for you."

"If I didn't adequately express the love affair I had with your food it was simply because I was rendered speechless. Your cuisine not only pleased my palate but spoke intimately to my heart. It was not the kind of seduction that I'm familiar with, so forgive me for being overwhelmed and seemingly distant when we met."

"That's a nice compliment. Thank you. By the way, I have a confession."

"Really?" Intrigued, Madam folded her arms.

"I was told you were the special guest, and after stealing glances at you and being captivated by your beauty, I couldn't prevent myself from putting my heart on the plate." Nico flashed white, even teeth at Madam, obviously flirting with her.

She returned the bright smile, twirling a tendril of hair and gazing at Nico with a kind of yearning that the butler had never seen in her eyes. He'd never witnessed Madam acting so girly and coquettish before. There was a smoldering heat between her and Nico that made the butler uncomfortable. Was it possible that Madam viewed Nico as more than a potential pleasure-slave to worship at her feet?

It couldn't be possible, he assured himself. In his wife's mind, everyone was human chattel, and the chef was nothing special.

Madam suddenly cast a withering look at the butler. "Where are your manners, Butler? Take the chef's bags to the guest suite."

"Yes, Madam." The butler accepted the backpack that Nico pulled off his shoulder. With a forced smile and a head nod, he accepted the duffle bag from Nico's hand.

Madam glared at the butler's hands. "Where are your gloves, Butler?"

"They're in my bureau drawer." He clasped his bare hands together and bit his lip nervously.

"As you know, the purpose of a butler wearing white gloves is to ensure that his hands and fingers don't smudge precious items."

"Yes, Madam, you're right. It was negligent of me to forget my gloves today."

"It certainly was. Nico's belongings are much too precious to be touched by your grimy—"

"Listen, I can carry own bags. I didn't come here to cause problems," Nico interjected.

"No, you will not carry your own bags," Madam said firmly. "You are a guest in this house and you'll be treated as one. It is the butler's job to carry your bags and to wait on you hand and foot." She turned a harsh gaze on the butler. "Put Nico's bags down and march yourself to the attic and get your gloves."

The humiliation was almost too much to bear. Though he tried not to betray any emotion as he lowered Nico's bags to the floor, he couldn't help from swallowing anxiously, his Adam's apple bobbing up and down relentlessly.

"Go get your gloves," she repeated through clenched teeth.

"Right away, Madam," the butler said. He turned on his heels and headed for the back staircase that would take him to the attic. From the corner of his eye, he saw Madam loop her arm into Nico's as she began giving him a tour of the stately manor. Walking arm-in-arm with Nico, Madam pointed out her art collection that included a Picasso and a Rembrandt and was considered one of the most important private collections in Eastern Pennsylvania.

Upstairs in the attic, the butler yanked open the middle drawer and snatched up a pair of white gloves. He was a man in crisis… enraged and feeling on the brink of committing murder. It was heartless of Madam to humiliate him in front of that arrogant chef. The emotional pain was excruciating. Yet, at the same time, his dick throbbed out of control.

There was no way he could return to the foyer for the chef's bags without relieving himself first. But he had to be quick about it. Madam would be livid if he left the bags sitting for too long.

The remedy for his condition was in his middle drawer. Tucked inside one of the many pairs of white gloves was a worn pair of Madam's lace panties. Holding the panties reverently up to his face, he took a deep whiff of her intoxicating scent. His cock pulsed and became so engorged that it pushed powerfully against his zipper, and seemed quite capable of breaking through the metal.

He quickly liberated his rebellious manhood. Riotous dick in hand, he wrestled with it, yanked the rock-hard phallus roughly inside his fist. The way he was forced to live was so unfair. His wife wouldn't give him any pussy, and yet the bitch wouldn't even allow him the necessary amount of time to hand-stroke his cock at an unrushed pace.

A pity he didn't have time to conjure up a detailed fantasy of Madam groveling on the floor, begging for a taste of his juicy dick meat. A fleeting image of her in a submissive position brought him to a swift orgasm. With a roar, he gushed out so much semen, it saturated his hand. Grunting and breathing hard, he wiped away the evidence from his palm with Madam's frilly panties.

While zippering himself back in his pants, he planned to redeem himself by making a late-night visit to the pleasure-slaves' dormitory. There were several new recruits on the premises, and he was in the mood to force his enormous cock down the narrow passage of a virgin throat while beating a plump ass with the leather belt he kept handy in his room.

After delivering Nico's bags to the guest suite, the butler was put to work in his office. Wanting to surprise Nico with visits to farmers' markets, Madam requested that he compile a list of not only farmers' markets, but also butcher shops within a thirty-mile radius.

Resentfully, the butler logged into his new computer and began searching.

Only a week ago, Madam had caressed his face and given him her palm to kiss, and he'd been hopeful that her fondness for him would soon lead to them finally consummating their marriage. But that wasn't possible now. Not with Nico living under the same roof as Madam.

The butler headed for the kitchen to warn Azalea about their common enemy. If he could convince Azalea that Nico was a threat, perhaps she and the butler could combine their energy and figure out a way to sabotage the young chef.

Upon entering the kitchen, it seemed as if he'd entered a different universe. Madam was sitting casually atop the island with her legs crossed and smiling happily as Azalea and the girls showed Nico around the kitchen, pointing out its many features. It didn't surprise him that Edwina and Darcie were falling all over each other trying to impress Nico, but Azalea should have been seething with anger and bitterness. But she seemed as enamored with Chef Nico as her two helpers and, of course, Madam.

It was obvious in the way Madam was preening and evident in the gaiety of her laughter that she viewed the chef more as a potential lover than a soon-to-be pleasure-slave. Had the butler known that Nico's arrival would cause such an upheaval in the household, he would have never hunted the man down.

"Whatever you need us to do, we'll be more than happy to help with," said Azalea. "This will be my first time working alongside a trained chef, and I'll be taking lots of notes."

The butler was flabbergasted. How could Azalea be so stupid as to brownnose the man who was going to boot her right out of her position and on to the unemployment line?

Noticing the butler, Madam's smile vanished. "Did you print that list for me?"

"I did. It's in my office. I'll go get it." He turned to leave.

"Not so fast, Butler. Speaking of *your* office. You can handle the guest list on a laptop in the attic. Nico, on the other hand, needs a quiet space to work in outside of the kitchen."

"No, no. I'm fine. I don't need his office," Nico protested.

"Nonsense. I wouldn't dream of allowing a butler to have an office while a top chef has to find an empty corner in a busy kitchen to jot down ideas for the menu." Madam settled her gaze on the butler. "Go get that list and bring back the office keys for Nico."

"Wait," Nico said. "I actually don't need a list of your local farmers' markets. There's a searchable database of farmers' markets that lists almost six thousand farmers' markets in the United States."

"Well, that settles that. We don't need your list, Butler. Now, go get the office keys and turn them over to my chef."

Nico lowered his gaze guiltily, and studied the kitchen floor.

"As you wish, Madam. I'll go get the keys." The butler bowed and backed out of the kitchen. Alone in the hallway, he raked a gloved hand down his face. *What have I done? I was so close to gaining respect, trust, and maybe even the love a husband deserves from his wife. Now I've lost it all to a novice chef. I bet he's not even a real chef. He probably made up his credentials. Lied about attending a prestigious culinary school. I'd bet good money that Nico is an imposter—nothing more than a short order cook.*

CHAPTER 25

"You look disappointed," Madam said to Nico as they browsed the aisles of colorful produce inside the farmers' market at Suburban Square Mall.

"I have to admit I am a little disappointed."

"What's wrong? Everything you need is here. Fresh produce. Fresh meat and seafood—all under one roof."

"I was expecting to meet the actual farmers who sell the produce they grow. This place is a little too commercial for my taste," Nico explained.

"But the sign says that everything is organic. Isn't that what you wanted?"

"Yes, but for all I know, this stuff was flown in from California or driven all the way from Florida. Food that's traveled halfway around the world in a cargo hold is not my idea of fresh produce. One of the secrets of good cooking is working with fresh grown local products. Also, I enjoy chatting with the farmers and finding out all I can."

Madam laughed. "Conversing with a farmer seems like it would be the most boring conversation ever."

"It's not boring at all. You can get a lot of valuable information. Some of the farmers grow some pretty unusual fruits. Ever tried a Bavarian Saturn Peach?"

"Can't say I have."

"It's one of the biggest, sweetest peaches that you could ever eat. I'd love to get my hands on some. In my travels, I've talked to farmers that are on the cutting edge of hydroponic growing technology," Nico said, his eyes sparkling. "When talking with the farmers, I like to find out things like whether or not they offer wholesale pricing for restaurants, and it's always a good idea to exchange contact information with vendors I haven't worked with before. You can always tell when you're at one of the top farmers' markets in an area."

"How so?"

Nico laughed. "When you're at a really superior farmers' market, there's always a plethora of white chef jackets clogging up the aisles," he said with laughter.

"I see," Madam said dismally.

"Hey, I hope I didn't offend you. If so, that wasn't my intention."

"No, I'm not offended. A little irked with myself for revealing my major flaw."

"And what's that?"

"My need to control every situation," she said with a shrug. "I should have butted out and let you select one of the markets you found on that database."

"You're the kind of woman who's accustomed to giving orders. I get that."

"You do?"

"Sure, but if you expect me to create a scrumptious meal for the Equestrian Festival, then promise me you'll allow me to do my work, my way."

"I promise."

"Good. Now, let's get out of here and try this place in Lancaster County."

"Lancaster County? Do you realize how long that drive is?"

Nico gave her a look and Madam laughed and then pantomimed zipping her lips. She handed him the keys to the Escalade and climbed in the passenger seat.

During the long drive, Nico told Madam a little about himself. That he was the youngest of three boys and that both his older brothers were serving prison sentences. He said he came from a normal middle class family, two-parent household with both parents holding down government jobs. But the neighborhood changed, he explained, and his brothers were lured into crime.

"In an effort to save me from the same fate as my brothers, my parents decided to send me to stay with my grandparents who lived in a rural part of upstate New York. From the time I was twelve until I graduated high school, I spent every summer in farm country."

"You're not in prison, so apparently it was a good decision."

"Yeah, I suppose so, but back then being shipped off to the middle of nowhere seemed like a prison sentence to me. I would have much rathered been in the city shooting hoops and running around with my friends and getting into mischief than schlepping around farm county where there were miles and miles of cornstalks. Being woken up by roosters at the crack of dawn is not pleasant.

"Still, I made the best of it—what else could I do? My grandma was a devoted cook, baker, grill master—you name it and she could do it," he said with a beaming smile that was contagious. "She was always dragging me to country fairs where she competed and always won first place for the best pear berry pie or the best chicken chili or barbecued ribs. What I learned from Grandma was to be very particular about ingredients—to use only the freshest and the best. All the herbs and every piece of produce she cooked with came from her own garden. And if she didn't grow it herself, she got it from a farmer in the nearby vicinity—straight off the tree, vine, or out of the ground. I was the only kid from my 'hood who ever got his hands dirty from pulling potatoes straight out of the ground." Nico gave a hearty burst of laughter and Madam laughed along with him.

"You're laughing but digging for potatoes is hard labor." He shot a look at her hands. "Judging by those soft, pretty hands, it's obvious you don't know anything about hard work."

"Consider yourself fortunate that picking potatoes was the most difficult part of your childhood. Believe me, I know all about back-breaking labor. I've done more than my fair share of drudgery," she replied.

"Yeah, I bet," he said skeptically.

"I'm not kidding," she responded, laughing.

"If you're serious, why are you laughing?"

"I don't know. I suppose I can laugh at my dirt-poor beginnings because it was so long ago, it's like a vague dream now," she said with nonchalance.

Nico was not only easy on the eyes, he was also a good conversationalist, keeping her interested and providing humor during the lengthy drive.

"One summer when I was around fifteen, Grandma encouraged me to enter a grill-off at the county fair," Nico continued. "First prize was two hundred bucks. Money I could use for a couple pairs of Nikes instead of going back to school in the corny sneakers my parents expected me to wear. My mom and dad were good providers but they didn't believe in wasting money on designer sneakers."

Madam chuckled. "So don't tell me you started your culinary career because you wanted expensive sneakers."

"Yep. To this day, I'm a sneakerhead. My kicks have to be tight. But getting back to the story, back then I didn't have a passion for cooking or grilling or anything that dealt with gastronomy. But I knew I could win that money because I'd watched my grandparents grill every summer for most of my life. I also knew the ingredients in Grandpa's special sauce."

"So, you cheated," Madam teased. "You used your grandfather's recipe."

"I wouldn't call it cheating; at least I didn't think of it like that."

"I'm joking."

"Anyway, I won the money and the next two summers, Grandma and I drove all over upstate New York entering cooking competitions—and we both always returned home with wads of cash."

"That's a heck of a story, Nico. So, did you go to culinary school right after high school?"

Nico's expression darkened. "No, I took a detour—didn't go to culinary school until I was twenty-six. The short version of why I delayed my career is that I fell in love and got married young. Ended up working for a host of horrible bosses doing work that I hated. And you can imagine how my marriage turned out."

"Any children?"

Nico sighed. "Luckily, no. But I would like to become a parent before I get too old." He laughed, lightening up the mood.

"How old are you, by the way?" Madam held her breath, hoping Nico was at least in his thirties.

"I'll hit the big three-O on my next birthday."

"You're still a baby," she said, pinching his cheek playfully.

"Sometimes I feel like an old man." He stared ahead as if deep in thought. Then he suddenly turned to Madam and asked, "And how old are you, if you don't mind my asking?"

"Uh…" Madam shifted in her seat. *Should I lie?* The age issue was something she wasn't comfortable with. "I'll be forty-two on my upcoming birthday," she admitted, deciding she had no reason to be ashamed. She was a survivor and an accomplished woman who was considered beautiful, so why lie about something she should be proud of, she told herself.

"Wow, you look half your age. You must have good genes," Nico complimented. "Anyway, enough about me, tell me about you. What drove you to become such a successful businesswoman?"

"Luck, I suppose," she answered. "I was born on a little island in the Caribbean that you probably never heard of…a place that's merely a dot on the map. The term dirt poor doesn't begin to describe the circumstances of my youth," she began weakly. Frowning, Madam closed her eyes and shook her head as if trying to rid herself of ghosts of the past.

"Listen, I didn't mean to pry. We can drop the subject and talk about something more pleasant."

"No, it's okay…I want to talk about it. I survived conditions and circumstances that would have broken the average person." She paused, staring ahead. After a few moments, she took a deep breath and said, "I don't have any memories of my parents. I was told my mother died and that shortly after, my father found work in Miami, Florida. The people he'd left me with grew tired of waiting for a support check from him, and when I was only five years old they told me they were sending me to a better life with a wealthy family in Jamaica." Madam sighed heavily. "What a joke. I ended up spending the next nine years of my life doing forced domestic labor for a family that didn't have much more income than the family that gave me away."

"That's disgraceful. What kind of labor could a five-year-old do? And how did that family get away with something so outlandish for that many years?"

Madam made a scoffing sound. "Free child labor is a common practice not only in the islands but in many places."

"Jesus, I never heard of anything so horrible. How'd you escape?"

"When I was fourteen, I met a man while I was at the grocers purchasing a few items including a seven-pound bag of rice.

"The man, a tourist, was amazed at my ability to carry my bundle of purchases on my head. He asked if he could take pictures of me and offered to pay me twenty American dollars.

"I would have posed for free. The attention he devoted to me as he clicked away on his camera was worth more than money to me."

"This is so sad," Nico muttered. "Please tell me that the man didn't also exploit you. Tell me that meeting the tourist was the beginning of your happy ending."

"Sort of."

Nico groaned dramatically.

"Suffice it to say, that I never went back to the home where I'd been kept as a child-slave and I was brought to the United States."

"And you lived happily ever after, right?" Nico added, hopefully.

"I suppose you could say that."

"You sound like an American; I don't detect any kind of Caribbean accent."

"I worked very hard to get rid of my accent. But I suppose it will always be with me, resurfacing on the rare occasions when I have my guard down," she said, sadly.

"Are you saying you make a point of keeping your guard up?"

"Wouldn't you, if you'd endured what I had?"

"You have a point."

"By the way, you don't conduct yourself or talk like a street thug from the 'hood."

"Well, I was never a street thug, but, uh, like you...I have my lapses. When I'm really comfortable with the person or people I'm with, I don't enunciate. I slip into jargon and curse like a sailor."

Madam laughed, and it was a tinkling, melodic, carefree sound. "I can't imagine that."

When they pulled into the lot of the farmers' market, Nico seemed to have taken on a protective demeanor toward Madam. Walking with a hand at the small of her back, pulling her close to him when distracted workers rushed past pushing stacks of unsteady boxes on a dolly.

"I'm not fragile, and you don't need to shield me," she said when Nico kept his hand clutched around her arm in the midst of examining cantaloupe.

"Oh, sorry," he apologized, removing his grip of her arm. "I didn't even realize I was holding on to you. Your story about Jamaica messed with my head, and now I feel like I need to keep you close to me."

"It's a sweet thought, but not necessary. It all happened a very long time ago. Obviously, along the way, I developed the skills to take care of myself. So, let it go and let's enjoy this market we drove a hundred miles to visit." She produced a brilliant smile that put Nico at ease.

"A hundred miles! Stop exaggerating, we didn't drive any further than fifty…fifty-five miles," Nico said with a grin.

Among the crush of merchants and shoppers at the Lancaster County farmers' market, Nico was in his element. He strolled through the sprawl of stalls rubbing his hands together boyishly as he approached a display of zucchini.

For Madam, watching him was mesmerizing. He constantly picked up items of produce, smelling and squeezing them to determine their freshness. He cracked jokes with farmers, asking them a myriad of questions. And as he'd predicted, there was a sea of men and women in white chef jackets browsing the open market.

After the shopping was done, she and Nico, laden down with bags of groceries, were on their way back to the parking lot when Nico spotted a merchant's sign that boasted: Dre's Homemade Water Ice & Ice Cream.

"Aw, yeah, we gotta get some of that," he said, tugging her along. "It's a black-owned company; the brother's from Philly."

Madam couldn't have cared less about homemade ice cream or any other kind, yet she went along with Nico. She struggled to recall the last time she'd allowed anyone to take the lead and decide how she spent her time or select what she ate—but she couldn't remember.

Nico ordered a double dip of homemade sweet potato ice cream on a waffle cone, but Madam wasn't interested in anything on the menu. "I'm not a dessert person," she divulged with an apologetic expression.

But Nico kept pestering her to try it, claiming it was the best ice cream he'd ever tasted.

"God, I never met anyone so persistent," she said, shaking her head in mock exasperation. Giving in to the pressure, she accepted a lick of ice cream. While her tongue was embedded in the creamy treat, Nico ducked down and licked the other side of the cone. His lips and Madam's, both covered in sweetness, found their way to each other.

Their lips pressed together were soft and gentle and as sweetly innocent as the first kiss of adolescence. Yet, at the same time, the kiss was dizzying in its intensity, and Madam had to hold on to Nico to remain upright and steady on her feet.

He clasped her hand, leading her to the Escalade, but Madam pulled her hand away and stopped walking.

"What's wrong?" Nico asked.

"Everything."

"Everything? I thought we were having a nice time."

"We are and that's the problem."

"How's that a problem?"

She shrugged.

"Let's talk about it."

"There's nothing to talk about."

"All right. I won't touch you…I won't try to hold your hand again. Let's just keep it moving and pretend like nothing happened between us."

Madam scowled. "The only thing that happened was a stupid kiss."

Nico held up both hands. "Hey, I misread the signals. But you don't have to worry about me getting out of line again. We'll keep it strictly business—client and chef." With a hardened expression, he took the keys out of his pocket and pressed the keypad, which alerted them to the location of the Escalade.

The drive home was quiet and tense and without any more recollections of their pasts. Madam stared out the window watching billboards flash by.

Nerves frazzled and confused by her deep feelings for Nico, she refused to look at him.

Being dominant and demanding had been her reality for the past thirteen years. Being cuddly, giggly, and girlish was foreign behavior, and it frightened her. She resolved to visit the stables as soon as she arrived home.

She was a dominatrix and Brynne was a pleasure-slave who was trained to release her tension without Madam having to utter a word of instruction. That was the only reality that made sense to her.

She glanced at Nico and her heart fluttered, causing her to wonder if indulging a fetish was the answer to her problem.

In the past, commanding another human being to worship her usually fed her ego, but today such fervent adoration would only make her feel empty inside. Being worshipped wasn't real. It was a consensual game between two individuals who weren't satisfied with their own personal reality.

She shouldn't have discussed her devastating childhood with

Nico. The conversation had triggered a part of her that was vulnerable and weak. Usually when she thought of her unholy youth, it was as if she were remembering fragments of someone else's life—someone unrelated to her, yet remotely familiar nonetheless.

But this time the memories were clear and the wounds were painful and raw. It was reckless to have spoken so cavalierly of circumstances that had left her so emotionally broken. Now she felt defenseless. Absolutely helpless. It was such a hopelessly debilitating feeling, she began to tremble and her eyes glistened with tears, which she promptly wiped away.

Post traumatic syndrome is real. The terrors of the past can come back to haunt you when you least expect it.

"Are you crying?" Nico inquired.

"No," she said, sniffling.

He took his eyes away from the road and briefly searched her face. "You really are crying. Damn, what did I say? What did I do wrong?" he asked, one hand on the wheel the other extended toward her, attempting to touch her comfortingly, trying to reconnect.

But when he returned his focus to the busy stretch of highway, she leaned away from him and sobbed with both hands covering her face.

It was a gut-wrenching sound. Her crying was loud and uninhibited, as if she were alone in the privacy of her bedroom.

He pulled over on the shoulder and put the Escalade in park. "Hey, whatever I did to cause this, I'm really sorry. Okay?"

This time when he extended his arm, she didn't push it away. Sniffling, she gathered herself, and then turned toward him and buried her face in his chest, crying all over again. He embraced her, his muscled arms, engulfing her.

"You're okay, now. That life is behind you. They tried, but they didn't break you, and that's because you're stronger than most people. You're much stronger than me with my stupid potato story. You persevered, Quintoria. Is it all right if I call you by your first name?"

She nodded, still crying, although the sound was softer now.

"You're an amazing woman, and you should be basking in triumph, not wallowing in self-pity. You're better than that," he said softly in her ear.

She snuggled closer to him, and for first time in her life, she felt protected and safe inside someone's arms.

CHAPTER 26

Lyza drew Madam's bath and then clicked on the switch that would fill the spacious bathroom with soft music to help soothe Madam's agitated nerves. Realizing that her mistress appreciated quiet when she was in one of her moods, Lyza didn't say a word. There was only music and the therapeutic sound of tinkling water as she joined Madam in the enormous sunken tub. Slowly she washed Madam's feet, her smooth long legs, and her firm thighs. When she moved the cloth toward Madam's pleasure center, Madam stiffened and pressed her thighs together.

"Wash me, nothing more," she told Lyza.

"Yes, of course, Madam." Though her response was respectful there was a trace of resentment. Part of Madam's bathing ritual was to be pleasured by Lyza's fingers while in the water and then her lips while being toweled dry.

"Are you upset with me for some reason, Madam?" Lyza asked as she soaped her mistress's breasts, bringing the dark nipples to a peak as she circled them with her thumbs.

The sensations aroused her and Madam released a deep breath. "You've done nothing wrong, Lyza. I simply don't have time to play with you, my pet. Maybe later tonight I'll be more in the mood."

"I'm always at your service."

Madam patted Lyza's hand appreciatively. "Towel me off and then get my clothes ready. The new chef has put together a meal that he wants me to consider for the Equestrian Festival."

Lyza nodded and buffed Madam's body with an ultra-thick and soft towel.

Dressed in a satin layered skirt that showcased her fabulous legs and a vintage bustier, acquired from Dior's couture collection during Paris Fashion Week, Madam descended the stairs. There was power in the echoing sound of her stilettos clicking against marble, and she felt much more like herself than she did during her mini breakdown in the Escalade.

While passing a French mosaic wall mirror, she glimpsed the diamonds that graced her neck and earlobes, shimmering gloriously as they caught the light from the chandelier above. She swept into the dining room and sat at the head of the long, elaborate table, which was set for one.

She gawked at the unusual centerpiece. There was a tall heap of dirt-covered potatoes on white linen, smack in the middle of the table. It was artsy. A truly creative display of potatoes in their natural state, ranging in color from white and brown, to red.

The display was an homage to the only way Nico had ever gotten his hands dirty. Recalling their conversation of earlier in the day, it was also a touching way of acknowledging Madam's strength— her ability to overcome severe hardship.

Judging from the music that piped from the sound system, it was eighties night. Prince was singing "Little Red Corvette," giving Madam the impression that it was going to be a fun night. Instead of being served by the pleasure-slaves that were at her disposal, it was a delightful surprise when Nico himself emerged from the kitchen and placed before Madam a tasting menu. All the dishes had zany names and Madam sat back and sipped water, waiting for the culinary show to begin.

The first dish called *Gremlins* was a beautifully plated dish of lamb wontons with salmon roe and sprigs of dill. The wontons, of course, featured Nico's flair for Asian cuisine while the salmon roe, yogurt, and dill garnishes gave the dish a fun Scandinavian twist. Crunchy, paper-thin slivers of fried potatoes were added on the side, and the dish was paired with a glass of Chardonnay.

Next on the playlist, Madonna sang "Crazy for You," and Nico delivered Japanese red snapper glazed in truffle mushroom sauce with a dollop of creamy mashed potatoes and wonderfully paired with Cabernet Franc. The third course was a whimsical play on French fries and ice cream. Vanilla ice cream was piped inside a fried potato strip that was formed into a cylinder shape. The whimsical potato/ice cream wonder was set on a bed of shredded leeks and placed in the middle of a bowl of satiny potato-leek soup and paired with the perfect wine.

Ordinarily, Madam would have been stuffed at this point, but Nico, a food-wizard, served perfectly sized portions that prevented her from being stuffed too early in the foodie escapade.

Next, Nico's creation of an herb-encrusted pork loin made quite an impression. Of course, potatoes made another appearance. This time, roasted fingerling potatoes with fresh herbs and garlic and the dish was paired with Sonoma Zinfandel.

The parade of scrumptiously prepared and innovative cuisine kept coming and the music continued to evoke pleasant memories. LL Cool J's "I Need Love" brought back memories of a cherished pair of huge gold bamboo earrings, a gift from her first and only boyfriend during the brief period when her life had been normal. But there was no need to think about ghosts from the past when Nico, without a doubt, a culinary master was here right now, romancing her with his palate-pleasing cuisine.

The dinner service offered by Nico was a culinary extravaganza that offered a unique experience with imaginative cuisine that was at times quirky, but always amazingly divine.

Nico asked her to pick a few items from the tasting menu to serve at her big event, but with such thoughtfully prepared and delicious food, it was impossible to select only a couple of courses. Madam told him she wanted to replicate the entire menu along with the eighties theme and music of that era.

"Your playlist reminded me of the time period when I first arrived in the United States. How did you know which music would evoke fond memories for me?"

Nico shrugged. "You said you left Jamaica at age fourteen, and so I went online and found the popular music during your teen years."

"That was very thoughtful, Nico. It seemed as if I should have been wearing a tiara tonight—you made everything so special, as if it were my birthday, or prom night, or my wedding day," she said with wide smile.

"I'm going to make every night special during the time that I'm here."

She gazed at him curiously. "You've already been hired to cook for my event, so why go out of your way to continue to impress me?"

"Why not? Now stop questioning me and prepare yourself for dessert."

Protesting, she shook her head and turned up her nose. "No dessert. I'm more than satisfied, and I've really had quite enough."

"I won't take no for an answer," Nico said as he gently placed a blindfold to her eyes and forbade her to remove it. Realizing it was easier to play along than to disagree with him, Madam settled in her seat, groped blindly for her wineglass and once the glass was located and secured in her hand, she couldn't help from smiling at the intrigue and mystery that Nico had created.

Perfectly timed, the creepy opening bars of "Thriller" filled the room at the exact moment that Nico returned and announced in a theatrically spooky voice that the dessert that concluded the tasting experience was next. The last course was called *King of Pop* and consisted of a balsamic-roasted cherry brownie with coconut-lime sorbet on top and resting in a pool of cherry soda pop glaze.

Madam parted her lips and took in the combined rich and tart sweetness of balsamic vinegar and roasted cherries with the dark fudgy texture of classic brownies. It was an explosion of mind-blowing awesomeness. The interplay of warm brownies and cold sorbet was intriguing, especially with her eyes covered and not knowing what temperature would delight her tongue next.

Being fed such scrumptiousness while blindfolded was magical. It was utterly divine.

"Mmm." The sound was an admission that she had been converted and could no longer claim that she was not a dessert person. She fell back in an exhausted swoon, smiling with happiness.

Nico used a thumb to wipe a crumb from her lip and she felt a jolt of exhilarating sensations surging through her—sensations that both thrilled and terrified her. His thumb that sensually outlined her mouth was soon replaced with his soft lips. His kiss caused a slow burn that started the moment he caught her lower lip and sucked on it gently. Somehow her arms wound around his neck without her quite knowing how they got there.

He touched her lips with the tip of his tongue and her mouth parted for him. His hands went to her waist, urging her to stand, which she did without hesitation. Madam inhaled sharply as his middle finger slowly meandered along her cleavage—softly, teasingly, so maddeningly, her breaths were coming in ragged gasps.

Being only seconds away from clawing open her bustier, she sucked in a burst of air, panting with gratitude when Nico's fingers made their way to the back of her garment and began to slowly slide the zipper down.

The bustier fell away and her breasts were exposed. Stripped bare from the waist up while blindfolded was exhilarating. Excitedly, she waited for the next phase of the seduction. First, Nico had seduced her taste buds, then he'd captured her heart, and now he was going to possess her body.

It was the time for her to turn things around and take control of the situation, yet she sat there without uttering a word of protest, doing nothing except shuddering in fear and allowing herself to be vulnerable. Oddly, it felt okay to simply let go. To submit to the possibility of love.

"I Wanna Be Your Man" by Zapp & Roger poured from the speakers and it seemed the lyrics had been written especially for this moment—an ode to love from Nico to her.

With his lips close to her ear, he said, "Your breasts are beautiful—a work of art, like a priceless ebony sculpture. I want to touch them…" His voice trailed off and he became silent while the music continued to play. The singer's plea, *I wanna be your man*, sounded heartfelt, creating a sexual tension that was swiftly becoming unbearable.

Madam's back arched, urging Nico to touch her. To maul and manhandle her until she cried out in sexual agony. But he didn't lay a finger on her.

"Touch me," she whispered, her voice cracking and revealing how urgently she needed him.

"I want to but—"

"Do it. Please."

"How do you want to be touched? Tenderly? Do you want me to show you with my hands and my lips how much you deserve to be cherished and revered?"

"Yes." Her hand reached for the blindfold. "I want to see you."

"Don't take it off. Not yet." His voice was low and gentle, yet firm, and it seemed to echo loudly once the music stopped. There was no longer a soundtrack playing behind them. The only sound in the quiet house was Nico's soft voice and Madam's jagged breathing.

"I…I want you so badly," she said with a whimper, as if it broke her heart to admit her fierce desire.

"You have me."

"But I'm scared."

"So am I."

"Why won't you touch me? You shouldn't tease me like this."

"I'm not teasing. Only taking my time. Admiring someone who has me mesmerized. Your body is the very definition of beauty. With all its classical perfection, it's like a museum piece that should only be admired—never touched."

"But I want you to."

"If you want me to touch you, then offer those luscious tits to me. Show me how much you want me to touch and taste them."

She cupped her breasts, leaned forward and said, "Touch them, Nico; they're yours."

She expected to feel his caress or the suction of his lips on her nipples, but what she experienced was startling. Something hot and creamy trickled down one of her breasts while a cold, thicker substance drizzled down the other. She gasped at the shock of the unexpected dual sensations of what she suddenly realized was hot, melted chocolate and chilled sorbet.

Her entire body felt primed for attention. Her skin felt like it was alive and buzzing with electricity. Every inch of her ached for Nico's touch.

She squeezed her breasts, rubbing what felt like fire and ice onto her skin, concentrating on spreading the gooey goodness all over her rigid nipples. She was ready to come out of her skirt now.

Ready to get on the table, naked, and let Nico cover her with everything he had cooked tonight. She wanted his food on her stomach, her legs, her face, and her pussy. She wanted to be dressed in his cuisine, her body perfumed with the co-mingled aromas.

The mixture of chocolate and sorbet were smeared on her breasts and across her chest, and she waited anxiously to feel the heat of his tongue licking through the sweetness and swirling around her nipples, causing them to become as hardened as black diamonds.

Instead of his tongue, Nico's fingers sliced through the sugary varnish, tracing letters across her chest: M-I-N-E.

CHAPTER 27

"I am yours…completely!" She hadn't meant to speak, but the words had tumbled out of her mouth, unbidden. My God, how long had it been since she'd known this kind of passion? Had she ever? The answer was "no." She'd experienced all manners of lustful scenarios and had indulged every freaky urge her twisted mind could summon. She'd always been the seductress—or most often, the demanding dominatrix flaunting her power over sniveling, eager-to-please submissives.

Nico had been lured to House of Stevens for the soul purpose of being systematically stripped of his power and brought to his knees as an addition to her collection of pleasure-slaves. But Madam hadn't even made an attempt to break the spirit of the strong-willed chef. Instinctively, she realized he'd never bend to her will or anyone else's.

She was the one who was blindfolded and willing to do anything commanded of her. It was a classic case of the hunter being captured by the game. It was almost comical, and she would have laughed at herself were she not in such discomfort. So strong was her desire for Nico, it brought a throbbing to her very core that was unrelentingly painful in its intensity.

Damp heat blossomed between her thighs and her heart raced in a panicked rhythm. "I want you, Nico. I want to be possessed by you, even if it's only for one night," she said in a voice that was sure and unwavering.

"Let's possess each other for as long or as short of a time as we make each other happy."

"Do I make you make you happy, Nico?"

"You make me ecstatic," he replied, removing the blindfold.

She blinked, adjusting her vision to the warm light of the chandelier. Settling her gaze on him, she glimpsed the raw emotion on his face, which incited her to reach out and touch his cheek with a trembling hand.

"The skirt I'm wearing was purchased in Paris. For such a small quantity of fabric, I paid an indecent amount of money."

"You wear it well. I'm sure it was worth whatever you spent," he replied, his serious dark brown eyes never leaving her face.

Her touch drifted from his cheek to his neck and flitted down to his chest, rubbing circularly, her fingers yearning to delve beneath the stiff fabric of his chef's jacket.

"Show me how much you want me, Nico. I don't have on panties; this skirt is the only thing that's preventing you from getting to my hot pussy."

Nico winced as his hands banded around her waist, at first caressing her buttocks, then suddenly ripping open the delicate fabric, shredding it away from her body, and then flinging it aside as if the couture skirt were nothing more than a worthless rag.

Naked except for her heels, Madam took steps backward and then hoisted herself up on the dining table, frenziedly knocking over bottles of wine and sending Waterford crystal glasses crashing to the floor. She had a savage lust for him, and in her shameless haste, she overturned the elegant silver containers of melted chocolate and creamy sorbet, spilling their contents as she cocked open her legs, putting her heated pussy on display. Lava-hot juices bubbled out and she stared at him with a feral look of need.

As Nico yanked off his white jacket and tore off his shirt, Madam probed her cunt with a long slender finger, stirring up the steamy juices that visibly spat and sputtered.

Keeping her eye on Nico as he stumbled out of his pants and kicked off his shoes, she emitted a husky groan as her finger sank deeper into the honeyed pond of lust.

At last, he was stripped bare. Stunned by her exhibition of raw sexuality, he stood motionless. She studied his powerful physique without blinking, her sexual desire heightened by the sight of his tightly muscled body. He was tall and magnificently sculpted, his looming presence giving the impression of an otherworldly being—a black god with supernatural powers who was capable of fucking her with such passion and intensity that he pushed her over the edge.

He took steps toward her, his thick dick-meat swinging heavily from one muscular thigh to the other, and she realized that this man, Nico, was capable of fucking her into a state of unconsciousness.

She didn't care. She was willing to risk everything, including her sanity. She plunged in another finger, fucking herself into a frenzy while desperately beckoning him with her free hand. Her lips moved anxiously as she murmured, "Take me, Nico. Fuck me without mercy. Rip me open, tear me apart!" She realized she must have looked half-crazed as the fingers of one hand spiraled frantically into her cunt while she tugged and yanked on her own tousled hair with the other.

With the ferocity of a wild beast, he leapt at her. He was all over her, biting softly on her neck, licking her breasts. His wide tongue swiped across her chest, symbolically staking his claim on her as he ingested the creamy imprinted letters, M-I-N-E.

His tongue lashes taunted her breasts and then flicked playfully down to her navel, but Madam was not in the mood for fun and games. He wanted to tease and she was ready to get serious. Urgently, she reached for his thick, dark manhood and clamped her hand around it, enjoying the feeling of his dick pulsing in her hand.

It had been eons since she'd humbled herself enough to suck a dick, but the way her mouth was watering indicated how very much she hungered for him. Willing herself to calm down and enjoy every moment, she gently stroked it before kissing it all over—from hilt to head.

His dick stretched out, thumped, and thickened, and Madam scooped up a handful of melted chocolate and sorbet from the table, using the mixture as an edible lubricant.

With hazy eyes and lids at half-mast, Nico looked down at his chocolate-and-sherbet-covered dick and let out a groan, and then bit into his bottom lip as Madam's tongue glided through the sticky coating. Holding the base of his shaft, she swirled her tongue around the head of his cock as if licking a scoop of ice cream on top of a cone. She slurped, sucked, smacked her lips, and applied suction to the head, all the while moaning deep in her throat as she tenderly caressed his balls.

Humping, he grabbed for her head, urging her to open her lips wider. He didn't stop thrusting until he'd buried his entire dick inside the warmth of her mouth.

Tears formed in her eyes as she determinedly took in more cock than she would have ever imagined possible. Nico moaned as she sucked his dick clean, pulling on it greedily as if trying to extract the life out of him.

"Damn, Quintoria. You sucking the shit out of my dick," he said with a grimace of lust. "Stop, baby; that's enough," he said, slowly pulling out of her hot mouth.

Relishing the taste of him, she quickly sucked him back in.

"If you keep it up, I'm gonna bust, and I don't want that." Sitting upright, he cracked one eye open and glimpsed the messy table. "Damn, what the fuck?" he uttered, looking around in wonderment. "Oh, well, can't do shit about it, so fuck it," he conceded, reaching for her. "Come here, bae; I'm about to go to work on that sweet little pussy of yours."

The pulsing in the center of her cunt had become almost unbearable, and though she wanted to be somewhat ladylike, it was impossible. While he played with her pussy, stroking her clit with the pad of his thumb, and snaking a long finger, well past the knuckle, into her creamy hole, she laid on her back writhing.

She slithered and wallowed in puddles of chocolate, sorbet, and dark red wine, fighting the orgasm that had been building up from the moment she'd swallowed his long, tasty dick.

When he finally climbed on top of her, dick in hand, she clung to him, arms looped around his neck, her legs hugging his waist. He entered her slowly, the heat that radiated from his dick warmed her insides like a sweet flame.

"I'm gonna get all up in that pussy and fuck you deep and long," he promised.

Rotating her hips and clenching her cunt muscles around his long, fat shaft, she tried to keep up with his strokes, bouncing her ass and throwing her hips and pelvis into overdrive. But she couldn't keep up with him. Her emotions had taken over and she couldn't hold back any longer.

The realization that she wanted more than good sex from Nico was beyond scary. And she questioned her motives. Why did she want Nico when she could have practically any man she wanted?

She didn't have an answer for herself. All she knew was that she'd developed strong feelings for him. She'd felt a strong emotional connection the first time she'd seen his face.

"You're so sexy and beautiful, Quintoria," he whispered in her ear as he plunged into her depths.

She erupted with a plaintive wail that prompted Nico to hold her close until she calmed down. Afterward, she whimpered, speaking softly in island dialect.

"What are you saying? I don't understand," Nico said confusedly.

Relieved that he couldn't understand her, she continued speaking in rapid Jamaican patois, pouring out her heart as she expressed the joy of first love.

Most people experienced falling in love for the first time during their teens, but back in those days, Madam had been too busy trying to survive to be concerned with romance.

But she was ready now.

Letting him know that she wanted more, she climbed on top, kissing him while pressing her chest to his. Slowly, rhythmically she rolled her hips and smiled as his thickness thumped against her groin. His dick found its way to her cunt, demanding entry into the sticky-wet confines. His thickness invaded her and her pussy responded by possessively clutching his length, teasingly attempting to milk him with rapid pussy clenches.

With a grunt, he gripped her hips, his momentum increased. "I'ma beat this fuckin' pussy up," he said gruffly.

She matched his rough thrusts. Riding him and responding to what he'd said in a mixture of island languages. Galloping fast and determinedly. The friction from grinding her sensitive clit against his hard dick took her over the edge, once again. But this time, the orgasm was gentler, putting a blissful smile on her lips as she cried out in ecstasy.

Nico inhaled and exhaled, panting and puffing as if ready to explode. He mumbled something incoherent and then bit down hard on his lip as he filled her body with his passion.

For the first few moments, they held on to each other, kissing and squeezing tightly. When they disengaged, Nico glanced around at the wreckage. Scowling, he examined his gook-covered arms and asked, "Is this a dream or is my naked ass lying on your dining table, covered in chocolate and wine and shit?"

Madam examined the dregs of dessert that clung to her body and said, "We must be sharing the same dream." She swiped chocolate from her arm and said, "And it's the sweetest dream I've ever had."

As if by magic, the music began to play again. This time, "Sweet Love" by Anita Baker filled the room. The instruments and lush vocals concealed the butler's footsteps as he crept from the shadows after secretly watching Madam and Nico while jerking his dick in lustful silence.

Stealthily, he exited the dining room and returned to the attic.

CHAPTER 28

Awakened by voices and the sound of laughter coming from outside, the butler stumbled out of bed and positioned a stepstool beneath the high attic window. Hands cupping his face, he peered out the cloudy window and what he saw caused him to pound a balled fist against the window frame: Madam and Nico were walking across the motor court, hand-in-hand, as carefree as teenage lovers.

It was bad enough that they'd been flaunting their illicit affair in front of him, fucking like rabbits in practically every room of the mansion as well as outdoors beside the pool, and behind bushes. The butler had been reduced to stealing glances since Madam had not bothered to invite him to participate or watch. Since Nico had arrived, she'd been completely ignoring him. Now the two of them were frolicking beneath his window at the crack of dawn, waking him from a peaceful sleep.

They were despicable. Disgusting heathens. And he hated both Madam and Nico with a passion.

The butler gripped his head in anguish. It wasn't fair. It simply wasn't fair. He'd done everything for that bitch and this was how she repaid him.

Seething with jealousy, he imagined wrapping his hands around her long, elegant neck and happily squeezing the very life out of her.

Once again, he was responsible for running the household along with conducting the training for the pleasure-slaves while Madam and her boy toy ran amok, taking day trips to farmers' markets all over the tristate area and even as far as New York. And when they weren't hunting for the best, tastiest, most interesting, and freshest ingredients, they were traveling up and down highways visiting the trendiest restaurants with the most innovative chefs.

Everything Madam talked about these days seemed to be food-related. It would serve her right if she blew up as big as a house. Getting fat probably wouldn't even bother her. He'd never known her to be so contented and at peace with herself. It was nauseating to witness. The silly woman seemed to have lost her mind with her perpetual ridiculous smile and constant humming—of all things—reggae songs!

The wanton behavior he'd secretly observed in the dining room when she and Nico were rolling around in food and sauces and knocking Waterford crystal off the table was evidence that Madam had lost her mind. In his opinion, she was becoming a danger to herself and others, and as her legal spouse, it was his right to have her committed for psychiatric treatment.

From the little he'd gleaned from Azalea, it appeared that Madam had some sort of mental health history. Being locked away for a while might be exactly what she needed.

The butler was so disgusted by her behavior, he was of a mind to contact the owners of the pleasure-slaves and let them know that their property was being grossly neglected. But if he interfered with Madam's largest source of income, he'd be cutting off his nose to spite his face.

There had to be another way to get back at her. Something excruciatingly cruel and painful. He simply had to figure out what to do and when.

He looked out the attic window again, squinting as he struggled to get a clear view. The sun had barely come up and already, Madam and her hoodlum boyfriend were cruising out of the driveway. The ruffian was behind the wheel. This time, they'd left the Escalade behind and had elected to make use of Madam's Ferrari.

He wondered where they were headed. Was this another day trip or would they be dining in Washington, D.C. or Manhattan and then staying overnight in a posh hotel? Taking the Ferrari instead of the SUV suggested they were not going on a food-buying excursion, but were planning a romantic getaway.

Madam's behavior was an outrage and a personal affront to her husband. He turned away from the window once he could no longer see the taillights of the car.

With Madam flitting about away from mansion on a regular basis, Lyza had far too much time on her hands. She should have been assisting him with organizing Madam's Equestrian Festival instead of carousing around with Hugo. No doubt after getting Madam ready for her rendezvous with her thug-lover, Lyza had slipped away to stables. The romance between Lyza and Hugo had been irking the butler for some time now, and it was high time he put an end to it.

He quickly changed from his pajamas into his pristine uniform. Striding purposefully, he crossed the small room and yanked his looped belt from the hook on the wall. Belt in hand, he exited the attic and locked the door and set off for the dormitory. This time, he wouldn't wake them with the blaring sound of an alarm. Today, he wanted to see them jump high and cower in fear as he woke them with hard strikes across their asses.

Leather cut through the air as he swung upward and came down hard, waking each girl with a vicious thwack across her backside.

He wasn't prepared for the pandemonium that ensued. The cacophony of squealing, yelping, wailing, and crying that resulted from the group flogging session had given him an erection of monumental proportion.

With Madam away for the day, there was no reason to rush the girls to the shower. No reason for them to hurry to their work posts. He had all the time in the world to give each girl a sound spanking and to provide individualized training wherever he saw fit.

With the naked girls lined in a row, he looked them over with malevolence shining in his eyes. Merely raising a hand triggered fearful reactions in most of the trainees. Some flinched, some gasped, and others stared, bug-eyed with fear.

Taking his strap to pleasure-slaves was a thoroughly delightful activity, especially when it resulted in his victims jumping from foot-to-foot in a comedic dance. Each time the fiery sting of leather landed on their bare skin their hopping movements reminded him of a macabre version of an old-time dance called the hucklebuck.

The butler discovered that he particularly enjoyed spanking bouncy pairs of tits almost as much as he enjoyed lashing round, fleshy asses. Most of the pleasure-slaves were lithe and delicate little creatures with hardly any excess body fat. But there were a few fatties in the bunch who possessed meaty asses and big, beatable cow-teats.

Joslyn had been delivered to House of Stevens by a cigar-smoking oil-tycoon from Texas. Joslyn wouldn't have won any races as a ponygirl but he decided she'd be good company whenever Madam was out gallivanting with her boy toy.

He lined the eight maidens in a row, all of them naked as jaybirds. One by one, he insisted they stand with their legs far apart while he removed his glove and prodded them with a forceful finger as he inspected their private parts. Most of those secret compartments were tight and hot while a few were loose and cool inside. Some of the girls flinched or gasped, but most knew the drill and gyrated on his finger, as he'd trained them to do.

Bored with the inspection, the butler clamped a hand around Joslyn's wrist and pulled her next to him. Shaking the belt threateningly at all the others, he ordered them to assume the position of the perfect submissive.

Obediently, they took turns and walked over to the butler and with grace and dignity, each girl knelt before him, pressing her lips against his crotch and kissing his large, coiled cock through the light fabric of his pants.

They all put their hearts into the assignment, but there was a pleasure-slave named Emily who was tall and gangly (all elbows and knees, that one) who had a real talent for cock-kissing. It was the way she puckered her full lips, sneakily flicking her tongue against the head of his dick. Her technique always incited the butler to pull down his zipper. Emily's scrawny hand wasn't strong enough to control the butler's massive erection. At that point, he beckoned Joslyn to wrestle his big dick out of his pants and guide it to Emily's puckered lips.

Emily hadn't been properly trained yet to relax her throat and take in the entirety of his colossal cock. Due to her poor deep-throating skills, streams of jism always poured out of the corners of her mouth, trickling down to her plum-sized little breasts.

That's when Chloe's talents came in handy. Quick as a wink, Chloe left her place in the line and licked the semen from Emily's tits before one droplet had hit the floor. Freckle-faced Chloe with red, close-cropped hair was a devoted dick sucker, but sadly, she couldn't withstand much of a beating.

He shook the belt at the girls once more before dismissing them. The fear that shone in all their eyes assured him that they would all work tirelessly and he wouldn't find a speck of dust in any crack or crevice inside the mansion.

As the pleasure-slaves filed out of the dormitory, Joslyn stood next to the butler with her eyes down and her arms behind her back as per her training. He drew her toward him and softly pinched her clit, which caused her cunt to moisten and her cheeks to redden. Enjoying her reaction, he took it further and pinched the inside of her plump thigh. When she let out a yelp of pain, he shoved her across the room toward the door, and then followed her with his strap, whipping her fluffy buttocks all the way down the hallway and up the stairs to the attic.

If she couldn't hold up to a little pinch, he wondered how she would fare being sequestered with him in the attic for hours. Before she was returned to her master, Joslyn's tolerance for pain would be greatly improved and in due time, she'd thank him for it.

By lunchtime, the butler had grown bored with Joslyn. He left her in the attic restrained and with all her orifices filled with cruelly-shaped stretching devices. Clamps with sharp-cutting teeth were fastened to her nipples and clit. The extreme ass spreader was reminiscent of a medieval torture device, and by the time Joslyn returned to Texas, every big-dicked cowboy in the state would be able to make use of her anal cavity without the least bit of resistance.

And though she was uncomfortable and unhappy at the moment, she would one day thank him for the way he'd patiently opened up her ass.

With the thug-chef out of the house, the butler had access to his office. With a handy extra key ensconced inside his pocket, gaining entry would be a breeze.

There was so much work piling up, he really could use the help of an assistant, and why not Lyza? She wasn't doing anything worthwhile. In fact, her presence at the stables was probably a distraction for Hugo, who needed to concentrate on getting those ponies ready for the big day.

He considered returning to the attic to retrieve his leather belt, but climbing the several flights of stairs required to get to the attic would have sapped the strength he needed to whip Lyza into shape. Using brute force, he intended to teach her that he was second-in-command and she had to answer to him whenever Madam wasn't around.

Madam didn't want any marks on Lyza's pert little derriere, but what she didn't know wouldn't hurt her. Besides, she was too busy with the roughneck-chef to examine Lyza's body. And if Lyza was foolish enough to blab on him, he'd apprise Madam of the goings on between the crude stable boy and the supposedly refined Brazilian beauty.

If Madam knew what was best, she'd check her private chambers for bedbugs, ticks, and fleas. No telling what Lyza had brought back after lying around in the filthy stables with that dirt-kickin' country boy.

From a cubby in the pantry, the butler replaced his shoes with a pair of hiking boots he kept on hand for trips to the stables. Most hiking boots were scruffy and rugged, but the butler kept his glowing with a military-like mirror shine.

It was a long and hot walk to the track where Hugo was working with the pleasure-slaves, teaching them various hurdle-jumping techniques. He looked down at his boots and sucked his teeth. From tromping across hills and dales and fields, his boots had lost their shine and were coated with thick grime. The butler would have to speak to Madam about getting him a golf cart, at the least. It was cruel of her not to offer him a mode of transportation now that he was handling most of her affairs.

For now, he'd take out his discontentment on Lyza. He'd give her a good thrashing and if she held up to his satisfaction, perhaps he'd reward her by allowing her to lick his boots clean. The imagery of the pretty maiden groveling at his feet gave him a burgeoning hard-on. His stiffened dick impeded his usual impeccable posture as well as his steady gait.

The butler was quite a sight. Hunched over with sweat pouring down his face, he moved awkwardly, taking one unsteady step after another toward the track. With the lovely Lyza in his cross-hairs, he was panting and practically salivating with the need to fuck someone. He tried to hurry as best he could, but with a dick as hard and as big as a boulder stuck between his thighs, all he could do was stagger along while dragging a gimp-leg behind him.

CHAPTER 29

Madam had offered to use her connections to get them a reservation at one of the most exclusive restaurants in New York, but Nico insisted on dining at an eatery owned by a friend from culinary school. As long as they were together, Madam was content to spend the evening however Nico wanted.

Although the atmosphere in the restaurant was vibrant and the place was clearly a hot spot for the young and trendy, Madam wasn't impressed. The venue was small, crammed with too many tables and was too loud for her taste. Her drink was good, though. Something called a Moscow Mule that was made with ginger beer and vodka. Nico had ordered it for her, promising that she'd like it.

She took another sip and decided it was exceptionally good.

"Well?" he asked, waiting for the verdict.

"It's delicious. But why is it called a Moscow Mule?" she inquired. "With the ginger beer element, why not call it a Jamaican Mule?"

"No idea. But glad you approve," he said, gazing at her admiringly.

With her hair styled in a thick side-braid with loose tendrils framing her face, Madam was the perfect image of casual elegance.

"Did I mention how hot you look tonight, bae?"

"Thank you, my darling." She smiled and then frowned suddenly. "By the way, what does bae mean?"

Nico chuckled. "It's an acronym for 'Before Anyone Else.'"

"Oh!"

"It's 'hood talk; I told you I lapse into jargon whenever I'm comfortable." He leaned in and eyed her closely. "And you let loose with that sexy Jamaican accent when we're in bed together."

She lifted a brow. "Only when we're in bed?"

"No, lots of other places, too. Like dining tables, inside elevators, on top of flower gardens, and squeezed inside public restroom stalls. So many endless nights of lust, I can't keep track of it all." He flashed that killer smile that never failed to moisten her panties.

She glanced around the restaurant. "I believe the men's room is empty at the moment. Would you like to slip inside for a quickie?"

Nico grinned devilishly. "I'm tempted, but, nah. I'm good."

Madam gave him a skeptical look.

The server arrived with their appetizers—crab toast with lemon aioli.

Madam took a bite and smiled. "This is scrumptious. Absolutely decadent."

"I told you my boy, Fletcher, can throw down."

"So far, so good. Hopefully the entrée can compare to the appetizer. Now, young man, let's get back to the topic of making a pit stop in the restroom."

"I'm usually up for all kinds of sexual adventures, but I have to act like I have some home training when I'm around my colleagues."

"Don't be such a spoilsport, Nico." Madam inclined her head toward the area of the restroom. "Don't you want me to hold your cock while you take a piss?"

"Mmm," he grunted. "That sounds nice and dirty, but you gotta play fair. It's not cool to get Big Daddy all worked up when he's tucked inside my briefs resting comfortably."

"I want Big Daddy tucked inside me," she said sulkily.

Nico reached out and caressed her hand. "I'll tell you what. As soon as we finish this lovely meal, we'll take a carriage ride through Central Park."

Madam wrinkled her nose. "Though I appreciate the romanticism, I'd rather rush back to the hotel after we've dined."

"Who said anything about romance? You misunderstood my intention, Miss Know-It-All."

"What's your intention?"

He spoke slowly and in a whispery tone of voice. "I intend to get you in that carriage and fuck your brains out, so take 'dem drawers off and stuff them in your purse before we bounce outta here."

She began fanning her face. "I'm suddenly quite full and totally bored with this place. Would you ask the waiter for the check?"

"I can't do that to Fletcher; that would be rude. You have to be patient. All right?"

She shrugged and pouted. "I suppose I can be patient…if I absolutely must."

"You absolutely must," Nico teased. Edging closer, he narrowed an eye at her playfully. "But before the night is over, I'ma put so much dick up in you, you're gonna be walking gap-legged like you were riding a horse for two or three days."

They laughed together and Madam realized how infrequently she actually let go and laughed until she'd met Nico.

The plates were cleared and the entrée was delivered. Salmon salad with quinoa, mushrooms, radicchio, and garlic-lime vinaigrette. On the side were roasted Brussels sprouts with apples and herbs. The dish was ordinary—nothing to write home about in Madam's opinion.

The owner and chef, Fletcher Hudson, came to their table to greet them. After the introductions, Nico congratulated the chef and raved about his cuisine. Madam drifted into her own private thoughts, allowing the two chefs to talk shop.

Love! It was everything she'd heard it to be. With Nico, she was euphoric, happy all the time. Everything Nico said either made her laugh or made her horny. She had zero interest in her various corporations and had put all important business decisions on hold. Her every thought revolved around Nico. She was addicted to him. Her only regret was that it had taken her whole life to experience being in love.

From the corner of her eye she observed Nico as he conversed with Fletcher. He was so fine and such an interesting and amazing man, she found herself considering the possibility of having his babies. Well, not her personally, but via a surrogate and most definitely with her eggs. She still had a period and assumed she still had some viable eggs. She'd have to make an appointment with a specialist very soon. God, she hoped she hadn't waited too long to try to have a child of her own.

"What are you thinking about?" Nico asked, interrupting her musing.

Lost in thought, she hadn't realized that Fletcher had returned to the kitchen. "I was thinking about you."

"What about me?"

"How you should have your own restaurant. Your friend, Fletcher is a good chef, but not a masterful chef like you. His food isn't as refined. The things you do with food are more elevated, much more upscale."

"What are you saying?"

"That I would like to help you get started with your own restaurant."

Nico looked flabbergasted. "That's generous, but I don't want to screw up what we have by mixing business with pleasure."

"But it's not as if you asked for a loan. I'm making a no-strings-attached offer."

"And as I said, thanks, but no thanks," Nico persisted.

"Stop being difficult. Why should your slightly-talented friend have his own restaurant while you have to hop from one place to the other like a wandering gypsy?"

Nico winced. "That's cold."

"I don't mean to be cruel, but you know I'm speaking the truth. I believe that you roam from place to place instead of settling down in one place simply because you don't want to answer to a boss. You want to be your own man, and I don't blame you."

Nico held up his hands. "You're right. I'm constantly moving because when I cook I put my heart and soul into it, I'm not trying to stick in one place, using my talent to help another person realize their dream when I have my own. I'm very patient, though. My day will come. And when it does, it'll be on my terms."

"Your sense of honor is commendable."

"Now you're being sarcastic."

"No, I'm not."

"Yes, you are. I appreciate the offer, but I'm my own man. So, drop it."

"I realize you're your own man, but what you don't realize is that I have an ulterior motive."

"And what's that." Nico shook his head. "Let me guess…you've always wanted to be in the restaurant business. Look here…I'm not interested in hooking up with a partner. I have my own ideas and my own way of running things. Like I said, I'm good. Eventually, I'll get mine."

"I have no desire to be in the restaurant business. My ulterior motive is that I've grown attached to you, and I hate the idea that after the Equestrian Festival you're going to pack your bags and leave."

"I won't be leaving for good. With FaceTime and Skype, we'll stay in touch. You have an open invitation to visit me anytime you want, and I don't mind flying back to Pennsylvania to hook up with you between guest-chef stints."

Unable to conceal her disappointment, Madam sighed.

Nico touched her hand. "Lot of couples have long-distance relationships."

"Is that what we are?"

Confused, he crinkled his brow.

"Are we a couple?"

"Uh…yeah?"

"You said that with a question mark."

"I'm not seeing anyone else. Are you? Well, aside from those freaky folks in your fetish community."

She shook her head. "No personal relationships. The only person I'm emotionally involved with is you." She refrained from mentioning her marriage, deciding it wasn't important enough to bring up.

"Put it like this," Nico said, interlocking his fingers and assuming a serious expression. "We're not your average couple. But we've got love for each other. And we're exclusive…in a weird sort of way." He gave a wry laugh.

"I want us to be happy together. I've achieved many of my dreams, and now I'd like to help you realize yours."

Nico's features hardened. "Listen, let's enjoy each other and have a good time, but don't try to buy me. I have my own money—I'm not for sale." He beckoned the server to bring the check.

They left the restaurant in silence, and Madam was surprised to see that a horse-drawn carriage was waiting at the curb, as if by magic. Perplexed, she looked at Nico.

"I called and made the arrangements earlier today," he explained in a somber tone. "I can cancel if you'd like," he added glumly.

"No, don't cancel," she said, linking her arm in his. With the tension between them, she didn't expect them to have the kinky carriage ride that Nico had promised, but hopefully she'd be able to get him out of his miserable mood.

Nico tipped the driver and spoke in a low tone, giving him directions on the route he wanted to take.

With a set of benches facing each other, the canopy-topped carriage was spacious enough for four. As the horse clumped over asphalt, Madam and Nico sat together in tense silence. Madam moved closer, enticing him to put his arm over her shoulder or to take hold of her hand, but he sat stiffly beside her, looking straight ahead.

It was their first disagreement, and she didn't like it one bit. She wanted to make things right. To make him smile again.

"What can I do to improve your mood, Nico?"

"You can start by taking those panties off."

Her eyes widened. "Okay," she said, stretching out the word, eyes glancing nervously around the sparsely populated street.

After she slid her panties down to her ankles, Nico roughly grabbed her, pitching her forward and bending her at the waist. She braced herself by grasping the edge of the empty seat that faced them. Though they were partially concealed by the canopy, they weren't invisible, and the scant few people walking dogs or taking an evening stroll gawked at the sight of Nico spanking Madam's ass while verbally chastising her.

"I'm not your goddamn boy toy; I'm a grown-ass man. Don't you ever again come at me with your checkbook open, trying to coerce me into something I told you I'm not ready for."

"I'm sorry, Nico; I was only trying to help," she said breathlessly, her cunt growing moist with each heavy-handed whack.

"Shut the fuck up," he snapped, guiding his dick into the opening of her pussy, and then shoving it deeply into its clutching depths.

With power thrusts, he hammered into her body, while intermittently smacking her ass, rocking the carriage as the horse plodded along.

Not seeming to notice or care about the lewd sex show taking place behind him, the driver yanked the horse's reins, guiding it through the streets of New York.

CHAPTER 30

Madam awakened with a smile on her face in a stylish hotel room that smelled of roses. Rolling over in bed, she put her arm around Nico and pressed against his strong body. It was a glorious morning, and waking up next to Nico was heavenly bliss. She thought about scooting beneath the covers and rousing him from sleep with a blowjob—her way of saying thank you for a wonderful time last night.

The freaky carriage ride had brought them even closer together, and although Nico had complained that she was trying to control him with money, she denied the accusation vehemently.

"Why can't you accept that I've fallen in love with you? You make me so deliriously happy that it seems unfair for me to have such a tremendous amount of joy and not share it with you."

"But I am happy," he'd said.

"We're not on an equal playing field, Nico. I've already achieved financial freedom and you're still striving."

"I'm still a young man. There's nothing wrong with putting in the work to get where I want to be. I love what I do so much, I don't even consider it work. I've been enjoying the chase of going after my ultimate goal, and I have no doubt that eventually I'll own my own restaurant. But I'm afraid it'll make me lazy and weak if I accept handouts and take the shortcut you're offering."

His sense of honor and nobility had touched her heart so profoundly, she almost withdrew her offer. She'd been on the brink of letting go and letting him fly free. But her love was too strong and too selfish to let him walk out of her life. Sure, he'd promised that they'd maintain a long-distance relationship, but she had no desire to be separated by hundreds of miles. Madam wanted to wake up with him every morning and go to bed with Nico by her side every night.

She'd kept up the pressure throughout the course of the evening and although he was reluctant to accept charity from her, he'd eventually come around to her way of thinking and agreed to look at available spaces to open a restaurant—spaces within driving distance of Madam's home.

"I'm going to pay you back," he had promised.

"That's not necessary; consider it a gift," she'd insisted.

"But I have money saved, and you can have it all."

"Keep it. You'll need a nest egg…in case the restaurant fails."

"Failure isn't an option," he'd said in a harsh tone.

"Of course not," she'd soothed. But she'd done her research and had learned that restaurants failed at an alarmingly high rate each year. If and when Nico's restaurant failed, she'd be standing by his side ready to comfort him and mend his broken heart.

She was excited about their future. Realizing that their time together would be unlimited, she was ready to change her decadent lifestyle.

It was laughable that she'd once believed that associating with the royal family of Norway was the ultimate measure of personal success. It repelled her to think of any type of sexual frolicking that didn't involve her and Nico, exclusively. The very thought of him touching or being touched by anyone else infuriated her.

Sadly, she also had regrets. Why, oh why had she allowed Jamison to talk her into that stupid festival. She had to call it off and send all the pleasure-slaves back to their owners. Rejecting her major source of income would be costly. She'd simply have to put more energy into her mainstream businesses to ensure that she and Nico were able to maintain their lush lifestyle.

Last night Nico had asked probing questions, wanting to know what had attracted her to the fetish community in the first place. Although she'd only known him for a short while, she trusted him enough to be completely honest, and she'd admitted that she'd been a frightened child who grew up to be a frightened woman who masked her fear by instilling it in others.

"I arrived in the United States as shell-shocked as any war veteran," she had begun her tale. And then she told him that through a network of Jamaican-Americans, she was led to a kindly woman affectionately called "Aunt Nola" who didn't have much but was willing to share what she had with the orphaned Jamaican youth she took in and provided a loving home.

Madam told Nico how a brash Americanized Jamaican girl named Azalea who wore bold hairstyles and big clunky jewelry had befriended her and taken her under her wing, teaching her teen culture in Philadelphia during the late-eighties. Azalea had become Madam's best friend and confidante, and the person who helped her shoplift a fashionable coat during Madam's first experience with astonishingly cold weather.

Those first three years in America had been happy times, and Madam had learned to smile again by blocking out memories of the daily beatings and forced domestic child labor she'd endured her entire life.

While recounting the story of her life, she'd conveniently left out the tragedy that had occurred a few months before her eighteenth birthday. She didn't tell Nico about her psychotic break.

When Aunt Nola had pointed out that Quintoria had failed to

clean the bathtub properly after taking a bath, young Quinnie as she was fondly called, snapped. In her confused mind she believed she was finally protecting herself from the injustices brought against her by the cruel woman who'd beaten her mercilessly and worked her relentlessly all the years she'd lived in Jamaica.

But in reality, it was sweet Aunt Nola whose eyes she savagely clawed like a wild tigress. It was kindly Aunt Nola's head that she bashed repeatedly against the side of the porcelain bath tub. With her hands and clothing covered in blood, Quintoria fled Aunt Nola's house and ran screaming through the streets, believing she was being pursued by people who sought to enslave her once again.

Blind and brain damaged, Aunt Nola spent her remaining years existing as a vegetable in a care facility.

Quintoria was locked away in a mental institution for ten years. Before her release, an eccentric therapist suggested she take control of her life and regain her personal power by exploring BDSM and taking on the persona of a dominatrix.

Shortly after being released from psychiatric care, she went to work for Jamison Hardwicke as his personal assistant. Assuming the role of a dominatrix, she persuaded him to use his finances to provide Aunt Nola with the best of care, and was surprised that he actually obeyed her.

Dominating Jamison had been so easy. On a lark she decided to see how far he was willing to go and she agreed to marry him when he asked. She had kiddingly asked him to assume the role of her butler and was pleasantly surprised when he agreed to every outlandish request. Over time, what began as merely a mind game became a lifestyle, and her therapist considered her a success story.

Madam had come to realize that she'd never actually had any power until now. There was power in love and she no longer needed the advice of a quirky therapist. From now on, Quintoria Stevens would be guided by the power of love.

Of course, her epiphany would not be received well by Jamison. For him, losing her would be a harsh blow. He'd be hurt and bitter, but would have to accept that their lives together had been nothing more than a game of dominance and submission—a game that he'd been all too willing to play.

She'd divorce him. Give him back the money she'd taken from him, and send him on his way.

Lyza wasn't going to like being shipped back to South America, but Madam had no more use for the beautiful girl.

Her lifelong friend, Azalea, would hopefully be satisfied with a generous severance package. If not, they could talk it over and come to an agreement. Madam was willing to give Azalea whatever she wanted…within reason, of course.

The exhaustive amount of changes that were necessary in order to begin a new life with Nico were simply too much to think about right now.

As Nico slept, she glanced at his handsome profile and felt her heart flutter with joy.

Slyly, she lifted the covers and shimmied downward until her face was flush with his cock. She covered his limp meat with kisses until it jerked upward, stiffening and thickening as it bobbed against her lips.

Greeting her with a soft moan, Nico began gently thrusting until his hardened cock was totally entrenched inside her warm, welcoming mouth.

The drive from New York to Pennsylvania was bittersweet. Madam was chattering happily while Nico was pensive, not saying much.

"What's troubling you, my love?" she asked.

"I'm not troubled about anything. But I am little anxious about finding the perfect spot for my restaurant. I never thought about narrowing my options to any particular location, and not knowing much about Pennsylvania puts me at a disadvantage."

"You're not limited to my exact neighborhood. Driving distance includes New Jersey, Delaware, and parts of Maryland. I have no doubt that you're going to find something amazing. Why don't you get in touch with a realtor and start looking at locations right away?"

"Good idea, but I need to stay focused until after your event. I want the food to be so delicious and so memorable, that your last freaky event is talked about for years," he said jokingly. "Seriously, though, I want everything to turn out perfectly. Wouldn't want to embarrass my bae in front of her rich, weirdo friends."

Madam let out a sigh. "I've decided to call off the Equestrian Festival."

His eyes widened in surprise. "Why? I thought it was an important event."

"As I told you last night, I'm ready to distance myself from that lifestyle. It doesn't represent who I am anymore."

He shot her a quick look. "I want you to know that I was willing to try to accept that part of your lifestyle. I told myself that all those freaks-in-the-sheets were consenting adults, and that I had no right to judge them. But I'd be lying if I said I was okay with it. To me it's disgusting, and that master and slave shit freaks me out."

"You won't have to be around it, Nico. When we get home, I plan to make arrangements to send all the pleasure-slaves back to their owners."

"Their *owners!*" Nico shook his head. "I'll never understand why anyone would willingly allow themselves to be owned."

"It can be psychologically thrilling. An emotional release. Like what we did in the carriage last night. That was a consensual power exchange."

"Nah, I can't agree with that. Smacking an ass during sex is perfectly normal. Everybody does it."

"If you say so, Nico," Madam said with a sly smile.

"Yeah, whatever. But as far as your freaky friends go, to each his own. But as a black man from the 'hood, I don't see anything sexy about being restrained in a pair of handcuffs, so don't even think about bringing any shit like that into the bedroom."

"I wouldn't dream of it. That life is officially behind me."

"So, who's going to clean that big-ass mansion after you emancipate those folks?" Nico said lightheartedly.

"I'll hire people." Madam fell silent. It was the perfect time to tell Nico about her farce of a marriage. She opened her mouth to confess, but the words became stuck in her throat. She was too embarrassed to admit the degree of her depravity. That she'd married a man and then consigned him to a life as her butler seemed too much for Nico to have to digest, despite how understanding he'd been up to this point. There were certain matters that were too sensitive to discuss. For Madam, those topics were her marriage to her butler and the missing ten years that she'd spent in psychiatric care.

No matter how much Nico claimed that he cared for her, she doubted if he would look at her in the same way if he had any idea of what she'd done to innocent Aunt Nola.

It was her darkest secret, information that only her psychiatrist and her friend, Azalea, were privy to. Sure, her crime had made the news at the time, but it was old news now, and most people forgot that it had ever happened.

CHAPTER 31

That fucking Brazilian spitfire was more trouble than she was worth. The butler had tried to warn Madam that sneaking Lyza out of Rio de Janeiro without a green card was a huge mistake. But Madam hadn't listened to his advice. She said she'd use her connections to expedite the process, but had never gotten around to it. Foolishly, Madam had trusted Lyza with far too much sensitive information, and now that lapse in judgement had come back to haunt them all.

Such a hot-head and too arrogant for her own good, Lyza had refused the butler's order to lick his boots clean, and after he'd taken her over his knee, the fiery little vixen had thrown a hissy fit, shouting *filho da puta*, calling him a son of a bitch in Portuguese.

She flung an antique ashtray filled with cigar ashes against the wall, and then the temperamental hussy ran out of the office, kicking over everything in her path. Out in the corridor, she snatched a bucket of dirty scrub water from one of the trainees and flung the murky water everywhere, splattering Madam's priceless Renoir.

And if that wasn't bad enough, she was now ranting and raving about calling the authorities to report the butler. Claiming that he had personally smuggled her into the United States and was keeping her against her will as a sex slave, which was complete rubbish.

It was horrifying to be accused of something as vile as human trafficking. If the authorities decide to swoop down upon House of Stevens and discovered a dormitory full of young women bearing welts and bruises, the butler would have a lot of explaining to do. And God forbid if they searched the grounds and found Marnie, Brynne, and the twins living in horse stalls.

Though he was not guilty, proving his innocence would not only be time-consuming and costly, but would also dishonor his prominent family name. He couldn't let Lyza anywhere near a telephone. At present, he had her locked inside her bedroom, but was doubtful how long he could keep the snarling tigress caged. Though her window was barred, he wouldn't have been the least bit surprised if she found the strength to break down the door.

He ran a nervous hand over his perspiring face as he imagined a troop of police officers racing through the house, rescuing the horde of the girls who hailed from all over the world. And if they decided to search the attic and discovered Joslyn strung up and stretched out for the second day in a row of extreme torture training, the butler would be put underneath the jail, and the media would have a field day. He'd be labeled a monster or worse.

Without Madam corroborating his story that all the girls in the house were there on their own accord, the butler would be in deep trouble. The authorities would consider him to be a babbling lunatic as he desperately tried to explain that the girls were consenting adults who lived and breathed to be pleasure-slaves and whose true masters had paid excessive amounts of money to have them properly trained at House of Stevens.

The butler could picture himself, sitting behind bars for hours—maybe days or weeks—trying to explain the sordid story. Meanwhile, Madam, free as bird, would be enjoying life to the fullest. It was possible that at that very moment, Madam was sailing on a yacht in St. Tropez, smiling adoringly at her boy toy.

What a fine mess Madam had gotten him into. All because she

had to have the beautiful and exotic Lyza as her personal hand-maiden. The butler had suspected from the start that Lyza would be nothing but trouble. And he'd been right.

He heard a thud from upstairs, something else being thrown, a shoe perhaps. The distant sound of Lyza's ranting was faint but audible as she continued her tirade in part English and part Portuguese.

Sitting behind the desk, he regarded the trashed office: a broken lamp, an overturned waste bin and computer printer, a broken ashtray, cigar butts and ashes scattered about on the desk and the carpeted floor, a dent in the wall, and paintings hanging askew.

He hadn't heard Azalea's sneaky footsteps, but out of nowhere, she appeared in the doorway of the office. "What the hell happened in here?"

"Mind your business, Azalea. Don't you have work to do in the kitchen?"

"Those trainees have all been fed, and Hugo came and collected the sacks of horse food for those pitiful folks you have locked up in the stables," Azalea said, eyeing the butler accusingly while shaking her head. "Quinnie's not here and she didn't say what time she'd be back. And since she only wants Nico preparing her meals from now on, I figured me and the girls would hang up our aprons and call it a day."

"If you're requesting an early dismissal, the time will have to be deducted from your check."

"I'm not asking *you* for a damn thing. You don't sign my paycheck, Quinnie does. Besides, with all the nonsense I put up with around here, I defy anyone to deduct one red cent out of my check. You got that, Jamison?" she said, poking him in the center of his forehead.

Of all days, Azalea chose a moment in his life when he felt the most vulnerable and frightened to put him in his place. Being poked in the forehead was deliciously degrading, and there he was, sitting behind the desk with a hard dick, and unable to do anything about it.

Azalea swished out of the office, and the butler dropped his head in one hand and soothed his swelling cock with the other.

The flagrant disregard for his authority had gotten completely out of hand. The household was quickly going to hell in a handbasket because Madam's attention was focused on Nico instead of handling the domestic staff and the pleasure-slaves she was in charge of.

The butler rarely imbibed of hard liquor, but he needed a stiff drink to calm his rattled nerves. Appreciative that the quick-tempered dirty slut (or *bardajona* as they said in Portuguese) hadn't gotten her hands on the bottle of Rémy Martin and used it for batting practice, he picked up the cognac that was stashed in a drawer with tremulous hands. After uncorking it, he drank the bitter libation straight from the bottle.

Something had to be done. Although he dreaded having to contact Madam with such unwelcome news, he had no choice. It was time to call and apprise her of this most unfortunate situation.

After checking out of their hotel, Madam lured Nico into Barneys New York. When she offered to pay for a super expensive pair of Valentino camouflage sneakers that he'd been admiring, Nico declined, stating he was grateful she was willing to put up the money for his restaurant, and that when the day came that his restaurant started turning a profit, he'd buy his own fourteen-hundred-dollar sneakers. Until then, he was happy wearing Nikes and other brands that cost no more than three or four hundred.

Softening the blow of what he realized she perceived as rejection,

Nico hugged her close and then said softly, "I'm not some broke dude looking for a come up. I love you for you. Not for what you can buy me." Then he kissed the tip of her nose. "Did I ever mention that you have a sexy nose?"

Madam giggled and beamed at him with love shining in her eyes. Still, her disappointment had been profound. Was it her fault that she loved him so much she wanted to show it by showering him with all the material things he could ever hope for? There were so many opportunities and luxuries she could provide for him if he'd only let her.

At her age, when love came into your life, you didn't waste time analyzing it or playing coy; you grabbed it and held on with all your might. And you showed how much you cherished that love with an abundance of expensive gifts.

As they left New York and entered New Jersey, Nico suggested cheerfully, "Let's take the scenic route."

"Sure," she agreed. Whatever made Nico happy was fine with her. With the help of the GPS, he discovered quaint towns with breathtaking pastoral scenery, expansive vistas, and rolling hills. The backroads were also sprinkled with roadside stands where farmers sold bushel baskets of tomatoes, huge ears of sweet corn, peppers, apples, and eggplant. Of course, Nico couldn't resist pulling over to sample what the Garden State had to offer in the way of fresh ingredients.

The excitement in his eyes told Madam to get comfortable because they'd be in farm country for quite a while. He was the only person she knew who'd pass up an exclusive shopping spree to browse produce and haggle with a merchant over the price of hand-gathered eggs.

As Nico inspected the goods and struck up conversations with other patrons, Madam stood near the car and observed him. There was no pretense to Nico. She admired his bright mind, quick wit, and his honesty about himself was endearing. He was warm and attentive toward her in a confident, masculine way, which convinced her that it was possible, even this late in the game, to have an idyllic life with a wonderful man.

More now than ever, she wanted to help him become a restauranteur, and she made a mental note to take matters into her own hands and call a realtor first thing tomorrow.

While in the midst of putting the first half of the bounty into the trunk of the car, Nico plucked a large tomato from the bag. Wiping the dirt that clung to the tomato onto the leg of his ripped jeans, he bit into it with all the enthusiasm of taking a bite out of a delicious apple.

"Try one, they're delicious," he said, tossing a tomato to Madam. For a moment, she stared curiously at the vibrant red produce as if holding a foreign object that had fallen from the sky. It had been a lifetime ago, in fact she still lived on Cat Island when she'd last eaten a tomato straight from the vine and speckled with bits of soil.

She would have preferred to have at least washed the dirt off before sinking her teeth into it, but throwing caution to the wind, she brushed the bits of soil on her Roberto Cavalli jeans and took a bite out of the juicy Jersey tomato.

"It's really good!" Madam acknowledged with a smile.

"Told you," Nico said, leaning in and giving her a quick kiss.

As Nico headed back to the produce stand, Madam leaned against the Ferrari, content to linger in the background, fondly observing the way he seemed to glide when he walked, the easy manner in which he interacted with people—and that thick, muscular body should have been a crime. Her breath caught and she couldn't look away. He had the most incredible ass, she acknowledged, wanting to slither up behind him and grope his manly buttocks right then and there. If there was ever a male butt competition, Nico would win, hands down.

Her phone vibrated inside her clutch bag, and she briefly took her eyes off Nico's lusciousness to give her designer clutch a sneering look. She'd been ignoring the constant vibrating ever since they'd exited the Holland Tunnel. She didn't have to take her phone out and gaze at the screen to identify the impatient caller. No one other than Countess Hedvig would have the audacity to harass her with nonstop calls.

Ordinarily, when the countess's constant calling become unbearable, Madam would instruct the butler to placate the woman. But now that she no longer desired to be a guest at the Royal House of Norway, Madam couldn't think of any good reason to continue putting up with nuisance calls from Countess Hedvig. It was time for her to put the obnoxious countess in her place, but not wanting to ruin the mood of such a wonderful sunny day, she opened her purse with the intention of turning off her phone. She'd have harsh words for the countess when she had a moment alone later tonight.

But it wasn't Countess Hedvig's name on the screen. It was Jamison calling. He'd made seventeen phone calls. The situation had to be urgent for him to call with such frequency. By nature, the butler was not an alarmist, something had to be terribly wrong for him to pester her with such persistence.

Had there been a tragic accident? Frantic with worry, she immediately thought of Azalea. Her dear friend suffered from hypertension, but no amount of coaxing had persuaded Azalea to monitor her blood pressure regularly, to try to stay calm, or to make wiser food choices. Madam's heart began palpitating as she envisioned Azalea lying dead in a morgue, her life cut short by a stroke or a massive heart attack.

Despite the harsh heat from the sun, she felt a sudden coldness on her flesh. *Please let Azalea be okay,* she thought as she pressed the butler's number.

CHAPTER 32

The butler picked up on the first ring.

"Madam, we have a serious problem," he divulged in a grave tone.

"Is Azalea okay?" She braced herself for the worst.

"Of course, Azalea's okay, but Lyza has lost her mind."

Oh, thank you, God. Azalea's all right! Though not related by blood, Azalea was the closest thing to family Madam had. Life was too short to live with regrets and Madam went silent as she made promises to herself to start treating Azalea with the kindness she deserved. She'd reduced her sister/friend to being nothing more than hired help, but that ended today.

"Are you there, Madam? Are you listening to me?" the butler said, sounding frantic. "Lyza is threatening to destroy everything you've built; she's trying to take us all down."

"What are you talking about, Jamison?"

In a breathless rush of words, the butler explained how Lyza's insolence and refusal to accept his authority had left him no choice but to discipline her. And after going on a destructive rampage, breaking things and destroying priceless works of art, the volatile little diva had threatened to involve the authorities. "She is planning to tell the police that we're running a sex trafficking ring and that I personally kidnapped her from Rio de Janeiro and brought her here."

"Lyza is devoted to me. She'd never tell such a horrible lie. Put her on the phone, Jamison."

"She's sequestered in her bedroom and has made it clear that she doesn't want to speak to you. She wants a hundred thousand in cash and the title and keys to the Escalade, which she intends to give to Hugo."

"Why would she want to give my SUV to *Hugo?*"

"They've been conducting a torrid affair for quite some time."

"And you didn't think that was something I should have been made aware of."

"I didn't want to trouble you, Madam."

Madam sighed. "I don't know what possessed you to put your hands on my personal property, but I'm going to deal with you as soon as I get home."

Oh, goodness. Listen to me, lapsing right back into the role I no longer want to play.

"Jamison, I apologize for raising my voice and for threatening you. I didn't mean what I said."

"No need to apologize. I deserve to be chastised. I'm the scum of the earth, the dirt beneath your shoes. I'm the most loathsome—"

"That's quite enough, Jamison. Listen carefully. I need you to follow my explicit instructions and handle this sensitive matter for me."

"Anything, Madam."

"I want you to go to the bank and withdraw the money Lyza asked for from the household expenses account," Madam instructed, relieved that she wouldn't have to personally handle paying off the bribe.

"Another thing, Jamison. As you know, the keys and the titles to the vehicles are locked inside the safe. Give those to Lyza also. Additionally, I want you to draw up some type of contract and have her sign it before you hand everything over."

"Yes, Madam. I'll work on that right away."

"Of course the contract won't be legally binding, but Lyza won't know that."

"You're so clever, Madam. And again, I'm so very sorry for bringing shame to this fine household." The butler stroked his dick as he groveled, hoping to keep Madam on the phone long enough to jerk himself off.

"I know you're sorry, Jamison. Now, let's forget about it and move forward. We have to get ahead of this in case Lyza decides to resort to blackmail again. So…I want you to contact the owners of all the pleasure-slaves and let them know there's been an emergency, and that their property will be returned to them ASAP."

"What about the Equestrian Festival?"

"It's canceled."

"No, that can't be true. I've worked so hard on organizing the event." His dick instantly went limp.

"We can't finish training without Hugo. Besides, I want my home and those horse stalls cleared out, just in case…"

"You're right, Madam. I'm being emotional right now. I'm so upset with myself for allowing that stupid little twit to outsmart me."

"How long do you think it'll take to return the twins and all the girls to their owners?"

"I have no idea. A couple of days at least to make the travel arrangements for all those people going in different directions. Marnie's owner is not going to be happy about this. He was expecting her to be ready for the auction block. I'm sure he'll do everything in his power to try to ruin your good name.

"It's important that we appease all their masters, so I want you to print graduation certificates for all of them, sign my name and send them on their way."

"I shall, Madam. I certainly shall."

She was merely placating the butler. She no longer cared about her reputation as the finest trainer of pleasure-slaves, and felt an enormous amount of relief to do away with the Madam Midnight persona. Lyza's tantrum was a blessing in disguise, and it was as if the universe was cooperating with her desire to lead a normal life.

Nico wasn't comfortable with the pleasure-slaves being in the house and this disaster with Lyza presented the perfect opportunity to clear out her home and start fresh.

But Jamison wouldn't be as easy dismissed as all the others. After thirteen years of waiting to consummate their marriage, he'd be thoroughly disappointed and quite possibly enraged. She'd have to give a great deal of careful thought regarding the matter of dissolving her loveless marriage. She'd speak to a good divorce attorney as soon as possible. Meanwhile, to keep the butler from being suspicious, she'd have to continue to behave as his stern mistress.

It would take a toll on her to have to behave as an unforgiving dominatrix when she'd prefer devoting all her time being warm and loving toward Nico.

Nico laughed as he crammed two more large bags of produce into the small trunk of the car. "I doubt if the Ferrari manufacturer envisioned the trunk of this luxury car being filled with fruit and veggies."

Leading her to the passenger's side of the car, he took her hand in his, his touch like fire, sending thrills through her body. Before opening the door, he leaned into her, kissing her fully on the lips, unconcerned that they had an audience of produce shoppers.

"I'm feeling so inspired, I can't wait to get back to your spot and whip up something scrumptious for my bae." Nico brushed his lips against her cheek, his nearness and the feel of his lips causing her to tremble.

"Uh, I spoke to Jamison a few moments ago and there seems to be a problem at home."

"What sort of problem?"

Madam grimaced. "It's embarrassing, but apparently we have a bed bug problem."

"You're kidding. They really exist? I always thought bed bugs were a myth."

"No, they're very real and apparently the house is infested with them. I'm so sorry, Nico, but we can't go back there. Jamison is sending the maids back to their masters while he gets the place fumigated, and replaces all the mattresses. It's best if we stay at a hotel until it's safe to return."

She was surprised by how fast the lies rolled off her tongue.

Nico looked disappointed. "I won't need the ingredients I just paid for. But I haggled so much with the vendor, I'm ashamed to return the goods and ask for my money back."

"You don't have to return anything. We'll book a suite in a hotel that has a full kitchen."

CHAPTER 33

Instead of going to a hotel, Madam had a better idea. She texted Jace Johnathan, a location scout she'd hired on several film projects in the past, and asked him to find her a vacation rental—a beach hideaway in New Jersey. Jace assured her that he'd find her something as fabulous as she was. She'd always been fond of Jace. He was free-spirited and bold. He told it like it was, sugar-coating nothing except his lips, which always shimmered with Love Nectar lip gloss by MAC. He also wore eye makeup that was expertly applied—all while sporting a mustache and close cropped beard. Yes, Jace lived in his truth as a man who unapologetically indulged his feminine side.

And when Jace said he could find her the perfect place to get away from it all, she believed him.

Two hours later, Madam and Nico pulled into the driveway of an amazing beach house in quiet little beach town along the Jersey shore called Breeze View. Nestled between Cape May and Sea Isle City, the shore town offered peaceful living with the opportunity for a wild night of fun by visiting the rowdier neighboring municipalities.

The property was ultra-modern. A mini-mansion that rented for six thousand a week and was well worth it in Madam's opinion. Nico may have been able to prevent her from buying him expensive personal gifts, but he couldn't stop her from spending her money on luxurious lodging.

There was a spacious garage equipped with his and her bikes, and in a text message, Jace had encouraged her to park her car and leave it since all the shops and restaurants were only a short walk from the home. And the beautiful beach was right outside her back door.

Jace was so thoughtful. Such a sweetheart. He was so vibrant and colorful, he was clearly wasting his talent being a location scout. Jace's star quality couldn't be denied, and Madam made a mental note to find an exciting part for him in her upcoming film project.

The beachfront property was beautifully decorated with every imaginable amenity, and it offered numerous decks and windows providing picturesque ocean views.

But Nico was most impressed with the accoutrements of the chef-worthy kitchen: double convection oven, a Sub-Zero refrigerator and a Thermador Pro-Style gas range. He rubbed his hands together, ready to get to work in the kitchen.

"You're full of surprises," he said to Madam, a smile curving his luscious lips. That smile warmed her inside. Made her want to do everything in her power to keep him smiling like that all the time.

After they'd settled in, Madam blocked the butler's number from her phone. This unexpected beach retreat was a slice of seaside heaven, and she didn't want to be disturbed with more bad news. She and Nico had the place for one week and that gave Jamison ample time to deal with Lyza and clear out the pleasure-slaves.

A week was more than enough time for her to consult with a divorce attorney who'd advise her on how to get rid of Jamison, whose presence in her home was as unwelcome as an infestation of bed bugs.

She wanted the butler to pack his things and go quietly into the night, and allow her to live the rest of her life happy and in love with Nico. Intuitively, she knew he would never go quietly. He'd throw himself at her mercy and beg to stay. She would not only need a divorce attorney but also an armed sheriff to get him out of her home.

She wondered if she should be honest and tell Nico about her bizarre marriage to Jamison. Absolutely not, she quickly decided. That disclosure could potentially lessen Nico's opinion of her, and that was not something she was willing to risk.

They enjoyed a candlelit dinner on the deck outside the kitchen, and afterward, beneath the moonlit sky, Madam and Nico strolled barefoot along the stretch of pristine sand that was accessible from their back door.

After all the years of island living, Madam had never taken a leisurely stroll on the beach. Had never been allowed any free time of her own that would grant her the opportunity to skip and scamper playfully along the water's edge. Her childhood had been a long blur of harsh words, hard fists, and grueling labor.

She drew a long ragged breath. No more self-pity. No more guilt or blame. What was done was done, and if she wanted to be truly happy, she had to be willing to let the past go.

The swirl of rushing water around her ankles felt like a caress, and she enjoyed the tickling sensation of seaweed sticking between her toes. She looked down and marveled at the sight of a spider crab skittering across the sand and foam line.

For so long she'd sought to overstimulate herself with wanton sex merely to feel alive. The discovery that a walk on the beach at night was so divine—so completely satisfying filled her with emotion. Tears sprang to her eyes and she tried to furtively wipe them away, but Nico caught her.

"What's wrong, Quintoria?"

"Nothing," she said, shaking her head adamantly. She wanted so badly to tell him about the missing ten years of her life, but she wasn't ready. Maybe one day, but not yet.

Nico tucked a finger beneath her chin, forcing her to look him in the eye. "Tell me what's bothering you." The care and concern in his voice were reasons to trust him with her darkest secrets. She was ready to tell him about Aunt Nola, and confess the truth about her twisted marriage, but when she opened her mouth nothing came out. The words caught in her throat, strengthening her belief that some things were best left unsaid.

"I'm feeling emotional…about us. And a little nervous," she confided.

"If you're nervous about the restaurant…or having second thoughts about getting involved, I fully understand. It has to be mad scary to invest in someone you've only known a short while."

"It's not about the restaurant. I'm looking forward to helping you attain that dream. And it hasn't been only a short while, I've known you for a very long time, Nico."

He looked at her curiously. "What do you mean you've known me for a long time? I don't get it."

"Maybe not you, per se. But the idea of you. Do you know what I mean?"

He shook his head. "Can't say that I do."

"Okay, let me try to explain." She took a deep breath and released it. "My whole life, I've been waiting for someone like you to come and rescue me. I finally gave up, and then here you come on your white horse. You're my knight-in-shining-armor, Nico."

"I don't know what to say. I haven't done anything to deserve that admirable title."

"You have no idea how much I've changed for the better in the short time I've known you. You bring out the best in me. I've never been in love before and until I get used to the feeling, I suppose you're going to have to put up with these little outbursts." She laughed a little, but was soon crying all over again as she flowed into his arms.

He wiped her tears, made comforting sounds. His kiss was soft and light, a mere brushing of his lips against hers, yet for Madam his kiss was achingly sweet, causing her to release a deep moan as if he'd penetrated her very soul.

Inspired by her restless hands that urgently traveled the length of his back, Nico's mouth began to rove all over, tickling her eyelids, her earlobe, and caressing her neck, and then traveling back again to her hot, opening lips.

They locked eyes and he took her hand. Words were not necessary as he guided her downward to a pristine blanket of sand. His hands stripped away the last vestiges of her defenses as he peeled off her clothes.

Completely naked and vulnerable, tears welled in the corner of her eyes. "I trust you with my heart, Nico. Please don't make me regret it."

He stroked her cheek tenderly. "I adore you, Quintoria. By now you should know that I'd hurt myself before I'd cause you any pain. We have to trust each other," he said, tearing off his clothes.

Bathed in moonlight, Nico, in all his naked male magnificence, was surrounded in what appeared to be an ethereal glow. For a moment, she was awestruck. It was a miracle that even though it was her first time falling in love, she'd chosen the perfect man. Nico, with all his ambition, talent, and drive had such an enormous capacity to love, and he gave it so deeply and unabashedly, she felt safe enough to surrender completely.

His head ducked downward as he kissed every inch of her velvety skin, murmuring words of love before covering her naked body with his own.

CHAPTER 34

Their beach getaway had proven to be the perfect escape. For the past few days, she and Nico had been on such a high together. Their love, so fresh and new was the ultimate joy ride—more fun and thrilling than the roller coaster she'd allowed him to talk her into riding when they visited the boardwalk in nearby Sea Isle City.

As they slept together, their bodies entwined, a morning breeze swept inside the bedroom, rustling the sheets. The cool air smelled of ocean salt with a hint of chocolate (courtesy of the nearby fudge shop). The comingled scents were quite agreeable and had become familiar to Madam, arousing her appetite.

Smiling at how sweet her life had become, she fondled the necklace that hung from her neck, a gold oyster shell with a pearl inside—a gift from Nico. He bought it from a jeweler on the boardwalk in Sea Isle City and said it was an ode to the first dish he'd ever prepared for her, his divine oysters and pearls dish, the first course served at the Secret Sunset Gala.

Although Madam had innumerable diamonds and other precious gems, this present from Nico meant more to her than any of the jewels secured in her vault at home.

Nico stirred in his sleep and then mumbled groggily, "I'm starving."

"I'm hungry, too. Why don't I cook for a change," Madam suggested. "We'll have breakfast in bed today. I haven't cooked in a while, but I'm sure I remember what to do with a carton of eggs and a pack of bacon."

She turned to get out of bed and Nico bear-hugged her from behind. "What's wrong with you, woman? Who said anything about food…I'm hungry for you," he said, turning her to face him.

A grin curled her lips. "Oh! It's that kind of hunger? I felt a few pangs myself."

Their combined laughter filled the bedroom, soon followed by soft murmurs and gentle words of appreciation for each other.

One of the many things Madam appreciated about their sex life was how natural it had become. They were growing accustomed to each other's rhythms, and the various ways they made love depended on the mood of the day. Each time they made love didn't necessarily involve explosive fireworks and savagely tearing off each other's clothes. Moments like this morning, their lovemaking was tender and sweet—extremely cautious—as if the protective bubble that shielded them from the rest of the world might suddenly break.

Madam was so filled up with love for Nico, it was as if she sometimes forgot to breathe. The beach town served as the set for their love story, the houses, boats, and shops were the props, and the people around them, fellow vacationers and local townspeople, were merely extras, barely acknowledged by Madam and Nico.

For the first time, Nico didn't go out of his way to get into lengthy discussions with strangers. Seeming to know that their impromptu vacation was special and magical. It was their right to be selfish and block out the rest of the world while doting on each other.

Their tender lovemaking left Madam in such a dreamy state, she withdrew her offer to cook breakfast, preferring to sit on the sidelines, watching Nico put his skills to use in the kitchen.

After a big breakfast with the fluffiest eggs she ever eaten, spiced rum country bacon, banana pancakes with real maple syrup (not the flavored kind you bought from the grocery store, Nico had pointed out) Madam was stuffed and needed a nap.

"Wanna take a ride on those bikes in the garage?" Nico asked.

Madam made a face and shook her head.

"We could burn off a lot of calories," he said, trying to pique her interest.

"No, thanks. I think I'll nap instead." She hated all forms of exercising. The parents she'd never known had given her excellent genes that allowed her to remain naturally slender despite being a woman of a certain age. But if she continued to eat the way she'd been doing in Breeze View, she was definitely going to start packing on the pounds.

"I'll take a bike ride by myself this time, but tomorrow, you're riding with me," he said.

"Okay, I'll join you tomorrow. I promise."

"I'm only kidding. We're on vacation and you can do whatever you want. I don't mind bike riding alone. It's time for me to meet some of the locals, anyway. By talking with them, I'll find out if there's a market for an upscale restaurant in this neck of the woods."

"You'd consider opening a restaurant here? I don't think it's a bad idea, but business would only be seasonal. What will you doing the winter months?"

"Whoa, calm down. I'm not going out to write my name in blood or sign any legal documents," he said with a chuckle. "I'm merely going out to snoop around—get a feel of the community."

"Oops, there I go, blurting out my thoughts. You'll have to bear with me, Nico. It's challenging, but I'm determined to overcome my need for control."

"Is that what you were doing—taking control?" He shrugged.

"I didn't see it that way. I saw a loving woman who wants to be certain her man makes wise choices. I dig it. Every day, I'm learning something new about our relationship. We're a team, and as long as we're honest and considerate of each other, we shouldn't have any problems."

After Nico left, Madam didn't jump back in bed for a nap. She sat outside on the deck, sipping water and marveling at her new-found happiness.

But the tender moment was ruined when her thoughts turned to Jamison. Every day she told herself to live in the moment and not to look at the outlandish number of missed calls on her phone, but she always looked anyway.

As if holding a ticking time bomb or a hand grenade, she lifted the phone gingerly from her purse and powered it on. The butler had racked up another forty calls since she'd last checked. She didn't dare listen to the messages. She could not torture herself with the sound of his voice giving her more bad news, not if she wanted to continue living peacefully in paradise.

She really ought to come clean to Nico about her past instead of selecting the parts that would gain her sympathy. As badly as she wanted to start life with a clean slate, she simply couldn't bring herself to reveal how she'd unscrupulously married the butler for his money, and then tricked him into thinking that through his undying devotion he could earn his way into her heart and her bed.

Then there was Aunt Nola. What she'd done to that saintly woman was inconceivable. No man in his right mind would trust that she was completely healed and emotionally stable after suffering from such a violent psychotic break.

The past had to stay in the past.

More than anything, she needed to focus on her future with Nico. No more procrastinating. She had to sit down with an aggressive divorce attorney and set the wheels in motion to dissolve her marriage as soon as she returned home.

Although she'd stolen her husband's money and used it to buy her home and to seed her own endeavors, the majority of her fortune had been earned through her own hard work and business savvy. Still she was willing to give him half of her fortune if that was what it would take to get him rid of him.

Loading the dishwasher, she turned around in surprise when Nico returned from his bike ride.

"You're back much earlier than I expected," she said with a delighted smile.

"Can't stay away from you very long…I miss you too much." He buried his face in her neck and trailed kisses down to her cleavage.

"Aw, Nico. I missed you, too, which is why I was cleaning the kitchen. I had to do something to pass the time until you came back to me."

"Seeing you doing housework…making beds, and toiling in the kitchen is a sight I haven't gotten used to, yet. I'm surprised you haven't called a service and hired someone to come and clean this big house," he said kiddingly.

"I enjoy being a domestic goddess," she replied. "There's something spiritual about hard work…when it's done out of love."

When her eyes went misty, Nico decided to change the subject before her warm thoughts reverted to her tragic childhood, bringing back a flood of painful memories.

"I have some good news. I wandered into a small café called Viola's that's been in business for over seventy-five years. Passed down from one generation to the next. The proprietors—Mr. and Mrs. Ballard—are ready to retire but can't interest either of their two children in taking over the place. One kid is a hotshot on Wall Street and the other is a high-powered attorney in New York. Neither of the Ballards' offspring would dream of trading their fast-paced New York lifestyle for a beach town—not even for the summer."

"Uh-oh. I know what's coming next," Madam said.

"Nope, you have no idea," Nico replied with a grin. "I told them all about myself—painting a picture of what my culinary career has been like up to this point. I told them I was looking for a place where people would enjoy high-end cuisine and Mr. Ballard quickly let me know that their customers enjoy good surf and turf in large portions. Not that artsy crap that comes in meager portions served on a big plate with craftily swirled sauces and topped with a sprig of rosemary."

Madam laughed. "Sounds like Mr. Ballard knows his clientele, and he doesn't mince words."

"He definitely speaks his mind. But I convinced him to humor me by allowing me to guest chef for a few days. I asked him to allow me to dazzle his customers with a fine dining experience they wouldn't soon forget."

"So, you're going to cook your elevated cuisine for a bunch of folks dressed in Dockers and T-shirts bearing the image of dolphins?"

Nico chuckled. "Yes, and I'm excited about it."

"Why?"

"I love the challenge."

"Does this mean you're interested in buying Viola's?"

"I won't know until I get a feel for the place. I am interested, though. When I walked in merely to strike up a conversation with the owners, the place spoke to me. I pictured it completely reno-vated and reflecting my vision." Excitedly, Nico gripped Madam by the shoulders. "And here's the best part…if I take over ownership of the restaurant, I wouldn't have to take a dime of your money. I have enough saved to meet the Ballard's asking price."

"But…but what will you do at the end of each summer?"

"You know I'm a wanderer at heart, hate being stuck in one place, and so I'll continue to travel after tourist season ends. I'll continue to guest chef and continue to be inspired by different locations, new ingredients, and the cooking styles and techniques of master chefs around the country."

"I want to be happy for you, Nico. I really do. But the selfish side of me doesn't want you to leave my side…not for a month, a weekend, or even for one day."

"You're a businesswoman with various corporations, I get that. But now that you're getting out of the pleasure-slave trade," he said, smiling and shaking his head at the absurdity of the words that came out of his mouth. "Now that you're not in that business anymore, I figured you'd have more free time. I don't want to be presumptuous and I don't want to make everything about me, but I was hoping we could travel together—at least some of the time. I wouldn't mind learning some techniques in other countries like Thailand, India, and parts of Africa. If you were willing, we could travel the world during off-season, bae."

Madam exhaled in relief. "Nothing would make me happier. I'll travel wherever you want to go—as long as we're together."

CHAPTER 35

The butler came up with a plan that included Azalea.

Two years ago, Madam had paid for Azalea to spend sixty days at exclusive rehab facility in Colorado. Azalea was now clean and sober and had been faithfully attending AA meetings for the past year and ten months. Azalea's commitment to her sobriety was something that made Madam extremely proud, but she was also cautious.

Due to Azalea's propensity toward overindulging in alcohol to the point of reckless endangerment, such as the time she'd carelessly left the burners lit on the stove, setting the kitchen on fire, Madam kept all the liquor under lock and key—in case Azalea relapsed.

Back when she was drinking, Azalea had been a nasty drunk, and it wasn't beneath her to take a shortcut to the bathroom by squatting over a potted plant. She'd been flagged over by the police on several occasions for speeding through red lights while wearing only flip flops and her underwear and holding an open bottle of gin in her hand.

With Madam being incommunicado, the butler felt he had no choice but to pick Azalea's brain. The woman kept her mouth shut as tight as a steel drum when it came to divulging information about Madam. A little alcohol was exactly what he needed to pry Azalea's tight lips apart.

Darcy and Edwina had already gone for the day when the butler took a seat at the table.

"I'm worried about Madam," he said, reaching into the inside pocket of his jacket and retrieving a flask filled with gin.

"There's nothing to worry about. She's a grown woman and, from what I can tell, she's in good hands with Nico," Azalea said with her back toward the butler as she busily wiped down countertops and appliances.

"But it's not like her to ignore my phone calls or to pull a disappearing act. Suppose he's holding her against her will…keeping her captive in some underground hell hole."

"Sounds like you've been watching too much of the ID channel," Azalea said, amused.

"It's not funny. We don't know Nico's true identity. He could be one of those professional con artists who charm older women and then empty out their bank accounts. Or worse, he could be a serial killer, slowly torturing her to death while we sit here doing nothing." The butler mimicked crying sounds though no tears fell from his eyes. He turned the flask up to his lips and took a deep sip.

The familiar smell drifted to Azalea's nostrils and she whirled around. "Don't tell me Madam's love affair has caused you to start drinking!"

"What else can I do but drink? I feel so powerless. So damned helpless."

"Don't worry about Quinnie. She's tough and can take care of herself. Knowing her, she's lying low until she's sure the coast is clear, and that all those freaky slave folks have carried their behinds back to where they came from.

"I can't believe that girl, Marnie, was actually walking around with a horse's tail stuck up her ass," she continued with a frown. "She was waving her graduation certificate around and talking about how her master would be able to get more money from her auction sale now that she was a ponygirl. And that other one, Brynne…she wouldn't talk at all. Would only neigh like a horse."

Azalea shook her head. "I was happy to see all of 'em get the hell out of here." She let out a long sigh. "I wish I knew how Quinnie got mixed up in this crazy lifestyle of hers, but I have my fingers crossed that Nico can help get her mind right."

The butler scoffed with indignation. "Nico doesn't even have a stable job, so what can he actually do for her?" he said with venom and took another swig from the flask.

He noticed Azalea behaving fidgety, her hand shaking as she wiped the same spot on the counter over and over, while her eyes darted to the butler's flask each time he turned it up to his lips.

"Would you like to join me?"

"You know I can't drink. I'm an alcoholic."

"Oh, I thought that rehab place cured you," he said, feigning ignorance about the disease.

"It's not something that can ever be cured."

"Too bad. I could really use a drinking buddy right now."

Azalea crept over and pulled out a chair. "I don't think one little drink will hurt me."

"I don't think it will either," he said, handing her the flask.

Two hours later, Azalea, stupefied with drink, was stretched out on the kitchen floor, drooling and lying in a pool of urine. Indeed, she was a nasty drunk, but she had provided the butler with a wealth of information about the ten years Madam never talked about. And the juicy details she'd shared about 'Aunt Nola,' the so-called relative whom Madam had been so concerned about when he'd first hired her, made him view Madam in an entirely different light.

Nico ought to have been a lot more careful about the company he kept.

He considered his sleuthing skills to be only average, yet it was fairly easy to track down Madam's whereabouts. All he had to do was follow the money. She was strict about keeping her banking information private, only allowing him access to the household expenses account, yet he'd managed to figure out the passcodes to her various accounts and was fully aware of every dollar she spent, right down to the penny.

For years he'd been extremely considerate with regard to his spending habits. He'd been so very cautious and low maintenance, he didn't even own a car.

Apparently Madam was no longer satisfied to carry on her illicit affair in the confines of her home. She needed a secret love nest for adultery and fornication. A six-thousand-dollar-a-week love nest, at that! The gall of that ungrateful woman. For thirteen years, he'd sat back and had never voiced a word of complaint while she fucked around with everything in a skirt and in pants—under the sacred roof of their marital home.

It had always been part of her cruel nature to flaunt her lovers in the butler's face—to make him watch her being sexually satisfied by the endless parade of nameless, faceless lovers with whom she'd shared her body—moaning, writing, and crying out in passion, all the while spurred on by the pain in her husband's eyes.

Oh, she was a heartless bitch, but she'd miscalculated how much abuse the butler could withstand. She should have never slinked off to fuck that gigolo outside their home.

Out of the hundreds of lovers that she flaunted in his face, what was it about this one that she didn't want him to see?

That she required privacy with her new lover infuriated the butler so much he came to the conclusion that it was high time that he upheld his honor. In olden days he would have had to challenge the disrespectful young man to a duel. But in these modern times, he'd simply show the thug-chef who the better man was by out-maneuvering him.

CHAPTER 36

I n a short span of time, Madam and Nico had fallen head over heels in love with Breeze View, and both regarded the beach house as a refuge. Taking late-night walks along the beach, watching the colorful sunrise together, and biking around the lovely community had become daily rituals.

There was a tremendous amount of buzz about Viola's after a food critic from the *New York Times* had written a glowing review, describing Nico's cooking technique as a balancing act of showmanship and culinary skills. The critic raved about a well-chosen cut of tenderloin that was balanced with a robust sauce of wild cherry brandy and Jersey-grown cherry preserves.

The review brought in customers from the neighboring shore towns, and the long lines of far more customers than could be accommodated compelled the Ballards to enforce a reservations-only requirement for dinner service. The review also confirmed Nico's belief that tourists were willing to spend extra cash for a fine dining experience.

When it was time to return the key to the realtor, neither Madam nor Nico was quite ready to say goodbye to their summer paradise. Nor was Nico willing to turn the kitchen back over to Mr. Ballard just yet, and Mr. Ballard, happy to sit among the customers and enjoy Nico's cuisine, didn't mind at all.

Thankful to put off the inevitable *divorce discussion* a little while longer, Madam arranged to rent the house for another week.

While Nico was putting in twelve-hour days at the restaurant, Madam decided to throw herself wholeheartedly into her next film project. After ducking Gary, her production partner's calls for weeks, she poured herself a glass of wine, sat on the deck outside the master bedroom, and powered on her phone. Her heart sank and she bit her lip in despair when she observed the high volume of missed calls from the butler.

I'll call Jamison after I talk to Gary. I've been selfish and inconsiderate. Jamison doesn't deserve this kind of treatment. At the very least, I should abate his worrying by letting him know I'm all right.

She called Gary and what she thought would be a quick conversation stretched into hours. She'd been so caught up in her decadent lifestyle with the pleasure-slaves and then she'd become so absorbed with Nico that she'd neglected her own passion for filmmaking.

In addition to bringing her up to date on the film's pre-production particulars, Gary also dished the latest scintillating gossip. The rumors involving actors were endless.

"Speaking of actors, have all the parts been cast?" Madam asked.

"All the major roles have."

"Any juicy minor roles left?" Madam inquired, thinking about Jace Johnathan.

"There're a couple of parts—a hotel clerk and a hit man, but I don't think I'd call either of the parts *juicy*. Both characters are only on screen for a few minutes."

"A few minutes is all the actor I have in mind needs," Madam replied. "A good actor can make any part juicy," she said with a smile in her voice.

The sudden chime of the doorbell jolted Madam. Having had no visitors, it was the first time she'd heard the sound since renting the place. "I have to go, Gary. Someone's at the door. I'll give you a call in a few days. Smooches," she said and hung up.

Padding down the stairs, it occurred to her that a tourist or someone new to the area had mistakenly rung her bell. But when she peeked through the eyehole, her mind did not immediately register what it was seeing. She blinked a few times before realizing that Azalea, of all people, looking drunk and haggard and barely standing up, was leaning precariously against the railing on the front porch.

Madam quickly yanked the door open. "Azalea! What are you doing here, and how did you find me?"

"When you're desperately worried about someone, you'll move heaven and earth to find them?" said the butler, emerging from the shadows.

At the sight of the butler, her heart nearly stopped. "Jamison, I, uh…"

"You don't seem happy to see me," he said, noticing the distress on Madam's face. "May we come in?" Without waiting for an answer, he stepped inside, tugging a stumbling Azalea along and guiding her to a stylish chair in the living room.

"What happened to her?" Madam asked, her surprised gaze sweeping from Azalea to the butler.

"She was so crushed after being abandoned by her dearest friend in the world that she resorted to drinking again. She has absolutely no willpower. The poor thing has gotten hopelessly drunk for five days in a row." The grin that formed on the butler's face was so wickedly triumphant, Madam found herself fearing him—an emotion she'd never felt during their marriage. Her jaw tensed and her stomach coiled tight with tension.

"I've been inconsiderate and I'm sorry, Jamison. I was going to give you a call but I haven't been feeling well." A shaky half smile lifted the corners of her mouth.

"You look perfectly healthy to me. In fact, you seem to have picked up a few pounds since I saw you last. I suppose all those creamy sauces and gooey desserts have found their way to your hips, my dear." He smiled a serpent's smile that caused her to back away in fear.

He advanced toward her, his very presence, terrifying and oppressive. The man she'd controlled and instilled fear in for so many years had somehow turned the tables on her.

Nico! She screamed his name in her head while trying to give her best interpretation of grace under pressure.

"You look a bit peaked, my dear. Are you feeling okay?" Arranging his features into a look of concern, he placed a hand against Madam's forehead.

Grimacing, Madam recoiled from his touch.

"Don't shy away from me, my dear. I've come to rescue you from that brute who calls himself a chef." This was said with such venom, his face twisted into a mask of fury.

"Nico is not a brute, and I don't need rescuing from him."

"Nico is pure scum; he's not fit to kiss your shoe. Or your ass. And he most certainly isn't good enough to stick his dick in your pussy, is he, you slut?"

Her hand covered her mouth in horror.

The butler towered over her. He raised his large hand, allowing it to hover in the air, prepared to strike her down. "Answer me, Quintoria. Is Nico good enough to stick his dick in the pussy you've been denying me all these years?"

"No," she said in a stunned whisper.

"I can't hear you."

"Nico isn't good enough to fuck me," she murmured, her eyes fixed on the floor.

"Good answer." He crossed the room and took a seat on the couch and patted the cushion next to him. "Come sit beside me. We have much to discuss."

Madam joined the butler, sitting stiffly next to him.

He clasped her hand and placed it in his lap, stroking her skin while moaning. "It feels so good to feel your skin again. The touch of you drives me insane." He began licking his lips in a most disgusting way. "I thirst for you, my dear. It is the kind of thirst that can only be quenched by drinking from the divine fountain that flows between your legs." His voice emerged in a timbre that was deep and rich, his words flowing like poetry.

He rose to his feet and then crouched down, burrowing his head between Madam's legs.

The moment his slimy tongue touched the crotch of her panties, she screamed and pushed him away. Jumping up, she ran toward the powder room and locked herself inside.

The butler pounded on the door, threatened to wring her neck and to crush her like a fly. She didn't doubt him. The man was insane, she now realized. She desperately needed a phone to call Nico, but she'd left hers upstairs on the deck. There was a small window in the powder room—too high to reach without climbing on the counter surrounding the sink and then hoisting herself upward. She had to. Climbing through the window was her only option—the only way to reach the safety of Nico's arms.

With one leg balanced on the sink and the other perched on the ledge of the window, she was moments away from freedom when the door suddenly burst open, and the butler, with his eyes blazing in fury, forcefully yanked her down. A sharp pain blossomed in her ankle when she collapsed to the floor, and she wondered if her ankle was broken. Lying in a crumbled heap, Madam gave in to helpless tears.

As she lay there, tears streaming, the butler stormed out of the powder room and quickly returned, dragging a semi-conscious Azalea.

In three swift motions, he palmed the back of Azalea's head with his huge hand, lifted it upward, and then with all his might, he banged her face against the granite counter.

The sound of bones crushing reverberated in the powder room. Blood spurted all over. The ceiling, the floor, the walls, the toilet seat and tank, the mirror, the faucets, the light switch—there was blood everywhere.

Madam screamed and nearly vomited when she saw what was left of Azalea's face. Her features were caved in and mushed together in a hideous distortion. What was left of her nose, mouth, and eyes were lumpy globs of skin, bone, and tissue.

Yet somehow, Azalea was still alive. Barely, but she was alive and she was suffering terribly. Madam noticed Azalea's left hand twitching and she pleaded fervently with the butler to help Azalea when she heard her friend making random sounds—a warble from her throat and a raspy hissing noise that was so pathetic and animalistic, it sounded inhuman.

She began to rage at the butler. "Help her! You can't let her die, you sick son of a bitch!" With awkward movements, she attempted to stand but the burst of pain that shot up her leg was so severe she became dizzy and collapsed.

With a vile look in his eyes, the butler smashed Azalea's head against granite once more. And this time Azalea went ominously silent and still.

CHAPTER 37

Madam couldn't run, and she feared that screaming might incite the butler to bash her head in, too. There was nothing she could do except remain huddled on the floor, and quietly await her fate. If he planned to kill her, she could only pray that her death would be swift.

"This brutal crime against Azalea brings back memories of poor Aunt Nola, doesn't it, Quintoria?" he said, laughing manically. "It's a pity you've snapped yet again and this time you've killed your best friend. I tried to duplicate the ghastly scene in the bathroom of your dear aunt's house, but without a bathtub in this powder room, I had to improvise and use the sink."

How'd he know? She'd so carefully hidden that part of her life. There were no words to express the depth of her remorse and sorrow. She hadn't meant to hurt Aunt Nola. The night it happened, her mind had gone fuzzy, and it was as if she were watching someone else avenging the stolen years of her childhood.

"Apparently, those ten years in the psych ward didn't satisfy your lust for blood," he said with his head tilted, eyeing Azalea's lifeless form as if observing a curious piece of modern art.

The butler lifted Azalea's limp body and her head lolled to one side. Through the mess of pulpy, bloodied flesh, Madam was able to discern an intact eyeball, which, although unfocused, was directed upward as if sending up a final prayer before meeting her maker.

The butler dumped Azalea like a sack of potatoes next to Madam. "You two cunts deserve each other," he spat.

"Azalea, oh, Azalea," Madam cried, pulling her friend close and wrapping her arms around her, smoothing her blood-clumped hair.

The butler washed the blood from his hands with fastidious care. Observing Madam through the mirror above the sink, he said, "With your history of violence, it'll be easy for the authorities to believe that you've struck again. You're going back to the loony bin, my dear. As your legal spouse, it's within my rights to make sure you're taken off the streets and confined in a strait jacket to keep you from being a danger to yourself and others."

"But I didn't do this. You know I didn't." Her words sounded hollow and empty. It was useless to have a rational conversation with him. But maybe if she engaged him in conversation, if she could only keep him talking long enough, there was a chance that Nico would come home and save her.

He turned around and faced her directly. "The last time you struck, you claimed that something beyond your control took over your mind and made you beat that woman within an inch of her life." The butler held out his hands and looked around in wonderment. "So…if you didn't do this to Azalea, then who did? Certainly not me. I'm a harmless butler, incapable of committing such a heinous crime. But you, on the other hand…" The butler's voice trailed off ominously.

Keep him talking, she thought while still clutching Azalea's dead body.

He took out his pocket watch and checked the time. "I've been tracking the chef's routine for the past few days and according to my calculations he'll be arriving at this love nest you two share in another hour or so."

The idea that he'd been watching Nico's movements caused her to shudder. Her skin prickled and dribbles of sweat began running down the sides of her face.

"You're sweating, my dear, and it's most unbecoming." The butler snatched a tissue from the blood-spattered tissue box on the counter and then kneeled in front of her, carefully dabbing perspiration from her face with tissue that was stained with Azalea's blood.

She wanted to attack him. His hand was close to her mouth and she wanted to rip into his wrist with her teeth and tear his flesh to shreds. But she didn't dare. He was liable to pummel her so violently that he'd easily beat her to death with his bare hands.

"I have a driver waiting to take us home. We have to get going, my dear."

"I can't leave without saying something to Nico."

"You can and you will," he said firmly. "I am your husband and he's nothing to you." The butler reached inside his inner pocket and pulled out an envelope. "This letter to Nico will bring him up to speed regarding your mental history and criminal past. The news article written about the heinous crime is accessible on the Internet, and I've provided the chef with a printout and also a copy of your mugshot."

"Oh, God," she murmured in anguish.

"I've also provided him with a copy of our marriage license and informed him that the woman he thought he knew is an incredible liar and is criminally insane."

"Don't do this, Jamison. I'll give you back every dime I took from you. If it's money you want, you can have it all. But please let me have this one chance at happiness. I'm begging you. Please."

The smirk on his face quickly informed her that her words were falling on deaf ears.

"After all these years of waiting on you hand and foot, and not even getting so much as a kind word or a pat on the head, I'd say that I'm the one who deserves a chance at happiness. Now, gather yourself and let's go home and resume being man and wife."

"I can't walk. My ankle…I think it's broken."

"Then I'll have to carry you, my dear."

"What about Azalea? You can't leave her body here for Nico to find."

"Nico has a right to see the degree of violence and rage that you're capable of."

"I didn't do it," she whimpered.

"Shh. Shh. Of course you did, but you don't remember," he said in a gentle tone. "Your mind gets so fuzzy sometimes. But everything is going to be all right. I'm taking you home and I'm going to protect you. I'm not going to allow anyone to take you away from me…not the police and certainly not the men in white coats. This time around, they'd most likely try cranial electrotherapy, and who knows how you'd come out of that. No, no, no. I'm not going to let them touch your brain, unless I find you to be uncontrollable and you leave me no other choice," he said threateningly.

"Tonight is the night, Quintoria. After all these years, we're finally going to consummate our marriage."

"No!" She shook her head. "I was never really your wife. Not ever, and you know it. We were both playing a stupid game. I love Nico and he loves me. And none of this staged mayhem is going to change that."

The butler chuckled. "Thank you for your earlier offer of money, but it won't be necessary being that I emptied out your bank accounts. We're a married couple, and being old school, I'm of the belief that the husband should control the purse strings. I took the liberty of offering to deposit a million dollars in Nico's bank account if he'll follow my implicit directions."

"What directions?" she asked nervously.

"Using your vast connections, I contacted someone who knew someone who had a cousin from Russia or maybe it was the Ukraine…anyway, I located a 'cleaner.' In the letter, I've provided Nico with the guy's contact info and instructed him to give him a call. I've bequeathed him the Ferrari and of course the generous monetary offer. It's the least I could do for all the trouble my psychotic wife has caused him.

"If Nico loves you the way you think he does, he'll man-up and walk away. I made it abundantly clear that if he sticks around and stirs up trouble, you're going to end up living out the rest of your life drooling in a psych ward. Or worse; they'll dismiss your claim of insanity and put you out of your misery with a lethal injection."

Madam sighed hopelessly.

"After Nico gets here and discovers the grisly tableau that awaits him, I'm sure he won't hesitate to pick up the phone and call Vladimir or Sergei or whatever the guy's name is. Whether he's in love with you or not, Nico would be a fool to get involved in a mess like this. I understand that the good folks of Breeze View have been coming out in droves to taste his fine cuisine. The popularity he's been enjoying won't last much longer if the police take him in to question him about the murder that took place in the vacation home where he was residing. Any involvement with Azalea's grisly murder would be a terrible PR move on Nico's part."

"You're a sick man, Jamison. Conniving and spiteful," Madam said with venom.

"I'm no more conniving than you, the unscrupulous woman who preyed on my weakness, took all my worldly goods, and then employed me as her lowly butler."

"And I'm sorry for that. I was misguided by a therapist I trusted."

"That's a bunch of crap. You never take responsibility for any of your wrongdoing," he shouted. "Always blaming someone other than yourself for your unscrupulous and reckless actions. Well, this time you're being held accountable…by me! You owe me, you bitch," he yelled. He was so filled with rage, he was wild-eyed and frothing at the mouth.

"You took everything from me. My self-respect and dignity and then you turned me into a caricature of my former self. You owe me for all the years I devoted myself to you."

"You're right. I do owe you, and I'll be happy to pay you back."

"You can't repay all those years of dedication and servitude. Anyway, I have no doubt that Nico will see things as I do. He's making quite a name for himself, and I can't think of any reason that a sane person with a bright future ahead of him would throw it all away by becoming entangled in a brutal murder committed by a bitch who's a certifiable lunatic."

He blew out a long breath and regarded Madam. Hands folded, fingers entwined, he rocked back and forth on his heels for a few moments and then said, "If you love Nico, you won't drag him into this mess that you created. It doesn't matter who's responsible for the actual killing of Azalea, when it comes down to it, it's all your fault. Had you treated me with even a shred of human decency, it would have never come to this."

He suddenly smiled at her with warmth shining in his eyes. "Come, Madam. Allow me to help you to your feet. Once we're back in our marital abode, we'll put all this behind us and never speak of it again." He held out his hand.

Madam recoiled, looking stricken. She thought of Nico and how bright his star would shine as long as he wasn't tarnished by the scandal of Azalea's murder—that kind of scandal in a quiet, small town would be dragged through the media for years to come.

Thinking of Nico and having his best interest at heart, she accepted the butler's hand.

CHAPTER 38

In the back of the limo she sat in a daze, staring vacantly out the window throughout the two-hour ride home. She was barely aware of the butler attempting to comfort her by stroking and caressing her hand. Growing bolder, he brought her hand to his lips and kissed her knuckles, licked between her fingers, and at one point he got so carried away, he began aggressively sucking each of her fingers.

Madam sat motionless, seemingly unperturbed by the molestation of her hand and fingers. Had she been more aware of what was occurring, she would have been sickened and appalled. But Madam had checked out. Her body was in the vehicle but her mind was back in Breeze View, sitting on the deck, dressed in sexy lingerie while enjoying a late-night cocktail with Nico.

Reality set in when the car pulled up to the gate. The first thing that struck her was that her precious oyster and pearl necklace was no longer around her neck. She frantically groped around the seat and looked down at the floor. But it was nowhere to be found.

The butler carried her from the limo to the front door and it was a jolting surprise to see that he'd placed bars in front of every window in the house.

He planned to keep her as a prisoner in her own home.

No more bike riding, no more walks on the beach at night. No more scrumptious meals prepared with love. No more passion-filled mornings and nights. No more laughter. No more joy.

Azalea! The sense of loss was so devastating, Madam clutched her chest and let out a heart-wrenching moan.

"Let's get you to bed, my dear," the butler said and then carried her up the staircase. "I've already moved my personal belongings out of the attic into *our* private suite of rooms.

"It was my plan that we'd consummate our marriage tonight, but due to your ankle, I'm willing to wait until you're feeling better." He placed her on the bed, sat next to her, stroking her hair and rubbing her back consolingly.

She didn't want his monstrous hands on her. She wanted to be enfolded inside Nico's loving arms. But that was something she'd never experience again. By now, Nico had stepped into the nightmare that the butler had left behind in the beach house. Right now, he was probably in a state of shock. Frantic and bewildered, and feeling so betrayed by the woman he loved.

I'm sorry, Nico. Unable to hold back the tears any longer, she collapsed on her pillow and sobbed.

"Now, now, my dear. Everything is going to be fine. I bet a nice cup of tea would make you feel better. Would you like your loving husband to make you a cup of tea?"

She nodded her head. Continuing to whimper and sniffle, she said, "Yes, I'd like a cup of tea." But she didn't want tea. She didn't want anything except to be alone for few moments to mourn the senseless death of her friend and the loss of the greatest love she'd ever have.

"Before I make your tea, I have a small request."

"Yes?" she said in a weak voice.

"I realize that your sprained ankle has put you out of commission, but in the meanwhile…" He paused and looked down at the floor as if overcome with bashfulness. "What I'm trying to say is that there's nothing wrong with your mouth and I'd appreciate it if you'd kiss my cock."

Madam gasped.

"Before we retire for the night, I expect a full-on blowjob from you." His expression changed from kindly to a look of outrage. "I want you to put the same effort and enthusiasm into blowing me as you did when you sucked that young thug's dick." He grabbed a handful of her hair and gave her head a hard yank. "Have I made myself abundantly clear?"

She nodded briskly.

"You don't call the shots anymore, I do. So don't give me a head nod, answer me appropriately."

"Yes, master," she said and then broke down crying.

He released her hair. "Now, now. Don't cry. I realize it's going to take some getting used to, but in time you'll enjoy having me as your master and you'll feel a flush of shame and thrill pass over you each time I debase you. Oh, my dear, you can't begin to imagine the wonderfully wicked things I'm going to do to you every single day until death do us part."

Wearing a sinister smile, he looked off in thought, and then turned his gaze on her. "By the way, I'm planning to sell this house very soon. It has too many memories that I'd prefer to forget. When we move into our new home, I'm going to throw a big party in your honor. I'll invite all your friends from here and abroad. I want everyone to be here for your debut as my personal pleasure-slave.

"You and I will make a grand entrance. On your hands and knees and attached to an eighteen-karat-gold leash, you'll be walked into the center of the room. So beautifully naked and submissive, you'll dazzle them all, my dear.

"Imagine the shock of all your friends when they discover with their own eyes that the great Madam Midnight has finally been tamed."

He can't make me stay with him. I'll pretend to be weak and docile, and I'll withstand every word of degradation and every brutal beating exactly as I did when I was a child. But the minute he lets his guard down, I'll escape from here!

Madam smiled faintly. Planning her reunion with Nico was the only thing that would keep her sane.

EPILOGUE

For Nico, the past two years had been a blur of activity with a procession of achievements and awards that didn't typically happen for the average young chef who'd opened his first restaurant. Part of his good fortune came from his talent, his unique culinary identity that set him apart from competitors in the area. But for the most part, Nico's streak of success was a result of the almost reckless way in which he took risks in developing cuisine.

Sleep didn't come easily for him anymore. Every night he stayed up hours after the restaurant closed thinking of new items for the menu. New ways for creative expression.

The menu, that changed weekly, was based on anything that came into his head. After the gruesome scene he'd come home to last summer, his thoughts tended to lean toward the bizarre and macabre, which was often reflected in the cuisine he served.

A signature dish, most beloved by the clientele was called *Murder Scene*. The meal consisted of braised halibut, grilled prawns and tiny new potatoes dotted with a small circle of caviar in the center. A red wine sauce that resembled blood spatter was splashed craftily on a white plate. It was edible art and the customers loved Nico's bravado and flair.

The customers enjoyed trying to interpret the dish, but no one picked up on the fact that the potato resembled an eyeball emerging from gore. Nico didn't expect anyone to. The Russian clean-up crew had been thorough. Their work ensured that none of the customers would ever understand Nico's interpretation of Azalea's battered remains.

Though it wasn't obvious to anyone except himself, he'd lost his passion for cooking on that fateful night when he'd lost Quintoria. Now his food was an emotional response to the events that occurred during the time he'd spent with her, and he was driven by the compulsion to express the thoughts and images that constantly plagued him.

What caused her to snap and kill her friend, Azalea? She'd confided intimate details about her wretched childhood in Jamaica so why hadn't she trusted him enough to tell him about her tragic lapse from reality when she was eighteen?

Another big shocker was learning that the butler was actually her husband. That discovery was so far-fetched and mind-boggling, Nico was left feeling off-kilter, and not sure whether or not his own feet were securely planted in reality.

Had Quintoria's entire life been a lie? Had he ever really known her?

Nico would never know. He'd gone back to House of Stevens, but the mansion was boarded up. He'd called mental hospitals but couldn't get any information on the patients. He'd even done an inmate search online, but nothing turned up. It was as if she'd fallen off the face of the earth. All he had left of her was the car she'd left behind, some of her clothing, the necklace he'd given her, which he'd found on the powder room floor, and a grainy mugshot of Quintoria at around age eighteen.

Nico greeted customers at the end of each dining experience, posed for photos and signed menus. He was an affable guy. Good looking and personable. Although easy to like, he was much too guarded to allow anyone to peel away his layers and get to know him on a deeper level.

Once the doors were closed and the patrons and staff had all gone for the evening, Nico would sit in the restaurant, drinking alone, and berating himself for not being there when Quintoria had needed him most. No matter what the butler had said in that letter, Nico refused to accept that the woman he'd left at home, happily planning their future together, had suddenly snapped and killed her dearest friend in the world. No amount of damning evidence would ever make him believe that.

After locking up the restaurant, instead of going home, he took a late-night stroll on the beach, the way he and Quintoria used to do.

A haunted man, hunched with his hands stuffed in his pockets, Nico walked barefoot along the wet sand, missing Quintoria so much; the loss was visceral and a physical pain in his heart.

Far off in the distance, he saw a lone figure—hair blowing in the night breeze, long skirt billowing.

Quintoria!

She was the reason he'd stayed in Breeze View. Being where Quintoria could find him was the only reason he'd moved forward with his plan to purchase Viola's.

Her inevitable return was exactly why he'd never touched the money that was deposited into his bank account. It belonged to her…not him, and he wanted to give back every cent to her.

Making sure he wasn't seeing things, he squinted in the dark. Yes, it was unmistakably Quintoria. Nico would know her anywhere.

His heart thumped at the sight of her familiar form, tall and sleekly feline with the grace of a panther.

It was instinctual to run to her as she stood waiting in the moonlight, but the part of him that was protective and considerate of how fragile her nerves must be after all she'd been through, decided that a gentler approach was more thoughtful.

With the biggest smile he'd worn in a long time, Nico strode swiftly, making deep footprints in the sand.

Don't ask her any questions, he cautioned himself. *Don't push! Let her take her time explaining what happened. Just hold her and be strong for her.*

He hastened his steps, eager to swoop her up in his arms.

She began moving in his direction, and the closer they got, the more faltering his footsteps became.

Finally, they were face to face. She gave him a faint smile. He nodded his head curtly and kept going.

It wasn't her.

This was the second time this week he'd mistaken someone else for her.

She was everywhere. Parked next to him at red lights. Seated in an obscure table at the back of his restaurant. Bent at the waist inspecting strawberries at the farmers' market. Peddling a bike on a sandy trail.

Yes, Quintoria was everywhere, but in reality she was nowhere.

Nico stuffed his hand deeper into his pocket. Wrapping his fingers around the oyster and pearl necklace, he pulled it out of his pocket. Enraged, he released a string of profanity as he raised his arm to hurl it into the ocean.

But he couldn't do it. The necklace was a part of her and he couldn't let it go.

Quintoria Stevens had touched his heart and soul like no one else had ever done. Nico would never accept that the love of his life was lost to him forever. How could he when he could still feel her, smell her, and taste the sweetness of her kiss? She was out there somewhere and he vowed to scour the Earth until he found her and held her in his arms once again.

ABOUT THE AUTHOR

Allison Hobbs is a national bestselling author of twenty-six novels and has been featured in such periodicals as *Romantic Times* and *The Philadelphia Inquirer*. She lives in Philadelphia, Pennsylvania. Visit the author at AllisonHobbs.com and Facebook.com/ Allison hobbseroticaauthor.